Breaking Badlands

Also by Scott Reintgen

Saving Fable
Escaping Ordinary

Breaking Badlands

~ Talespinners Book 3 ~

SCOTT REINTGEN

Crown Books for Young Readers
New York

Text copyright © 2021 by Scott Reintgen
Jacket art copyright © 2021 by Maike Plenzke

All rights reserved. Published in the United States by Crown Books for Young Readers, an imprint of Random House Children's Books, a division of Penguin Random House LLC, New York.

Crown and the colophon are registered trademarks of Penguin Random House LLC.

Visit us on the Web! rhcbooks.com

Educators and librarians, for a variety of teaching tools, visit us at RHTeachersLibrarians.com

Library of Congress Cataloging-in-Publication Data
Names: Reintgen, Scott, author.
Title: Breaking Badlands / Scott Reintgen.
Description: First edition. | New York : Crown Books for Young Readers, [2021] |
Series: Talespinners ; book 3 | Audience: Ages 8–12. | Audience: Grades 3–7. |
Summary: Indira accepts an undercover mission to infiltrate Antagonist Academy and unwittingly becomes a pawn in a devious plan to upset the balance between good and evil.
Identifiers: LCCN 2021004778 (print) | LCCN 2021004779 (ebook) |
ISBN 978-0-593-30720-5 (hardcover) | ISBN 978-0-593-30722-9 (ebook) |
Subjects: CYAC: Books and reading—Fiction. | Adventure and adventurers—Fiction. |
Good and evil—Fiction. | Honesty—Fiction. | Heroes—Fiction. | Fantasy.
Classification: LCC PZ7.1.R4554 Br 2021 (print) | LCC PZ7.1.R4554 (ebook) |
DDC [Fic]—dc23

The text of this book is set in 12-point Cochin.
Interior design by Ken Crossland

Printed in the United States of America
10 9 8 7 6 5 4 3 2 1
First Edition

For Granddaddy and Mama. One of you taught me how to work, and one of you taught me how to play. Writing is a unique spoon-stir of both of those qualities. All the grandchildren miss you in their own way. For me, it's not being able to see you on the back row at my events, smiling like that's the only place you wanted to be.
Thanks for all the laughter, all the love, everything.

Contents

Breaking Badlands

1

Peeve Meadows

*S*he wasn't much at first glance, but then, most people aren't.

Peeve Meadows watched the progress of a small boat as it made its way through a treacherous cove toward the shore. The Words echoed in her head, as they had since she'd first arrived in Fester. Her teachers had taught her that the words were sort of like a prophecy. She was supposed to treasure them. If she was lucky enough to get into a story of her own, those words would be the beginning. Except, she didn't *like* the words she'd been given.

Wasn't much at first glance? That didn't sound very flattering. It sounded like she was destined for a story where people underestimated her. Which was how her time in the world of Imagination had gone so far. First she'd arrived in Origin, where Indira had pretty much ignored her efforts to be friends. And then Peeve's attempt to steal Indira's invitation to Protagonist Preparatory had completely backfired. She'd ended up being forced to attend Antagonist Academy instead.

While Indira was off saving the world, Peeve had struggled through her first semester in the city of Fester. Life there was a slow descent into questionable morals. Peeve was taught how to lie, steal, cheat, and swindle. Her teachers encouraged her to be crueler and less merciful. Most of her teachers, however, had the same response to her efforts in their classes.

Peeve just wasn't *evil* enough for their tastes.

She lacked some unspoken quality. She wasn't as big as some of the other baddies. She wasn't as mean. She wasn't as sly or maniacal or two-faced. One teacher had even asked whether she had the heart to be bad. Peeve hadn't known what to say. She hadn't chosen this.

But now she intended to prove everyone wrong.

The small rowboat finally reached the rendezvous point. Peeve drew her hood up to fend off the biting wind. She started walking down the beach to where sea met stone. Even wearing her best boots, Peeve felt the cold sting of the water as she raised a hand in greeting to the two rowers. Great waves crashed around them, but she could still hear the sound of their dark cackling.

"Skeletons," she muttered. "Always laughing at nothing."

Time in Fester had introduced Peeve to every sort of monster. There were werewolves and vampires and people who talked too loud in the morning. Of all the creatures she'd met, skeletons were the least reliable. Peeve had chosen to work with them because there had been no other way.

She knew the taller skeleton was named Tempest. He waved at her from the back of the vessel like a pageant queen. The other skeleton—Bertram—could not wave, as he was holding his own skull in his hands like it was a dish he was bringing to a potluck dinner. Peeve stood there, a shiver running down her spine, waiting for them to continue rowing. It took a minute for her to realize the two skeletons would come no closer.

"Seriously?" she called. "It's freezing. Are you really going to make me walk out that deep?"

Bertram lifted his head up to get a good look at her.

"There can be no reward without risk," he replied.

Peeve rolled her eyes. "You mean you don't want to get out of the boat?"

Tempest cackled. "No, we don't want to get out of the boat."

"But you're just bones! The water isn't even *cold* to you."

Bertram's headless shoulders shrugged. "True, but getting out would be a whole ordeal. It will be far easier to make the exchange from the boat. More efficient that way."

"Besides," Tempest added, "you're already standing in the water! No harm done!"

Peeve bit her tongue. There was no point arguing. If she said the wrong thing, they might pack up and start rowing away. She couldn't afford for them to leave. Not when she'd already risked so much to get her hands on the package they were delivering. There was nothing else to do but grit her teeth and start forward. The dark water was nearly up to her stomach by the time she reached them.

"Hand over the money first," Bertram suggested. "No funny business."

There were several sacks sitting inside the little boat. Peeve knew the skeletons often made trips into the Land of Forgotten Stories. They'd return with items of great value, but always for a price. Tempest fetched the nearest sack, straining to set it upright. Peeve shook her head.

"I don't think so." She'd learned to never give the money first in an exchange. Not with disreputable creatures like skeletons. "You give me the scepter first."

Bertram looked ready to argue, but Tempest let out a mad cackle and tossed the sack overboard without a second thought. The waves started soaking the fabric, threatening to drown it completely. Peeve snatched the package before it could sink and pulled it to her chest. With her free hand, she reached into a pocket and removed a single, glinting coin. Both skeletons leaned forward greedily at the sight of her offered treasure.

Peeve was about to toss the payment to them, but she caught a glimpse inside the sack and paused. The object it held was most certainly *not* the weapon she'd requested.

"Seriously? This is just a bunch of coat hangers!"

Tempest pretended to be surprised. "Really? How did *those* get in there? How bizarre . . ." He hunted back through the other items on their boat. "Oh yes. Here it is."

The gangly skeleton grinned at her.

"Now, we can't risk you running off with it. Bertram?"

The shorter skeleton let out a sigh. "This is always so humiliating."

Peeve flinched when he hefted his skull up and threw it at her. She barely reacted in time, snatching his head before it could land in the water. She stood there, staring down at the empty eye sockets, unsure of what to say.

"Ouch. Don't squeeze so tight," Bertram complained.

Back on the boat, the rest of his body settled into a hands-on-hips gesture of disapproval. Tempest cackled like a madman again. "Now you pass us the coin. And *then* we'll give you the scepter. And *then* you give us Bertram. It's a win-win-win."

Peeve snorted. "That's really unnecessarily complicated."

She tossed the coin. Tempest caught it gracefully, tucking it who knows where, before tossing the *real* scepter overboard. This time it really did sink quickly. Peeve didn't have a second to think. She leaped after the scepter, releasing Bertram's head in the process. She heard a little shout as the waves started tugging his skull out to sea. Peeve yanked the scepter up, feeling its weight in her hands, as the skeletons shouted at one another.

"Sharks! Hurry, Tempest! Use the oar, you buffoon!"

In any other moment, Peeve might have laughed at the unfolding scene. Tempest was using the oar in an attempt to corral Bertram's skull back toward the boat. Except his bony arms were not the most coordinated, so he kept accidentally pushing his friend's skull under the water. Peeve was too busy admiring the scepter to enjoy any of that.

It wasn't activated, but she knew it was the right one because the scepter had a twin. How often had she seen it in her dreams? Peeve had witnessed exactly what the other scepter could do, and she had high hopes this one was just as potent. The thought brought a smile to her lips.

After a moment, Peeve looked up. The skeletons were both back in their boat. Tempest was waving goodbye. Bertram sat up front, skull comfortably in hand, watching her with a curious expression. He looked like he was going to leave without saying more, but at the very last moment, just before they were out of earshot, he called to her.

"It's the wrong one." The words echoed. "For someone like *you*."

Peeve returned his dark stare before nodding.

"We'll just see about that."

2

En Garde

Indira could teleport across a room with a throw of her hammer. She'd defeated a rogue Author *and* a corrupt brainstorm. She'd now successfully navigated two stories as a protagonist without much trouble. It was rare that she faced a foe and felt unprepared. Until now.

Her current nemesis? A fancy table setting.

She took her seat across from Phoenix. The tablecloth was so bright and white that she couldn't help imagining that even the slightest stain would ruin the whole look. There were *four* different forks. Each one of them was apparently for her. Phoenix grinned, but Indira couldn't stop glancing down at the various plates and utensils. As a big fan of the spork for its two-in-one quality, she found the table setting a little aggressive.

"Nice, isn't it?" Phoenix asked. "I thought you'd like it here."

He was wearing a tie. Indira had never seen him wear

7

a tie. He looked really handsome, but she couldn't help tugging at the collar of her homespun tunic. It was the same light pink one she'd always worn. Nothing fancy about it at all. Indira managed to smile back.

"Very nice," she said, eyeing the table again. "So many . . . spoons."

His grin widened. "I know it looks fancy, but trust me, you'll like it."

Indira raised a challenging eyebrow. "Yeah? How do you know that?"

"Just wait for it."

There were five other tables in the room, all spaced out in neat rows, with people seated at each. Indira couldn't help noticing that everyone else was older. This did feel like a very grown-up thing to do. She'd much rather have just ordered a pizza or something. The lighting in the room was a low amber color. Mrs. Pennington would have said the place had good *ambience*. Which, as far as Indira could tell, was a code word for *romantic, but in a very gloomy way*. She glanced around the room before looking back at Phoenix.

"What am I waiting—"

There was a bang as a set of double doors burst open. Indira started to reach for her hammer when two waiters thundered out from a back room, both wielding swords. They took several swipes at one another, feet dancing, as the second backed the first toward their table. The swords were little slashes of silver, more for fencing than for actual combat. Indira admired the great sweeps of metal and almost clapped when the first waiter kicked the second one in the chest, clearing out just enough space for him to turn briefly in their direction.

"Good evening, sir and madam. Welcome to En Garde. Where everything fights back, except for the food."

Without breaking eye contact, he fended off several strikes from the other waiter. They watched him use his off hand to remove two menus from a pocket on his apron. He continued his introduction, speaking between blows.

"The special . . ."

CLANG.

". . . is a roasted duck . . ."

CLANG.

". . . with a jam-infused pan sauce . . ."

He rolled unexpectedly to his right and jabbed upward, catching the other waiter right in the chest. The tip of his sword flexed satisfyingly, and the waiter pumped a fist in celebration.

"Point!" he shouted, before turning back to them. "The soup of the day is a chowder. And you'll find a list of age-appropriate drinks on the back. Our hubris is especially delicious, though we don't suggest drinking any if you're about to work on a new story. While the drink does inspire an initial burst of confidence, it regularly leads to a tragic downfall afterward. My personal favorite is the hyperbole soda. It is the *best* drink anyone will *ever* drink in their *entire* lives."

And with that, he was thrown back into a second duel. The swords clanged and the waiters spun, and a moment later they'd disappeared back into the kitchen. Indira threw a grin at Phoenix. His eyes were bright with twin flames. "Told you," he said.

The two of them glanced through the menus, joking about the words they didn't recognize. This was one of Phoenix's greatest talents. He had a knack for making Indira feel comfortable. After all, they'd been together since the beginning. Back when she'd lived in Origin, Indira had first met Phoenix while standing in line to take a dragoneye to Fable. She'd liked him right away. A quiet boy with smoldering irises? What wasn't to like about that? Ever since then, she'd only found more reasons to spend time with him. Phoenix was such a big part of her life in Fable that she'd pulled him into her sequel. The two of them had solved riddles and pulled off cool action sequences. It felt like they were the perfect combination.

Until Everest Smith arrived.

Indira's other love interest. She knew that the two boys *didn't* get along. As they'd built their Story House, they'd butted heads several times. She also knew that Everest Smith was the reason Phoenix had been trying so hard recently. Asking to hang out every day. Arranging dates in fancy restaurants like this one. He was afraid of losing her. Indira wanted to tell him that it would all be okay—of course Phoenix had a special place in her heart. But to her continued surprise, Indira found she really liked Everest, too. She'd been struggling with making a decision for weeks now.

"... you know what I mean?"

Indira blinked. "Huh?"

Phoenix tried to hide his disappointment. He'd clearly been talking about something for a while now, and Indira had drifted off in her own thoughts. Again. She shook her head a little, clearing out the cobwebs, and smiled at him. "Distracted by the menu. Sorry. Tell me again."

He launched back into a description of a new dragon power he was working on. Indira loved this side of him too. Phoenix was never satisfied. Like her, he was always trying to improve on the skills he'd already learned. It made him really fun to work with in a story.

". . . I'm pretty sure that will let me dive even faster in my dragon form. Just have to figure out how to do that with a rider on my back. We might need an upgraded harness."

Indira nodded. "I'm always up for a little more speed."

A moment later the waiters came to take their order, halfway through an epic boxing match. All the food was delicious. Indira and Phoenix made a game out of using the wrong utensils, laughing when the waiter scolded them for eating soup with the dessert spoon. But in between those moments, Indira couldn't help noticing how anxious Phoenix was. It was like he was watching her to make sure she was having fun, instead of just enjoying their time together.

After they'd eaten dessert, the waiters performed a final duel that involved slapping each other with a fish that was covered in pudding. Indira wasn't sure what story that was from, but as they paid their bill and left the restaurant, it was the first time she was ever glad to not be involved in a duel.

"I've got one more surprise for you," Phoenix said.

Indira almost told him she was tired and ready to go home. Her face hurt a little from smiling so much. It'd be nice to curl up alone for a while, maybe read a good book before bedtime. But there was something about that glint of fire in his eye that she couldn't resist.

"All right, but just one surprise."

A horse and buggy escorted them through the bright afternoon streets. Fable had been in an older time period for a few weeks now. The drive took them down a winding road and through a thick forest before bursting out into a sunny field. There was a building in the distance that looked like it was made almost entirely of glass. Indira saw a few other characters coming and going by the entrance. Phoenix led her out of the buggy, and she finally spotted the sign for the building.

THE OFFICIAL FAN ART MUSEUM

Indira had never been a *huge* museum person, but she did think it would be cool to see readers' interpretations of the famous characters she'd met over the years. No doubt some of her teachers would be featured on these walls. She knew some fan art even inspired spin-offs for entirely new versions of books. She hid a yawn as they walked through the brightly lit entrance. Phoenix directed her to an elevator at the far end of the room.

"This way."

Indira nudged his shoulder. "Please tell me we're not going to see Merlin fan art. I get that he's your wizard crush, but I'm not sure I can take another history lesson on *how he changed the role of wizards in stories forever.*"

That earned an eye roll from Phoenix. "He *did* change the role of wizards in stories forever, but no. I found something else I've been meaning to show you."

The elevator doors whisked open with a short chime. She was surprised to find no buttons, no method for choosing which floor to go to. That was kind of odd. Phoenix waited until the doors were fully closed before clearing his throat. "Show us the Indira Story hallway."

There was a beep of recognition, and the elevator began sliding upward. Indira couldn't help frowning over at Phoenix.

"But I've never been here before. How could I . . ."

He grinned at her. The doors whisked open again. The path led them into a small art gallery. Once more, Indira felt that brief nervousness at being in a place that was far too fancy for her liking. She didn't eat at nice restaurants. She didn't stroll through art galleries. Most days she did her best to make sure there weren't any stains on her clothing before walking out the door.

The feeling that she wasn't welcome didn't last for long.

"It's you."

Phoenix was right. The entire hallway was full of *her.* Indira was lured forward like a moth to flame. There was a bright painting featuring a cartoon version of her, hammer in mid-swing. One display held a small statue made out of colorful blocks. There were watercolors and digital drawings. Some of the images were executed by serious artists, but the dearest ones were those that had been drawn by a less steady hand. Amateur work, certainly, but created with as much love and care as she could have ever hoped for.

"This is all the fan art that your books have inspired," Phoenix explained. "I'm really fond of this particular drawing right here. . . ."

She grinned. It showed Phoenix transforming into a dragon, his massive, scaled form bursting out of a bathroom stall. She recognized it as the very first scene of her sequel.

"You did such a great job on that scene. It only took you one try!"

Phoenix snorted. "I was so nervous. The only reason it looked so realistic was because I was already sweating when I walked into the room for the first attempt."

Indira smiled at that memory. They kept making their way around the gallery. The collection likely fell short of some of the most well-read series in the world, but Indira found herself treasuring every brushstroke. Eventually, her attention was drawn back to the boy who'd been thoughtful enough to bring her here.

"Thanks, Phoenix. This is really cool."

He turned to face her. The two of them were close enough that she could smell that campfire scent she'd always loved. Their sequel had involved several hugs. A few times, they'd even held hands. But thinking about actually kissing Phoenix sent Indira's stomach tumbling end over end. Phoenix must have been thinking the same thing, because he was currently looking anywhere but at her. She considered being brave. Why not just plant a quick kiss on his cheek and get all the nervousness out of the way? She was about to do just that when Phoenix said, "Oh."

They'd unintentionally stopped in front of one of the final paintings. The artistic style was a little exaggerated. Every feature of the character on the canvas was a little *too* perfect. Indira knew he wasn't *that* muscular. And certainly his eyes weren't *that* blue. But the drawing had managed to capture the dark hair and the sharp jaw almost perfectly. The person who'd drawn this one was clearly a fan of Everest Smith.

The sight of her other romantic interest looming over them sucked all the wind out of Phoenix's sails. He looked completely uncomfortable now. She saw sweat running down his forehead. He tugged at his collar, like it was choking him, before saying, "Maybe . . . we should go."

Indira stood there, her cheeks bright red, and watched Phoenix walk back to the elevators. And, just like that, their date was ruined.

3

The Boy and the Moon

Indira desperately needed some time alone.

She always debated between the Story Houses from her first two books—and then, every now and again, she'd have sleepovers at Mrs. Pennington's new place. After an awkward goodbye with Phoenix, Indira headed for the Story House from her very first book. She knew Mrs. Pennington would have a hundred questions about the date. Questions she didn't really want to answer. And she also knew that Phoenix sometimes slept in their sequel Story House whenever he wasn't out of town for special dragon training. It would be easier to avoid everyone.

She was settling in to her evening routine when she heard a rattle by the window. Indira thought it was just the wind and ignored the sound. But it slowly transformed into a more distinct pattern. A knock, knock, knock. Groaning, she set down her toothbrush and crossed the room.

"It's probably Detective Malaprop again. Solving another case about missing shrubbery or something . . ."

Outside, it wasn't fully dark yet. Dusk still streaked the horizon with fading golds and reds. She was squinting through the window when a face swung into view. Indira let out a cry that turned into a laugh. Everest Smith pushed dark hair out of his eyes and grinned at her. He didn't say anything, just smiled and waved for her to follow him. She watched as he started walking off down the hill.

Always so confident. That side of him had annoyed Indira when they first met. He'd always been so certain about everything. After getting to know him, though, she'd realized she liked that about him. His confidence gave her confidence.

Everest always reminded her of the first time she'd come to Fable. Her mentor—Deus—had invited her to leap blindly off a cliff, trusting that a bird would appear and catch her. Every moment with Everest felt a little like that leap. Adventurous and scary and exhilarating. Indira slipped out into the lengthening shadows. Her heart beat faster as she jogged to catch up with him.

"Everest! Wait! Where are we going?"

"It's a surprise," he called back.

The slight British accent always melted her. It had been a few weeks since she'd talked with him. That happened with Everest. He vanished sometimes—as a part of the story, she'd assumed—and initially she'd counted it as a mark against him. But he always came back, and the first person he wanted to see when he did was Indira. They walked up a winding trail. Everest slowed enough so that they were side by side, their shoulders bumping every few seconds. Indira had a hundred questions, but she also kind of liked how Everest sometimes didn't need to say anything at all. They walked in silence until the road led them to a small overlook. There was a lovely valley below. The last streaks of day were fading.

"I thought you didn't like sunsets," Indira said. "You said they were cheesy."

He smiled at that. "I said they're *overrated.*"

"And yet here we are, looking at a sunset."

"Not here for the sunset," he corrected. "We're waiting for the moon and the stars."

As the last light vanished from the horizon, pinprick stars began to appear in the looming black. They'd walked a decent distance from the nearest neighborhoods, which meant the sky was bright and clear and full. Indira admired the constellations, sneaking occasional glances at Everest. He'd joined their crew about halfway through the sequel. No one had known what to expect, because he was a plot twist from the Author. Indira was the only one who wasn't surprised. After all, Brainstorm Underglass had promised that a second romantic interest was coming. She just hadn't told Indira that he'd be someone like Everest. Indira *knew* it wasn't fair to compare him with Phoenix, but she had a feeling her third book was going to make her choose between them. How could making a choice like that ever be fair?

Everest grinned. "Indira Story. Always thinking."

She smiled back. "You give me so much to think about."

"Well, I'm about to give you a little more to think about. I've got a secret. Pretty sure it was meant to come out in book three. It's a bit of a spoiler, so make sure to act very surprised when it happens in the book. But I've been dying to show someone for ages now. And who better than you?"

"You have a secret? Everest Smith has a secret? How shocking."

His grin widened. They'd joked a lot about how the Author had made him so mysterious in the book. She watched curiously as he backed away a few steps. Clouds were drifting overhead. She saw the moon trying to peek through. Everest spread both arms wide.

"This is my secret. I am a *walshy*."

"Walshy?" Indira repeated. "That's fun to say."

Another grin. "We are an ancient folk. Three things in one. Part human. Part guardian. And part . . . well . . . it's best if I show you. . . ."

Moonlight filled the clearing. Indira was briefly blinded by a flash of silver light. She held her hand up to block the glare, and in that moment, the boy version of Everest vanished. A creature emerged where he'd been standing, padding around on paws nearly as wide as tree trunks. Indira had never seen anything quite so regal and majestic. A great white wolf sniffed the air. Its eyes looked like chips of blue ice. Indira stared for a moment before realizing she was looking at *Everest*.

"You can transform into a *wolf*?"

A low growl sounded. Indira knew it wasn't a threatening growl. It was an invitation. He huffed a little before lowering his right flank to the ground. Indira didn't hesitate at all. She climbed onto his fur-lined back and saw that his beaded necklace had transformed into a special collar. It offered her a place to slide her hands in for a solid grip. When she was settled and ready, she tapped his side with one knee. The way he sprang forward left her breathless.

Everest aimed for the nearest forest. Trees blurred on both sides of them. Every time he landed, it felt like they were already leaping again. She leaned down against his neck and let out a delighted whoop. It reminded her—with a slight jolt of guilt—of the first time she'd ridden on Phoenix's back. It was a very different experience, though. Phoenix had speed when he was diving, but for most of his flight he was sweeping through the air. A breathless glide. And being a dragon offered great heights and dizzying views. In contrast, Everest was pure adrenaline. The way he darted down the forest trail, barely missing the outstretched arms of trees, all purely by instinct. Indira loved how fearless he was.

They made their way through the Fable countryside for what felt like hours. A few times, Indira caught glimpses of Climactic Mountain in the distance. It was the highest point in all of Imagination. There were little towns, too, lit up like fireflies in the night. She wondered which characters lived there now and if they were dreaming of going to Fable, the way she once had.

Indira was almost disappointed when she realized their path had taken them in a wide circle, and her neighborhood loomed ahead. Everest slid to a stop outside her back window, panting a little. She climbed down and scratched him behind an ear. She laughed when he rolled over on his back, tongue lolling.

"Thanks for sharing your secret with me," Indira whispered.

He rolled back over and nuzzled her outstretched hand. For a second she stood there, one hand on the bridge of his nose, the wild eyes of a wolf staring back at her. Learning about this side of Everest explained a lot. He'd had a habit of disappearing during her sequel, sometimes when she'd needed him most. Now she realized he'd always vanished during the full moon. It also explained his lone-wolf attitude when they'd first met. Pretending like he didn't need her help, or even want her friendship.

But that had changed over the course of the story. By the end of her sequel, Everest was completely loyal to her. She wondered if that was because his pack senses had kicked in. As if Indira had become part of his crew, and now he'd do anything to protect her.

Indira was also painfully aware that her Author had set up two romantic interests, one who transformed into a dragon and one who transformed into an ancient creature

21

similar to a werewolf. It didn't seem fair. She liked them both.

Everest didn't transform back into a boy. Instead he nuzzled her hand one more time and loped off into the night. Indira stood there watching until the forest swallowed the sight of him. She was heading back inside when she heard a distant and wild sound. She smiled a little, knowing that that particular howl was just for her. The smile faded, though, as she got ready for bed.

There was the boy who always made her feel at home, the one who turned into a dragon. And then there was the boy who always drew her into adventure, the one who howled at the moon.

How was she supposed to choose?

4

Breaking Point

Unfortunately, the decision didn't get any easier.

The boys seemed intent on one-upping each other. When Phoenix heard that Everest was back in Fable, he planned another date for Indira. The two of them hiked over to Rhyming Canyon, where no matter how hard someone tried, they couldn't avoid rhyming with the person who'd spoken before them. Indira cleverly ended a sentence with the word *orange* and the two of them were promptly kicked out by a park ranger.

Not to be outdone, Everest took Indira to the very first "fourth wall" that had ever been broken. It was a great crumbled mess, and if they listened closely, they could hear the whispers of surprised audience members in the Real World. The next day, Phoenix took her to an escape room with famous symbolism from successful books. They got stumped by a random green light that some guy named Gatsby refused to stop staring at.

Next, Everest snuck Indira into a tavern called Epilogue. If you flipped a coin into a fountain there, he said, you could hear the last line of your very last story. Indira thought the idea sounded a little sad, but Everest flipped his coin and grinned back at her.

"The end of one thing is usually just the beginning of something else."

She liked that attitude.

But she *didn't* like the inevitable blowup that followed. She hadn't realized that the boys kept running into each other. Phoenix would swing by to see if Indira was home, only to catch a glimpse of her leaving with Everest. And Everest would be picking up something in town, only to spot her and Phoenix heading into the local ice cream spot. The tension between them grew and grew until it finally boiled over one night.

Indira was hanging out at the Story House when she heard raised voices, shouting back and forth. She walked out onto her balcony and found Everest and Phoenix standing nose to nose in the courtyard below. Phoenix already had fire in his eyes. And even from above, she could tell that the hairs on the back of Everest's neck were standing up.

"Do we have a problem?" Everest said, voice as calm as a breeze.

"I don't know," Phoenix fired back. "Do we?"

Feeling like they were on the verge of a fight, Indira ran back through the Story House, heading downstairs and out the front door. She found the two boys still sizing each other up. Phoenix's chest was pumping up and down in anger. Everest looked infuriatingly calm about it all.

". . . I was here first."

Everest snorted. "Since when does arriving *first* make someone the *best* fit for anything? That's not how it works."

"You're just a brooding side character. Someone the Author shoves into the story to complicate things. It's not like you're really *competition* for me."

"Oh yeah?" Everest replied. "Then why are you *so* worried?"

Indira was about twenty paces away. She felt her own heart racing. There were books that made it sound really fun to have two people fighting over you. But this was the opposite of fun. In fact, she felt anger building in her own chest. The way they were talking made it sound like it was up to the two of them to figure out who was the right choice for her. As if she didn't have a say in the matter. She was about to tell them to stop when Phoenix gave the slightest shove.

Everest stumbled back. She saw him transition smoothly into a fighting stance. He casually lifted his right hand up into the air, as if he was about to catch something. It looked strange—and Phoenix almost laughed at the gesture—but Indira knew exactly what Everest was about to do.

The two of them had a secret. It had happened at the end of their sequel. She hadn't told anyone else yet. After all the other characters had left, a final room had opened up for Indira and Everest. The very last scene in the book.

It was one of the reasons she'd been so conflicted. No one she'd ever met could lift her hammer. Not even Deus Ex Machina was powerful enough. It had always been attuned to her, and her alone.

Until Everest.

Now he called on that shared magic. The hammer at her hip trembled slightly before vanishing altogether. Power echoed between them like a strike of lightning. The weapon appeared in Everest's hand. He pointed it at Phoenix.

"If I'm not a threat, how is it that I can wield *this*?"

Indira's anger was a living thing. He'd revealed their secret to show off. Without even asking her. It didn't help that Phoenix was being a jerk too. It was all too much. As the boys circled, ready for a fight, she summoned the hammer back into her hand. Everest and Phoenix both looked up in surprise as she pointed it threateningly at them instead.

"I am *not* a prize to be won," she said. "I do not *belong* to anyone. You do not get to decide who is best for me. *I* get to decide that. And right now, I'm deciding that *neither* of you is good enough. Look at you. Fighting like a couple of low-level antagonists. You're better than this. Or at least I thought you were. Do me a favor and stay away from the Story House for a while. If I want to see one of you, I'll come looking for you. I need some space from . . ." She gestured at the two of them, frozen in their ridiculous fighting stances. "From whatever this is supposed to be."

Indira left them there, both stunned into silence. She really didn't want to hear any explanations right now. She was tired of thinking about what would happen in her third book, tired of wondering which boy was the right one for her. She hated to admit it, but she needed a vacation.

Her feet carried her to the right place on instinct. Up the stairs, third condominium on the right. She knocked a few times. The door opened and a powerful gust of cinnamon almost dropped her to the floor. She'd always been a sucker for Mrs. Pennington's baked goods. Her favorite mom stood there in pajamas, a mixing bowl cradled in one arm.

In the background, Patch was sprinting away from Mrs. Pennington's fiancé—Jack—and appeared to have underwear on his head. Jack lunged and missed, accidentally stepping on a toy as he did. He let out a cry of pain as Patch escaped, giggling his way into the other room. Mrs. Pennington looked about as exhausted as Indira felt.

"I think it's time for a vacation."

Mrs. Pennington was so shocked by those words that she dropped her mixing bowl, but Indira knew that was coming. The two of them had a history of surprises and broken baked goods. She caught the bowl mid-fall. Both of them laughed and went inside to make the necessary phone call.

Indira had been resisting an invitation to go somewhere for months now, thinking that vacation sounded a little boring. But now she thought boring was exactly what she needed. Their unofficial travel agent picked up on the third ring.

"Operation vacation is a green light," Indira said.

There was a loud *squee* on the other end of the line.

"I've *totally* got the perfect place," Maxi said. "What are your thoughts on massages? You know what? Don't answer that. You don't actually know what you want. I will be your tour guide through this strange and foreign world known as Relaxation. It is my home planet. I have lived there my entire life. Allow me to show you around. Can you leave tomorrow?"

Indira and Mrs. Pennington exchanged a glance. There was a loud boom in the other room. Patch came sprinting back out into the living room with a board game clutched in his little hands, pieces bouncing away every few steps he took. Indira nodded at her mother, who answered for both of them.

"Absolutely."

5

Vacation

Indira stood on an abandoned shore, tracing the progress of a small Jet Ski as it made its way across the sunlit cove. It was an absolutely stunning day. Sunlight chased across the crystal-clear water. A pleasant breeze whispered over the dunes. Indira dug her toes into the sand before squinting once more out to sea. The sight made her smile. Mrs. Pennington was on the back of the Jet Ski, whooping like a banshee.

So far it had been a wonderful vacation.

It was nice to have some girl time: just her, Mrs. Pennington, and Maxi. Indira eyed the rest of the beach. It really was *just* the three of them. Maxi had gone a little too far in her promise that this would be an exclusive vacation. She'd edited the other reservations and canceled everyone else's stay at the Chapter Break Resort for this week.

Other than the three of them, Indira had only run into

the hotel waitstaff. She could see them back on the terrace now, polishing glasses and plates that likely wouldn't be used.

"Relax," Maxi said, surprising Indira.

Her friend was lying on a towel to her right. Indira had thought — based on the slight snoring — that Maxi had drifted off to sleep. Indira frowned at her.

"I am relaxed."

"Yeah? Then why are you reaching for your hammer?"

Indira looked down and realized her hand had indeed been hovering at her hip, set right above the spot where her hammer usually hung. She was wearing a bathing suit now, however, and her hammer had been locked away in her room. Maxi had insisted that Indira not train while she was out here. There would be no fighting. No epic plots. No misadventures. Nothing to ruin their vacation. Annoyed at being caught, Indira distractedly ran her fingers through the sand.

"I've never done *nothing*," she replied after a moment. "It's weird."

Maxi smiled. "You mean it's *nice*. Tomorrow, *nothing* is a full-body massage. And the day after that, *nothing* is going to be us snorkeling off the coast there. You need a little *nothing* in your life."

Indira nodded. She was doing her best to feel excited about *nothing*.

"I'm trying, Maxi. It's just hard. What do you see when you look out there?"

30

Maxi followed Indira's gaze. "A pretty ocean."

"An ocean," she confirmed. "But I can't look out there without imagining someone standing on the other side of this ocean. Except they're not on vacation. They're plotting to ruin the world."

Maxi turned over on her towel, allowing the sun to soak her back.

"You have problems. There's no one out there. Everything is fine."

Indira let out a breath. "Right. You're probably right."

Mrs. Pennington was stumbling up the beach, her hair windswept from the Jet Ski. Indira was grateful her mother had been able to come. She'd left Patch with her new fiancé. Maxi had spent the previous two dinners at the resort extracting every single detail she could about how they'd met. Mrs. Pennington had explained what a "meet-cute" was. Apparently, she'd first met her fiancé in a hilarious but unfortunate laundry incident. Indira had never seen her so happy, and she was clearly comfortable enough to leave Patch with him.

"I wish my story had been set on a tropical island instead of in Chicago!" Mrs. Pennington said, beaming. "This is the best vacation."

Maxi made a noise. "Tell Indira that. She's too busy dreaming of fighting evil with that hammer of hers."

"Am not," Indira replied with a smile.

Mrs. Pennington swept that thought away with the back of her hand. "There's always time for that in your next story. Why not try Jet-Skiing instead? Far more exhilarating. And the good thing about Jet Skis? They can't hit you back."

Indira laughed. The three of them sat in the sun for a while, drinking in the rays, before heading back inside to get ready for dinner. The Chapter Break Resort was a famous rest stop for characters. The hotel claimed to be the very *first* chapter break to ever exist. I'm sure you're familiar, my dear reader, with that brief pause that you're offered between chapters. It's the spot where, late at night, a reader can comfortably set the book aside, if they so desire, to get some sleep. It's also a little marker of reward for both reader and writer. A reminder that we're progressing nicely through the book and deserve a pat on the back for how far we've already come.

You might not know, though, that those breaks are equally important for the characters in a story. It would be such a bother to run on from scene to scene, acting everything out, barely catching one's breath. A good chapter break really gives the characters a chance to sit back, gather themselves, and return to entertaining you with true gusto.

The Chapter Break Resort's motto reflected that idea: *When we rest, we're at our best!*

Indira had an entire suite to herself. It overlooked the shining cove below. She stood in front of a mirror, getting dressed in a slightly more formal outfit. She supposed it didn't matter much what she wore, given there were no other guests at the hotel. As she got ready, it was hard to ignore the little tingle that ran down her spine. A soft whisper that said she should open the room's lockbox and fetch her hammer. What would it hurt to tuck it into her belt? Just in case?

Indira ignored the voice, though. "No. I'm on vacation. No *plots*."

She was corralling her hair into a ponytail when she saw a flicker of movement. There—in the corner of the mirror—for just a whisper of a second. She stared at the spot, drawn curiously forward. But the longer she stared, the clearer it was that nothing was there. Her brain was so used to action scenes and hidden riddles that she was trying to force conflict into her own vacation.

A few minutes later, Maxi knocked at her door, shouting something about free appetizers down on the terrace. Indira laughed as she joined her friend.

"Why the rush, Maxi? There's no one to eat them except us."

"But still! We should get them while they're hot!"

And with that, the two of them started downstairs. Neither one saw the brief flicker of a shadow in the mirror. The form—so like a person—taking shape.

6

Stranger Things

Vacation continued on in a pleasant fashion.

Indira enjoyed the great food. After dinner, Mrs. Pennington arranged for them to make s'mores out by the firepit. The next morning, Indira enjoyed a massage, and the trio fell asleep in the shadows cast by a grove of palm trees on the beach. It was truly the kind of rest her body needed.

But Indira spent her early mornings—before the others woke up—pacing back and forth. Her eyes would dart over to the lockbox set in the wall, fingers itching to hold her hammer and run through practice exercises. She was built for saving worlds, not for little chocolates set on pillows each night, even if those were nice.

On her fifth day at the resort, Indira finally noticed the unwelcome guest.

She was pacing the room, from one end to the other, when she saw that flicker of movement in the mirror again.

Only this time it was more than a flicker. It was a shadow, shaped like a person. She watched as the shadow began to take on form and color. Alarm bells rang in Indira's mind. Her first heroic encounter had involved a magical mirror. She'd never forget that dark room and the disembodied voice and her classmates set out like dolls. Nor would she forget the dark laugh of Brainstorm Ketty as she tried to perform unthinkable magic using a mirror.

Indira set her feet, ready for anything, only to find herself staring at a monkey. She had certainly seen stranger things, but this still ranked high on the list. It was a rather odd sight for a number of reasons. First, it was clearly not a monkey. It was a person about the same height as Indira who was wearing an almost cartoonish monkey mask. Two eyes stared out from behind the painted features. Indira waited for the person to speak, but they stood as still as a statue.

It took a moment for Indira to remember that mirrors were reflections. She spun around, thinking the monkey was in the room behind her, but no one was there. Her attention swung back. Was this some strange magic from the hotel? The housekeepers folded the towels into snakes and other creatures each time they cleaned. Was this like that?

She approached cautiously, but the monkey didn't so much as blink. Its chest did not move up or down. It stood there like a still-life painting. Indira moved close enough to truly inspect the creature. It was a woman, she noted. There were a few blond curls running out just behind the mask, down to the shoulders. She wore a sort of farmhouse dress. After inspecting the woman from head to toe, Indira finally found her voice.

"Who are you?"

No response. The eyes did not blink. The head did not turn. Indira wandered off to the right. Then back to the left. She could not seem to draw a reaction. In a final effort, she darted forward, pretending she was going to poke the monkey right in the eye.

A hand shot up like a strike of lightning. Indira let out a gasp as the monkey's grip closed around her wrist. The woman set her feet and yanked Indira headfirst toward the glass. Indira's cry vanished with her, leaving the room empty and silent, except for the slight wobble of the mirror as it shook, then settled.

And just like that she was *elsewhere.*

———

Elsewhere might have been fine, if not for the sack someone jammed over her head. Indira squirmed a little, but a set of very strong hands guided her forward. She heard several voices now, and when she thrashed in earnest, a rather deep voice responded.

"None of that, Ms. Story. We need only a moment of your time."

For a while, Indira bumped along helplessly. She couldn't see a thing, but she did hear the sound of water nearby. No salt in the air, though, which meant it wasn't the ocean. At some point, she thought she could smell lavender. Then the warmth of the sun faded from the backs of her legs and she heard a door slam shut. She was forced to sit in a chair. Indira waited there for a moment before realizing the hand on her shoulder was gone.

She scrambled to take off the sack on her head, which left her as the only one in the room without a face-covering. Seven cartoonish animals watched her. She saw the blinking, human eyes that hid behind each mask. In the silence, she did her best to memorize eye colors and shapes. Little details someone else might not notice. Details that might help her later, if there ever was a later. The masked entourage sat around a half-moon table, some lounging comfortably, others sharp and straight-backed. Indira considered them all, one by one.

There was the monkey she'd seen in the mirror. It waved tauntingly. But there was also a baboon, two snakes, a lion, a wolf, and a bright bird.

"Welcome, Ms. Story," one of the snakes said, "to the Underground."

Indira glanced over one shoulder, considering escape routes. Unfortunately, a massive man stood behind her sporting a bear mask. It would be hard to get past him. Indira turned back, doing her best to remain calm. "You know, you could have just sent a normal invitation in the mail."

The monkey smiled. "We're not a normal group."

"And that gives you the right to kidnap people?"

"Kidnap?" The wolf laughed. "Not at all, dear. We were just curious to meet you."

"Yes," the bear added from behind her. "We're familiar with your heroics. We were also told that, once upon a time, you considered visiting our neck of the woods."

"Your neck of the woods," Indira repeated. "I'm assuming you're from Fester?"

Snickers sounded all around the table. So she'd guessed right. These were bad guys, antagonists. She wasn't sure why they'd go through all this trouble for her, but she knew that she couldn't trust anyone who'd made their home in Fable's rival city.

"Well, is it true?" the wolf asked. "Did you really consider visiting our wonderful school?"

Indira shrugged. "Yes, but I made the right decision. I stayed in Fable."

"Don't worry. We count the thought of coming in your favor," one of the snakes replied. "Some of your peers are so self-righteous. Pretending to be all good all the time. We were hoping to work with a hero who has a little more . . . gray, if you catch my meaning."

"I'm not like you," Indira answered. "I think my actions prove that."

The other snake giggled before waving a little folder. "Oh, I think your actions say a great deal. We've been going over your file for some time now. Quite a track record. Failing auditions. Blaming everyone else. Believing the worst about your friends. Breaking and entering the home of an advisor. Ruining someone else's dreams of starting a new life . . ."

Indira was speechless. She'd never heard someone interpret the events of her first year of school that way. None of what they were saying was *actually* true.

"Really? You mean Brainstorm Ketty? She abused her power and secretly sabotaged other characters. I didn't 'ruin' someone else's dream. I stopped her from destroying our entire *world.*"

The wolf shrugged. "You say tomato, I say to-mah-to."

Indira shook her head. "That's ridiculous."

"And quite the point," the bird interrupted, voice sharp as a knife. The other masked figures all fell quiet. Indira took note. They clearly respected this particular member. "Sometimes you have to be bad to do a little good. Don't you agree, Indira Story?"

Indira couldn't stop herself from nodding. She didn't trust any of them, especially not after being kidnapped this way, but she did agree with those words, at least. "It depends on the situation, but sure. Sometimes you have to do something that other people think is bad in order to help the greater good."

The eyes inside the bird mask sparkled a little. The others were leaning forward hungrily. Indira had a feeling she'd just said exactly what they were hoping to hear.

The baboon spoke. "And what would you say to an offer like that? To being bad in order to help the greater good?"

"Sorry. I'm on vacation."

The monkey snorted. "We've been watching you. You don't like vacation. You can't wait to get back into the action."

Indira bit her tongue. The monkey was right. What was the point in arguing? She'd been itching to pick up her hammer all week. "So, what's this *greater good* I can help you all with? Because I'm sure a group of antagonists have really pure motives. . . ."

The baboon answered again. "That requires a bit of backstory. Right now, Fester is run by the Demon Initiative. Bainrow and his crew of demons took over seven years ago. It was our own fault. We were getting lazy in how we ran the school. Not investing enough in our new characters. We had our worst year of auditions in almost a century. Very poor performances. Bainrow saw the scores and knew it was an opportunity to take control of the school."

The wolf nodded. "He stepped in and offered a solution to the problem."

"And what solution was that?" Indira asked.

The lion answered, "Evil. A purer kind of evil."

The baboon picked up the story. "And that is Fester's current strategy. Make characters evil. We no longer develop conflicted characters who are both good and bad. Bainrow and his sort believe a true villain is someone without any morals at all. Characters who are evil simply for the sake of being evil."

"And while we do need *some* of those villains," the monkey noted, "making *every* villain the same will ruin stories.

We've made efforts to reduce the damage he's created. Teaching different strategies to students when we're not being monitored. Recruiting characters to our cause who don't like his style. All of that has been working. Until now."

The baboon nodded. "Now he's performing the Final Boss Protocol."

A little shiver ran through the group. She saw uncomfortable glances being exchanged. "Final Boss Protocol? Like in video games? You fight little guys for most of the stage until you reach the final boss?"

"Exactly," the baboon answered. "Bainrow was in the Final Boss Faction when he attended Antagonist Academy. It's the kind of villain he believes in. Why be a henchman when you can be the boss? Why be a little bad when you can be *really* bad? We learned about the Final Boss Protocol at great cost. Lost several of our best agents."

Indira frowned. "But what is it?"

"A ritual spell," the lion answered. "He'll perform it a month from now. His plan is to start the spell on the anniversary of the day Antagonist Academy was founded. It will permanently change how our world works. Every antagonist will be powered up. Far bigger, far badder. His protocol will make every antagonist into a Final Boss."

Indira didn't like the sound of that at all. A bunch of bad guys with extra powers and extra strength? But there was one thing she didn't understand. "Why wouldn't *you* want that? You *are* the bad guys."

The baboon shook its head. "Haven't you been listening? Making all antagonists the same would ruin stories.

Not everyone needs a rocket launcher or a bone helmet to be a proper villain! We need rival basketball players who are just a *little* bad. Surprise enemies who only turn on the protagonist at the very end of the story. We need characters capable of small revenges and quiet villainy. Bainrow's spell eliminates all but one type of villain."

"Imagine a toolbox," the lion added. "Some tasks require a saw. Others need a hammer or a wrench. Every tool has its job. Bainrow's plan will reduce our toolbox to a single spiked sledgehammer. Chaos will follow. Bad stories always lead to bored readers. And a generation of bored readers? Our world's very existence is at stake."

Indira understood that much. Last year, in Ordinary, she'd faced a similar problem. A rogue Author named Joey had unintentionally altered stories so that they were all the same. Thanks to her crew, they'd avoided a similar fate to the one the masked figures were describing. Indira still didn't understand what they wanted *her* to do, however.

"Right, and how exactly do I come into the equation?"

"Bainrow's spell is powered by something called the Gemini Scepter," the baboon answered. "We want you to steal the scepter. That way, the spell can never happen. And when Bainrow is without his main source of power, we can overthrow him for good. We will get the school back on the right track. Which means you and your heroic friends get better rivals. Stories will improve. It's a win-win scenario."

That all sounded rather promising, but Indira couldn't help pointing out the flaw in the plan. "So . . . you'd like me to help you?"

They all nodded.

"A group who kidnapped me, won't show their faces, and haven't even told me their real names? Sounds like a great foundation for a relationship. A lot of trust."

The lion answered. "We're just being cautious. Bainrow has ways to . . . extract information from you. If you see our faces . . . it's necessary that we cover our tracks."

Indira frowned at that. "But you didn't answer the question. Who are you?"

The animals hesitated. One by one, they shot secretive glances in the direction of the bird. Indira filed that away with the rest of what she'd learned. Definitely the leader of the group.

"We're the Antiheroes," the bird answered. "We're good guys with a dark side. Bad guys with a soft spot. Not all dark. Not all light. We're somewhere in the middle."

Indira didn't hate the sound of that. It left just one more question.

"Why me? Why not some other student who's already at your school?"

"We've recruited other students to our cause. But . . ." The lion waved Indira's file in the air. "You've proven you're one of the best. Simply put, you get the job done. And, to be perfectly honest, we know you actually care about doing good in this world. A lot of our students struggle with the concept of good deeds. It doesn't come naturally to them. Our first attempts at a similar heist did not go well. The student tried to betray us."

"You can always say no. Go on, enjoy the rest of your vacation. Get a few more massages and go back to Fable." He shrugged. "But we're inviting you to save the world. Again. We're inviting you to be the hero you've always been. We're also inviting you to be . . . a little bad."

She could tell from their eyes that there were grins hiding under every mask. Indira knew she should tell them no. There was almost zero chance she could trust a single rotten one of them. But she'd been curious about Fester for a long time now. And the idea of going on a new adventure . . .

A grin spread over her face too.

"What do I do?"

7

Choices

Indira returned through the magic mirror with a few directives.

She also returned to a rather concerned pair of loved ones. Maxi thundered to her feet, ready to ask a million questions. Mrs. Pennington was pointing from Indira to the mirror and back again.

"I thought we'd sworn off magic mirrors!" Maxi said. "In fact, I very distinctly recall us agreeing that, like, we'd never use magic mirrors *ever* again."

"I can explain, Maxi. . . ."

And she did. She was definitely intending to work with the Antiheroes, but not before investigating them as thoroughly as possible. Maxi started casing the room immediately. She took a set of fingerprints off the mirror, which she noted was a different design from the mirrors in both her room and Mrs. Pennington's. Someone had placed it in Indira's room on purpose. After a rather long discussion, Maxi suggested what Indira had already been planning on doing.

"You should take this to Brainstorm Underglass."

Indira nodded. "I will."

Mrs. Pennington sighed. "So . . . our vacation is over?"

"You can both stay!" Indira answered quickly. "I mean it. Don't let me stop you from enjoying your vacation, Mrs. P. You deserve it. . . ."

But her mother was already waving the thought away. "I'm not sure I can sleep here thinking about monkey-masked individuals appearing in mirrors. Let's go ahead and get packed up. Besides, I'm pretty sure my backside is sore from all the Jet-Skiing."

Maxi let out a little hoot of laughter. "Okay. We go back together. I'll look into the prints I pulled off that mirror. I'll also check the database for everything we've got on the Antiheroes. Let's make sure you know what you're getting yourself into."

———

An overnight train brought them back into Fable's welcoming arms.

Indira smiled as they pulled into the station. The city had slipped into a new costume, as it always did. Now Fable looked like a sprawling farm town nestled in a lush valley. There were brooks babbling here and there. The buildings looked more like cabins, all with their doors brightly painted.

Instead of the typical exterior walls, the city was now enclosed by great groves of apple trees. All the Marks she could see from the station were going out, dressed in overalls and farmhouse dresses, to begin picking. The bright slashes of leaves proclaimed it was autumn, and the crisp air that greeted them on the platform confirmed that fact.

"It's so wonderful."

Maxi groaned. "Historical settings. Always makes the paperwork so much harder. All our computers vanish. Can't wait to thumb through dusty textbooks for the next few hours."

Mrs. Pennington was all smiles, though. "Patch will want to go apple picking!"

All three of them said their goodbyes at the platform. Maxi threw on her Editor's sunglasses, gave Indira a hug, and vanished with a promise to get Indira information ASAP. Mrs. Pennington kissed Indira lightly on the cheek. "Have fun, dear!"

Indira frowned at that. "No warnings about being careful?"

Mrs. Pennington shrugged. "I'm not sure if it's all the Jet-Skiing, or just the fact that you've already saved the world twice. You know what you're doing at this point, my dear. I could tell you to be careful, but you *are* careful. So why not just tell you to have fun instead?"

Her mother started walking off down the platform before remembering something. She turned back around, a little grin on her face. "Oh! And tell Phoenix hello for me!

Or Everest! You know, just go ahead and tell *both* of them hello. Such lovely boys!"

Indira hadn't mentioned that the whole reason for her vacation was to get away from both boys. Her cheeks colored a little, and she was thankful when Mrs. Pennington turned around and kept walking toward the exit. It gave her a chance to quietly recover. It was ridiculous that she felt this way, that their names could have this kind of effect on her. As she headed for Protagonist Preparatory, she couldn't help imagining the two of them standing side by side.

Phoenix had a flop of untidy red hair, freckles scattered across both cheeks, and sparks of flame that kicked to life in his eyes when he saw Indira. Then there was Everest, with his dark hair, deep-set blue eyes, and slight accent. Phoenix was down-to-earth, almost nervous at times. Everest was confident, on the verge of cocky. One was the friend who'd been there for her since the start. The other was the boy who could send a shiver down her spine with just a look. Each one had his positives and negatives.

"And neither of them will be in Fester," she whispered to herself.

Why worry about that choice now? A special mission in the heart of Fester was just what she needed. It'd be nice to focus on something meaningful before the final book in her trilogy came along. Before she had to choose. Indira shook herself. "You've got a job to do."

Distracted, she nearly walked right into the middle of a construction site. It was a little unusual to see someone making repairs to Fable, a city that repaired itself every few weeks. Indira saw a girl wearing a helmet and wielding a jackhammer. She was bent over her work, happily drilling into a small section of courtyard out in front of Protagonist Preparatory. It wasn't until Indira circled around the spot that she recognized the girl.

"Gadget?"

There was a brief pause in the jackhammer's repeating punches. Gadget looked around in confusion before spotting Indira. Her eyes went wide as she killed the power.

"Indira! What's up? Thought you were on vacation!"

She smiled. "I was, but it's good to be back. What are you doing?"

Gadget had marked off a small section with bright cones. The girl gestured nervously to the beginnings of a square-shaped hole she was hammering out.

"You know . . . routine city maintenance. I get to do the occasional . . . renovation."

Indira couldn't help smiling. Gadget was always so nervous, but she'd formed a deep bond with her during their Hero's Journey tutorial. It had helped to be partnered up with someone who was truly different from her.

"Looks great. I'm heading in to visit Underglass. Maybe I'll see you later!"

Gadget jumped a little. "Right, later, yeah!"

Half laughing, Indira turned back to the entrance of

Protagonist Preparatory. The school had been reshaped by the city's magic into one of the most massive farmhouses she'd ever seen. The entrance had been converted into a pair of giant barn doors. As always, they stood wide open in welcome. Indira walked through them with a smile.

This part always felt like coming home.

8

The Great Exchange

A knock at Brainstorm Underglass's door was greeted with a call to enter.

When Indira's previous mentor had hatched a plot to ruin her life, Brainstorm Underglass had been gracious enough to take Indira under her wing. The two of them had developed a close relationship since then. This office was a safe space, with a long-earned comfort that Indira always treasured. Not to mention it was twenty times neater than any other room Indira spent time in.

"Indira!" Underglass offered a rare smile. "I thought you were on vacation."

She nodded. "I just got back. It was . . . refreshing."

There was a moo from the corner. Indira raised an eyebrow, noticing for the first time that the city's farmhouse setting had extended into the brainstorm's office. A cow munched on something that looked like grass. It eyed Indira with disinterest, before mooing again and grazing in the opposite corner. Brainstorm Underglass offered the creature an annoyed look before picking the conversation back up.

"Refreshing?" she asked. "I know *you* don't think it was refreshing—no doubt you were itching for a little action the entire time—but I hope you know how important it is to turn off your mind from time to time. Just what the doctor ordered. I was thinking . . ."

Indira coughed, trying to interrupt as politely as possible. "I know what I want to do next."

Underglass paused. "Certainly. It's your time, after all. And you can do what you wish."

"What do you know about the Antiheroes?"

It took just a few minutes for Indira to relay the events that had occurred at the Chapter Break Resort. She did her best to include the most crucial details she could remember. The various animal masks. The general heights of the people seated around the table. Who'd talked the most and in what tone of voice. Brainstorm Underglass took rather thorough notes, choosing not to speak until Indira finished.

"Interesting," she said, leaning back in her chair. "I've heard of them. The Antiheroes have been on our radar for a few years now. We knew there was unrest when Brainstorm Bainrow took over as the head of the school. But we also knew that was normal. Not everyone was happy when I was appointed to my position. It is how life goes. People disagree, especially when power is at stake. But the reasoning in Bainrow's case is a bit clearer. He believes in a particular sort of antagonist."

Indira was nodding. "That's what they said. 'A purer kind of evil.'"

"Indeed." Brainstorm Underglass bit her lip. "I don't normally publicize this information, but you aren't exactly a *normal* visitor, are you? The girl who saved Fable twice now. I'd imagine you've earned the right to more information than most. Come with me."

Indira stood, but to her surprise, Underglass turned to the back wall. There was a lovely painting of a young girl on a swing, framed by a sunset. Indira had never noticed the painting before. A swipe of Underglass's hand made the painting vanish. In its place, a door into the dark.

"A secret door?" Indira grinned. "I'm a little wary of secret doors located in advisors' offices."

Underglass laughed. "Trust me, you'll enjoy this one."

The brainstorm entered a combination, turned a lock, and gave the door a polite shove. Indira couldn't resist the invitation to a new mystery. The room offered a trembling glow. Underglass and Indira entered together. What waited within left her in awe.

She'd assumed they were walking into a small space, a secret vault or a walk-in closet. Instead, an endless night sky sprawled above her. The floor was stone. Ahead she saw a great iron wheel turning. It was about the size of a house, and it was the source of the space's glowing light.

A countless number of smaller wheels and gears had

been attached to the first. Each one turned or spun, their patterns impacted by all the others. The gears glowed blue and red and green and purple. Trying to follow all the pieces was like trying to drink in an entire galaxy. Impossible to do in just one sip. As she watched, their light threaded in the air above the wheel, growing until they formed an image that Indira recognized.

"Is that the Author Borealis?"

"A smaller version," Underglass replied. "But indeed it is. Beautiful, isn't it?"

Indira could only nod. She'd seen the borealis before, but she'd never known how it was created.

"This is called the Great Exchange," Underglass explained. "I was permitted to see it when I first became a brainstorm, many years ago. More years than I'd care to admit. I have seen it hundreds of times since that day, but it never fails to take my breath away. I'm not sure who created it or how long ago. Some scholars think it was the result of the very first story ever told. Others believe it was the Raven King's work. It is a visual representation of our relationship with the Real World."

Underglass pointed to the left half of the turning wheel. There were, Indira noted, mostly cool colors there. Blues and purples and greens. "Those gears represent people."

Indira could just barely see individual gears; then they'd turn and merge with the blurring masses that made up the greater galaxy of the Real World, countless in number. Some of the gears glowed brighter and others dimmed.

"What's happening to them?"

"Every spark is a moment of imagination," Underglass answered. "Someone is reading or thinking or dreaming or writing. We are seeing acts of creativity, however small. Look."

As Indira watched, slivers of light chased from that half of the wheel to the other half. Impossibly brief flashes of lightning—spreading from gear to gear. It brought the warmer colors to life. Indira saw red and orange and yellow begin to glow.

"Their moments of imagination fuel our world," Underglass explained. "They create characters like you. Power brainstorms like me. We are inspired by their thoughts and dreams. By their best moments and their worst. Look in that corner. Do you see the two brightest gears?"

Indira nodded. In that section—the one that she thought represented the world of Imagination—were two particularly large stars. One was nearly three times the size of the other.

"Fable and Fester," Underglass explained. "We are the North Star that the world of Imagination centers itself upon. Fester is our smaller but no less necessary cousin. Good and evil."

Indira frowned. She'd always imagined that the two cities would be more balanced, a fifty-fifty split, but it was clear that Fable shone brighter and loomed larger than Fester. As she watched, the red-glowing gears began to churn.

Some winked out. Others bloomed with light. There were shifts in color and starlike streaks. The frenetic energy turned and turned until Indira saw the effect. Those same untraceable strikes of lightning swept across the wheel again. All the blue lights warmed to their touch.

"Do you see it now? This wheel turns and turns. It represents our worlds well. The Great Exchange is a circle. People in the Real World breathe life into our world. Characters arrive. They come to our schools; they grow and train. Then they appear in books or movies or plays, and return the favor by sparking life in them. And those sparks grow into ideas for still more characters. An endless and treasured cycle. It has gone on this way since the beginning of time."

Indira couldn't help admiring that thought. Her eyes traced the afterimages of light and she saw the endless loop that she got to be a rather small part of. But she'd never been a big fan of symbolism or metaphors. She was a girl with a hammer. She liked action, purpose.

"And what does this have to do with Bainrow?"

Underglass—who had looked lost in the lights cast by the wheel—came back to herself. Indira saw the business-like demeanor return.

"I'll explain back in my office."

Indira returned to her chair, blinking a little as her eyesight adjusted. Underglass carefully locked the door before taking her seat.

"Bainrow was already threatening the balance of our system with his methods. This Final Boss Protocol, however, would be truly catastrophic. We've had a dip in readership across all stories and genres. The trend has been distinct since he took over seven years ago. His policies already create antagonists that lack complexity, but to transform *every* villain into the exact same model? Any threat to the normal way of things is a threat to all of us.

"As such, I certainly see value in you pursuing this. If it were anyone else, I'd be concerned, but you're well equipped for the task. Naturally, we'd want trusted agents at your side. And we cannot actually *trust* anything the Antiheroes offer. Their contacts will likely be double agents. That's a standard in negotiating with anyone from Fester: trust no one. But the answer to your question is yes. Stealing the scepter and having Bainrow replaced would be a welcome change. Our stories would benefit. Readers would respond well. You'd certainly be doing a great service to the world of Imagination."

Indira stood, excitement thrumming in her chest. "So I can go?"

Underglass was too polite to snort, but the noise she made was as close as she'd get.

"Sit. Let's talk through the details. I'd want you to know some of the fail-safes we've created over the years to protect our students. That way, even if you find yourself in danger, you'll know what to do. Fester, for example, does not have access to the Ninth Hearth. We'll need to make alternative plans in case your life is in danger. You know what they say about backup plans. . . ."

Indira shrugged. "Have one?"

Underglass laughed. "It's a bit more eloquent than that, but yes. Have one. Let's begin."

Between

Indira found herself in the back of a wagon.

She'd been given *very* specific instructions, and as she bounced down the road, sweating underneath the blanket she'd been hidden beneath, Indira tried to remember all of them. First there were the directions given to her by the monkey-masked villain at the end of their first encounter.

"Hire a wagon to take you north," the monkey had instructed her. "Ask the driver to take you to the town of Between. You'll need to visit several locations there."

That had been strange enough, but Brainstorm Underglass hadn't offered directives that were any closer to normal. That was partially why Indira was having such a hard time keeping up with all of them.

"We'll be sending two agents, both undercover, to rendezvous with you in the town of Between. You'll meet up with them before following the final instructions from the Antiheroes. Look for the building with the red door."

Indira had nodded. "Cool. Like James Bond."

"Yes, but hopefully with a lot less *dying*," Underglass noted. "These are two of our best operatives. I have a feeling you'll like them both."

"Of course," Indira replied. "Anything else?"

Underglass made an unreadable face.

"What? Just tell me. What is it?"

"Your hammer."

Indira's hand had tightened on the grip of her weapon. The idea of parting with her hammer was unthinkable.

"At this point, it's rather famous," Underglass explained. "Don't worry. I won't ask you to leave it behind. Far too risky. But I've reached out to our contacts in the town of Between. Some of them will help your visual transition. You can't be a spy without a proper disguise."

Indira was smiling now. "Wicked."

"Not my favorite choice of words, but sure, it will look rather *wicked*. Just don't forget why you're going there, Indira. You are taking on the appearance of evil for the greater good."

As the wagon came to a stop, that reminder echoed in Indira's mind. She was grateful to escape her relationship troubles with Everest and Phoenix. Grateful to focus on a fun mission and go to a new place. But her mentor was right. She didn't want to be fooled by the city of Fester. She knew it would be easy to lose sight of who she really was. She needed to remember she was going for the greater good.

Outside, she heard the driver's feet crunching over

gravel as he approached the back of the wagon. By their arrangement, he knocked three times. A sign that they'd arrived and that the coast was clear. Four knocks would have meant guards were nearby. Indira slipped free of the blanket, wiped the sweat from her forehead, and leaped out of the back of the wagon.

An unexpected figure was waiting for her.

"David? What happened to my other driver?"

Her driver had been a short fellow—part goblin, she'd assumed. His face had been the last one she'd seen before crawling into her hiding place that morning. It was a shock to see David instead. Indira's eyes widened a little with realization.

"Are you part of my team in Fester?"

He shook his head. "No, I just volunteered to drive you. Underglass said I could come see you off. Felt like I should be here. Offer some brotherly advice. Like 'remember who you really are.' Or 'don't spend too much time around skeletons: they're all notorious pickpockets who want to steal your soul so they can come back to life.' It's our oldest tradition, right? Me offering advice. You mostly ignoring it."

Indira laughed at that. It had been a few weeks since she'd seen him, and it was obvious he'd been in training. David looked a little taller, his shoulders a bit broader. She was trying to think of a comeback when she noticed a huge gash between his thumb and forefinger.

"Whoa. What's that from?"

"Training," he answered, but Indira noticed how he

used his body to hide the hand from sight. "Just trying out new techniques, new weapons and all that. You never know what book three is going to throw at us."

"Yeah. Don't remind me. I'm here to get my mind off book three."

David nodded at that. It was deep afternoon, very nearly dusk. Indira knew she needed to get moving. Her brother sensed it too, and hooked a guiding arm around her, gesturing to the town like a tour guide.

"The town of Between, madam. It was an honor to drive you."

Indira grinned at him. "Any other brotherly advice?"

He shrugged. "Just know that I love you and I'm proud of you. Oh, and don't go outside on nights with full moons. Half of Fester's population transforms into something with sharp claws and teeth like this."

David used two fingers to mime a weird biting motion that had Indira cracking up. She squeezed him in a side hug before setting her eyes on the waiting town. "All right. Time to get moving."

"Godspeed," he whispered back. "That city needs a hero."

"Been working on your one-liners?"

He gave her a playful shove. "Maybe a little. Love you, baby sister. Have fun."

As David climbed back into the wagon, Indira strode into town. It was a decent match with Fable's current theme to the south. Between didn't have apple trees for picking, but there were old-school workshops on every street corner. Great rolling doors were thrust open, filling the streets with heat. Smoke rose from every chimney. Indira thought it a charming town, even if it was a little soot-stained.

A few workers nodded politely, but on the next street, everyone shot her looks of contempt. It kept happening as she walked. One store full of smiles. The next full of frowns. It wasn't until Indira reached the very center of the town that she understood.

There was a large plaque that marked the location. It read simply: A HOUSE DIVIDED. One side clearly represented good and the other clearly represented evil. She knew this town sat at the midpoint between the two towns, and it had a hard time choosing which side it was on.

Indira kept walking until she found the store that Underglass had mentioned. It was located on the northern side of town—the more "evil" of the two—and went by the charming name of *Badify*.

"Hello?"

The door was open, but the interior was unlit. Indira couldn't tell if it was a functional place of business, or if it had been abandoned. She'd just noticed a massive spiderweb in one corner when a throat cleared. A gruff, bearded man edged out into the light. He spat on the stones between them, as if spitting were an acceptable greeting at his store.

"Help you?"

Indira remembered Underglass's advice. This town would be a good opportunity to get used to people who weren't exactly *nice*. It would be a good time to brush up on her new role.

"I don't know, can you?"

He barked out a laugh. "Nice. Thought you were one of those goody-goodies from Fable. Always coming up here with their pleases and thank-yous." He spat again. "What'll it be?"

Indira did her best to keep up the act. "Stole this hammer." She held it out. "I need it . . . badified."

"Lovely craftsmanship," he said, running a finger down the length. "May I?"

Indira frowned. "Well, it's kind of attuned to me."

He gave a look of approval. "You earned its respect by stealing it, I'd guess. Interesting. Well, bring it into the workshop. I'll have you set it up on the table. Come back in an hour."

Indira hadn't thought to ask before, but now a little concern bubbled up.

"You won't . . . alter it too much, right? It has some pretty cool magic."

"Can't alter magic. My badification is more about aesthetics."

"'Aesthetics'?" Indira repeated.

"Appearances. Just trust me," he replied. "Uncle will take care of things."

And with that, Indira left her most valuable weapon in the possession of a man who she was quite certain had dried milk in both corners of his beard. She ignored that little detail, though, because she needed to meet with her *next* contact. This was actually the part she was most dreading. It was one thing to leave her hammer behind; she was pretty sure no one could actually steal the weapon. But the next contact involved something she'd never been overly comfortable with.

It was a meeting to discuss hair and makeup.

The sign above the store read: BAD CAN BE GOOD.

"Lovely," Indira muttered.

She entered. Rather than the usual bright chime, she heard a toll like an ancient church bell. Four hairdressers looked up at the same time. All four had a strange combination of pale skin and chic style choices. Indira could not help feeling that her light pink tunic was out of place. Three of the girls wore some kind of black, metal-studded leather. The fourth sported a shawl that was made of raven feathers. It was this particular hairdresser who glided forward.

"How can we help you, darling?"

The *w* in the word *we* sounded much more like a *v*. Indira couldn't quite place the accent. Nor was she sure if she needed to practice acting tough, or make contact with whoever she'd been assigned to meet. The girl saw her hesitation and gestured warmly to the nearest chair.

"Come into my workshop. We discuss."

Indira heard the other hairdressers sigh as she crossed the room. She decided to go with blunt honesty. "I'm heading north for the first time, and I need to look the part."

The girl's eyes narrowed. She gestured for Indira to

take a seat before replying in a quiet voice, no louder than a whisper. "You are Miss Story, no?"

Indira chewed her lip before nodding.

"I was expecting you. My name is Vera. Not to worry. I've got just the thing."

The girl wrapped her in a protective cover before circling, quietly assessing the angles of Indira's face. It was a relief that she'd found the right contact person, but that didn't make the next part easier. While Indira wanted to be fully committed to her spy mission, even she had limitations.

"No bangs, please."

In response, the girl snatched a pair of scissors and a spray can from her instrument tray. "Trust Vera."

The next ten minutes were a blur. Vera would spin her chair one way, set a hand on Indira's shoulder to stop her, snip twice, and spin again. Every few seconds she'd pluck up a canister and spray something overhead that smelled like something in an antiques store. The hairdresser did work on her eyebrows as well, plucking loose hairs as needed. Indira tried to sit back and remain calm. This was worth it. She was serving a noble purpose by going undercover.

Vera finally stepped back. "Perfection."

She spun the chair so that Indira was facing the mirror. Surprisingly, very little had changed. All that snipping and spinning had resulted in only two distinct alterations. The hairdresser had darkened her eyelids with some kind of black eye shadow. The dark color extended well beyond Indira's eyes, which made her look raven-like and brooding. The second change was a single purple streak of hair that framed the right side of her face. It was certainly pretty, but Indira thought the changes might be too small.

"That's all?"

She looked up in the mirror and received her second shock. A gasp parted her lips. There was no one standing beside Indira in the mirror. But she could *feel* Vera's hand still resting on her right shoulder. She could even hear the girl's shoe tapping the floor. Indira's eyes darted that way in confusion.

"You . . . wait . . . what?"

She looked back in the mirror. Vera wasn't there.

Vera spun the chair around and grinned. "Vampires, dear. No reflection."

Of *course*. Vampires were a lot more common up in Fester. It was only normal that a few would have made their home in the town of Between. Vera spun the chair back so that Indira could see herself again. "A little darker, but still you. Do you like it?"

Indira nodded. "You're sure it will actually hide my identity?"

"Only if you *sell* it," Vera answered. "That's why I chose the purple. You'll need a new name, yes? You can't call yourself Indira while you're up there. But you don't want to choose a name that isn't natural, either. If you pretend to be Amber, for example, someone will call you that name and you won't respond. Bad guys are clever. They search for weaknesses. You can't afford a slipup."

Indira reached up to touch the purple streak.

"So . . . you had a name in mind, I'm guessing?"

"Indigo," Vera answered. "It's close to your name. It fits your appearance. It even sounds a little . . . bad, yes? And you need to give off a vibe that says, 'I'm the baddest new kid in town.'"

Indira smiled at that. It was actually kind of perfect. No wonder Underglass had sent her to work with this hairdresser. She'd been worried at first glance that this wasn't enough to really hide her identity, but the longer she stared at the dark-lidded girl in the mirror, the more confident she felt this would actually work. She couldn't help wondering what Phoenix would think.

"I *really* like it."

Vera spun her chair back around. "Good. Then you're ready."

Indira hesitated. "Do . . . do you need, like . . . blood? For payment?"

Vera laughed, and Indira got a look at her two slightly sharper teeth.

"No, dear. We're not so crude. Money works just fine."

Indira settled up with the vampire hairdresser. She was also gifted a similar dress to the one she always wore, but in an ink-black color. It came with a sleek black belt with a blood-red buckle. Indira was sad to leave her pink tunic behind, but knew it would stand out where she was going.

Back in the streets of Between, the modification was

already having the desired effect. Now the "good guys" in the neighborhood ignored her; some even crossed the street to avoid crossing paths with her. And all the "bad guys" gave the slightest nod when they saw her. As if she'd been accepted into some secret club. All it had taken was a little eye makeup and a lock of purple hair? It was strange that all of them assumed they knew her at just a glance.

As she made her way through the town, she kept catching her own reflection in the various storefronts. She was surprised how much she *liked* this new look. Feeling a new kind of confidence, she headed back to Uncle's workshop. The owner of Badify came forward, beaming. Her hammer was right where she'd left it, but the man had covered it with a black cloth. He herded her inside before saying, "And now for the big reveal!"

A tug brought the black fabric sliding away. Indira almost laughed.

"You painted it black," she said, unimpressed. "And added one black spike to the top."

Uncle gave a chef's kiss. "Genius, no?"

She thought about her dark eye shadow and the purple streak, and how those simple changes had already caused people to assume she was a bad person. Indira reached down and lifted her hammer. It could still teleport her across a room or withstand a blow from an enemy weapon. But now? Now it was a little *bad*. Just like her.

"It'll work just fine," Indira replied. She was about to thank him, but that was something Indira would do. Her new identity—Indigo—would toss a few coins to the man and walk away without saying a word. So that was what she did. She didn't have to look back to sense his approval.

Indira was already making the subtle shift to Indigo. The thought put a new swagger in her step. Maybe it was good to be a little bad.

10

Two Unusual Rendezvous

The building was on the far end of town. There were no windows, no signs that anyone really lived there at all. But when Indira stepped up to knock, she could hear voices within. Underglass's two agents were there as planned. Except the voices didn't sound like they were discussing a mission. No, they sounded like they were in the middle of an argument.

Indira paused before knocking and pressed her ear to the door. She listened closely before shaking her head. Could she *really* be this unlucky? Frustrated, Indira lined up her shoulder and rammed the door. It swung inward on busted hinges. Two startled faces looked up at her. Both of them were very familiar to her.

Everest Smith looked as handsome as ever. The only slight alteration was a fur cloak that made him look like a brooding lord in some winter-bound army. Phoenix, on the other hand, barely looked like Phoenix at all. It was such a jolting change that Indira forgot what she'd been planning to say.

All that managed to come out was "Why?"

They started to explain themselves at the same time, then stopped long enough to throw rude looks at each other, then went right back to talking over each other. Indira struck the nearest wall with her altered hammer. It was kind of satisfying to see them both jump back in surprise. The indentation left rivers of cracks in the paint. Everest actually grinned at her after the initial shock faded.

"You look *really* cool, by the way," he said.

"Quiet," Indira said forcefully. "Please. Phoenix. You start. Why on *earth* do you look like . . . Are you supposed to be a zombie?"

He shrugged. "Undead, but same difference."

She couldn't help staring at him more fully now. His normally red hair was dyed raven black. It stretched over features that were, for lack of a better term, dead. All the little details helped pull off the look. The sunken eyes and rotting teeth and waxen skin. It was absolutely brilliant.

"You look *wicked*."

He was nodding. "It's a spell. Took forever for them to get it right. You look cool too, by the way. I like the purple highlight . . . and your eyes."

Indira blushed a little before Everest cleared his throat.

"Right. I kind of already said that, mate. You're stealing my words."

Phoenix turned on the other boy, a comeback on his

lips, but Indira hit the wall with her hammer again. When she was certain she had their attention, she pointed the weapon at the two of them.

"I am on a mission. If Brainstorm Underglass had told me she was assigning the two of you, I'd never have agreed to this. But here we are. Stuck with each other. If this is going to work, I'm going to need you both to treat this like a mission. It is *not* a chance to impress me. I am not here for either of you; I'm here to help the city of Fable. If you can't focus on that, I don't want you here. Is that understood?"

Both boys nodded. Indira was pretty sure she'd never have given that speech without the makeover. It was giving her the confidence to truly speak her mind. "Sorry," Phoenix said. "Won't happen again."

Everest nodded. "All good."

Neither boy would look at the other, but Indira supposed this was the best she could hope for. "I've got fifteen minutes. Tell me everything."

Phoenix would be using the nickname Phobia. An undead student by that name had disappeared during auditions, which had given Underglass a perfect cover story for him. The magic they'd done to adjust his appearance really was a work of art.

Everest, on the other hand, would be entering with students from the Menagerie. Every year, the school for animal characters sent story recruits down to both Fester and Fable. She wondered what kind of animals came to a city for antagonists. Evil cats? Hellhounds?

A boy who could transform into a wolf would definitely fit right in.

"The Menagerie?" Phoenix asked. "What's your connection to them?"

Indira started to answer. "Well, Everest is—"

"Good with animals," the other boy cut in. "Trained with them before."

She frowned. Why didn't he want to tell Phoenix about his shifting ability? Was he embarrassed by it? He offered Indira a secretive shake of the head and she realized that he was trying to spare Phoenix's feelings. All this time, one of Phoenix's advantages over Everest had been his ability to transform into a dragon. Who wouldn't like a boy who could take her soaring through the clouds? Everest's new revelation would make that seem a little less special. Indira offered him a subtle nod. She'd keep his secret to herself for now.

"And I'll go by Indigo. I've got a second rendezvous to get to. I'll see you inside Fester. Promise me now. No fighting."

Everest nodded quickly. Phoenix started to say something, but an actual bug crawled out of his mouth. He jumped a little before swatting it away, which had Everest cackling. Indira rolled her eyes.

"See you on the inside."

Trying to channel the confidence of Indigo, she turned on her heel and left them without another word. She'd barely made it halfway down the street before she heard another whispered argument break out between them.

"We're all going to get caught," she muttered to herself. "Great."

———

Indira's final directive from the Antiheroes was very specific. She read the note again, just to make sure she wasn't missing any of the details:

> Walk to the northern edge of town. Start at the base of the tree that looks like a grumpy ogre. Aim for the highest mountain peak and begin walking directly toward it. Once you find the hidden path, do not veer from it, or else you risk the attention of darker forces. You must walk exactly 2,331 paces before stopping.
>
> At that point, please await more instructions.

The specificity of how many paces she should walk was particularly interesting. How could they possibly know how long her strides were? Was she supposed to walk with big steps or small steps? Had the person who'd written the instructions somehow measured exactly how long her average stride would be?

Indira obeyed the command, though. She started counting her steps as the sun vanished from the sky. It had been a long day already, but she wasn't sure she'd be promised any sleep by the end of it. Really, she had no idea what to expect from Antagonist Academy. The rumors always sounded awful, but sometimes rumors were a far cry from reality.

On her 584th step, Indira finally found the secret path mentioned in the note. She kept on walking and counting, walking and counting. At the 1,783rd step, complete darkness fell. Indira noted how chilly the air had gotten. She also noted that the night noises in this forest were not the same as in Fable. They were more ominous. As she closed in on Fester's location, she heard the howling of wolves. There were great battle cries—human or animal, she couldn't say—that echoed out from every corner. Indira stuck to the instructions. *Do not leave the path. Keep counting.*

2,320...2,328...2,331.

Indira stopped. It was pitch-black now. She kept one hand tight on the grip of her hammer. Slowly, she turned in a circle. There were night noises in every direction but no sign of what was making them. *Await more instructions.* The letter had not mentioned how *long* she should wait. An hour? A day? Or maybe she'd messed up the count somehow? It was possible she'd been taking shorter strides as the day progressed, and somehow had ended up falling short of her target. Indira aligned herself again—using the stars as a guide—and took one more step.

Just in case.

Dear reader, have you ever been on a roller coaster? Do you know that feeling when you reach the very top and the world starts to peel away and gravity takes control?

It's a helpless feeling, because you are strapped to all that metal and there is nowhere to go but down.

Indira felt this exact feeling.

First, she heard the click. And then the earth beneath her gave way. She felt her body dropping through the trapdoor. Blackness rose up to swallow her. She didn't even have time to scream, which was rather lucky, because a pool of dark water broke her descent. It was shocking. Not for its cold, but for the sudden *everywhere* feeling of the water. Indira's eyes darted around, but the darkness was terrifyingly complete. She was forced to trust her instincts.

Three kicks—up and up and up—until she broke the surface of the water. Silence greeted her. Her eyes choked on darkness. Indira was not one to panic. She reached out. It took a few sideways strokes to find the wall. She carefully circled, fingers tracing the wall as she did. It was a tight loop. Her eyes darted upward, but the light from the trapdoor was so far above her that she knew she could not scale these walls—nor throw her hammer out. Her breathing was starting to quicken as she realized she was trapped.

Await more instructions.

That thought tickled the back of Indira's mind. She'd been sent to this location on purpose. This was where she was *supposed* to be. Slowly, Indira steadied her breathing and began searching the unlit pool again. Her hands finally found a small ledge. She probed a little before pulling herself up. Reaching forward, she discovered a very small tunnel that led out of the chamber. There were no other exits. It was the only way.

"Fester," she whispered. "Already living up to its name."

Carefully, Indira crawled forward on her hands and knees. She could feel cave moss and slime and mud caking onto her shirt. As she went, she kept one hand out, probing ahead. The coarse stones started to wear her elbows and stomach raw. Where was she? At some point, she noticed the tunnel starting a slight downward slant. She didn't count this as a positive development. She was already underground, after all, and going farther down didn't seem like the best strategy.

When the lights appeared, Indira thought she was imagining them. Little golden swirls in the unknowable distance. She blinked a few times, kept crawling, and startled when the lights were still there. She was so tired, so tempted to stop and give up, but the draw of that distant light pulled her on until the tunnel widened out, dumping her into a room of glittering piles.

It was a proper cavern with great vaulted ceilings and stalactites hanging down here and there. The place was *massive*, too. The size of a football field, at least. Every inch of the room was decorated with piles of hoarded treasure. As her eyes adjusted to the light, Indira mistook them for gold at first. Maybe this would be her supply? She'd use all this gold to make deals in Fester?

She'd gone from being trapped in a cave to discovering treasure. Things were looking up. But the thought made Indira pause. In every story, piles of gold came with guardians for protection. Dragons or pirates or some deadly curse. Cautiously, Indira set her back to the nearest wall and ducked into the shadows. Her eyes combed the heaped piles, but there was no sign of movement.

As she scanned the room, however, she did notice something. The individual items in those glittering piles were becoming clearer, and they weren't exactly typical treasures.

The nearest pile was made up completely of malformed kitchen mixers. Some looked broken, others chewed through by something with rather large teeth. In the pile next to those, someone had gathered fancy but clearly inoperable coffeepots. Next to that she spied vending machines stacked up like a makeshift fort. Indira laughed.

This wasn't a treasure hoard. It was a trash dump. Wonderful.

No longer fearing guardians or curses, Indira rounded the corner and ran directly into a dragon. It was a lot like running into a stone-plated wall. She stumbled back, her eyes crossing, and barely managed to slap a hand over her mouth to keep from screaming.

The dragon didn't have magnificent, colorful scales. It looked nothing like Phoenix. The scales were more of a muddy brown color. However, this dragon was almost three times larger than Phoenix. Indira noted that the great dragon was turning her way, too. She stood stock-still as a massive, triangular head hovered over her. A little rumble echoed up the creature's throat.

Indira could only stare as the great jaws opened.

11

The Sorting Hate

Thankfully, the dragon was opening its jaws to complain, rather than eat her.

"You smell *horrible*," it said to her. "Dog, come here. I've found the straggler."

A great stomping sounded from across the room. Indira tried to stop herself from trembling as the dragon's scaled body uncoiled. Great talons scratched at an itch under one of its membranous wings. The stomping grew closer, and—to Indira's surprise—a full-size elephant appeared.

The dragon sounded a command. "Sit, Dog."

Indira received a suspicious look from the elephant before it obeyed, plunking down beside the dragon. The room shook a little, and a pile of faded checkerboards crashed to the ground on their left.

"Welcome to the Sorting Grounds of Fester," the dragon said in a booming baritone. "I've been known by many names over the millennia: the Everhate, the Blind Hate, Bobby. In this time, however, I am called the Sorting Hate. Guardian of the city and decider of factions, yada yada yada. Allow me to introduce my most loyal companion, Dog."

Indira could not stop herself from asking the obvious question.

"Why is it named Dog?"

"I've never been very creative."

"But . . ." Indira eyed the creature. "It's an elephant. You can see why that's confusing."

The dragon frowned. "Don't be a fool. Dog is a dog. Thus the name: Dog. I bought her from a rather trustworthy breeder. You might find her a bit odd, but that's likely because you've never seen an Indian sheepdog before. They're beautiful creatures. Quite rare, I'll have you know."

For the first time, Indira noticed the dragon's eyes. They were narrow slits, but still bigger than her fist. Maybe once they'd been startling and colorful. Now a filmy white glazed over both irises, making them look more like frozen marbles. She thought that the dragon must be partially blind.

"Did I mention you smell bad?" the Sorting Hate asked bluntly. "What is that stench?"

Indira looked at her dirt-stained clothing. "It's not my fault. I had to crawl through a muddy cave to get here. It was disgusting down there."

"It's not the mud. Hmm."

The Sorting Hate lowered its head. Indira recoiled, but not before the beast inhaled deeply. The powerful suction of his oversize nostrils tugged her forward like a vacuum. The dragon sniffed a second time and one of Indira's arms was pulled up the left nostril. She cried out as the dragon sneezed. Actual flame snapped across her exposed hand. She was forced to roll on the floor to smother the fire.

The dragon snorted at her. "You ought to be more careful."

"What? That was *your* fault."

"No, it wasn't."

"Yes, it was."

The dragon smiled daggers. "Let's ask a neutral party. Dog, who is to blame?"

The elephant considered both of them before pointing its trunk directly at Indira.

"He isn't a neutral party!" Indira snapped.

"Nor is *she* a *he*! Don't be such a pig head." The dragon spread a translucent wing and petted Dog with a gentle talon. The elephant made a delighted trumpeting noise. Indira was starting to feel a little annoyed. Was this her next contact? Why was she here?

"That's the sound elephants make," she pointed out. "You know that, don't you?"

"Indian sheepdog," the dragon corrected. "And all of this is rather beside the point. You have arrived in Fester. It is time to be placed in your proper faction."

Before Indira could respond, the Sorting Hate turned and marched off in the opposite direction. Dog prodded her with a few forceful pushes and she followed. It was rather hard to keep up with the Sorting Hate, who, despite his old age, moved twenty or thirty paces with each step. The dragon's little pet followed behind, keeping an eye on her. Indira glanced back at the elephant. Big pet, rather. Definitely a big pet. It only seemed little when compared to a dragon.

They passed more piles of heaped trash. Empty picture frames. Dust-covered dressers. One pile was just a massive tower of barren tuna cans. Indira wanted to ask why they kept a room full of useless junk, but realized the dragon might take offense. After all, one dragon's trash might be another dragon's treasure. She decided to keep the question to herself.

Finally, they arrived at the opposite end of the room. The Sorting Hate rooted through a pile of rusted electronics before plucking out an item and turning to face her.

"All right. Name?"

"Ind—" She caught herself mid-syllable. It was an instinctual response. After hacking a pretend cough, she said simply, "I'm Indigo."

A little electric-blue light appeared. The dragon was typing on some kind of touch-screen computer. Its talons were too big, though, so she stood there patiently, watching the dragon delete letters and retype them over and over. Indira couldn't resist asking.

"How can you see that?"

The Sorting Hate frowned. "I'm not sure what you mean."

"Aren't you blind?"

The dragon harrumphed. "How presumptuous! I am merely, slightly, possibly nearsighted. And I'm asking the questions here!" The blue screen flickered. "What's your height?"

Indira didn't know her actual height. "Big enough to hold my own."

The Sorting Hate smirked, but recorded the answer. "All right. I'll convert that into demonic inches . . . very good. Any special powers?"

"I've got a . . ."

She trailed off, though. Was she supposed to tell him about her hammer?

". . . I've got a hammer."

"Hmm. That's a *weapon*, not a power. So . . . you are not special in any way, shape, or form. Noting that. Do you have any eternal grudges? Personal vendettas? Tragic backstories?"

Indira shrugged. "I just got here."

The Sorting Hate tapped a few buttons. "My sniffer tells me that your *core* is a lie. Any chance you remember what kind of lie you were born from?"

Indira raised an eyebrow. "There's more than one kind of lie?"

"Oh, of course. Broken promises, exaggerations, trickeries, and omissions. Not to mention bold-faced, compulsive, ironic, and even half-truths. I'm rather good at all of them." The Sorting Hate smiled down at her. "For example: your resume is very promising thus far, Indigo."

"Very funny." Indira scowled. "Any more questions?"

"No," the Sorting Hate replied. "You're a late arrival. Happens sometimes. We've already sent our crop of students to Fable for the traditional auditions. You'll have to hope one of the factions needs an extra body at this point. Might have to defer until next year. We'll begin with the tutorial introduction to Fester, and then we'll move into covering the factions you may choose from."

The dragon swiveled the screen around so she could see. There was a video ready and loaded. She tapped the play icon. Rather cheesy background music played as the camera panned across a desolate landscape. "The city of Fester was founded nearly a thousand years ago."

A map appeared. Indira recognized the marked mountains and rivers. There was a glowing dot that she knew was the location of Fable. The map showed a series of arrows moving from the city she loved to where Fester was located.

"We were driven from our home by the protagonists. Cut off from the city that we'd lived in for centuries. Fester grew out of necessity, a sore that would always remind us of the land we lost. Our founders came to these mountains because there was nowhere else to go."

Indira resisted rolling her eyes. There was no way that had really happened.

"But necessity is the mother of invention. Pushed

against the wall, we pushed back. Driven underground, we decided to rise." The video transitioned to a group of dark towers. Indira thought they looked more like a desolate castle than a school. "From tricked to triumphant, we now carry on the proud tradition of our forefathers at Antagonist Academy. State-of-the-art facilities allow us to teach the most developed story techniques available." She watched a montage of classroom scenes showing students participating in various exercises. "Thanks to the leadership provided by Brainstorm Bainrow and the Demon Initiative, our school is finally back to doing what it does best."

A well-dressed demon walked onto a clear greenscreen. Indira was surprised that she recognized him. This was the same demon who had overseen her very first auditions. Brainstorm Vesulias had been there representing Fable. This demon had been there to represent Fester. He was rather tall, and his entire body was made of a diamond-like stone. Veins ran down his forearms like trails of fire. Everything about him whispered power. This was her main target: Brainstorm Bainrow. He offered the camera a malicious smile.

"Our current motto at Antagonist Academy is 'Let's be the best at being the worst.' And I can assure you that our teachers and staff are committed to that goal. We are dedicated to unlocking your darkest secrets, your worst qualities, and more. Our new sorting system provides a better teaching experience for *your* skill set. And the new

Badlands competition will offer hands-on learning that previous generations never had. With our help, you'll find the very worst of who you are blossoming in no time. Guaranteed!"

The screen went blank. As far as advertisements went, Indira thought it was one of the weakest she'd ever seen. "Is any of that even true? About protagonists kicking you—I mean us—out of Fable?"

"The propaganda?" the Sorting Hate asked in a bored voice. "Yes, of course. It's all true. Now it is time for you to share your preferences, which will likely not matter. The device will show you the four factions that have been created for students at Antagonist Academy. You are allowed to mark your favorite. I will consider that in my sorting. Understood?"

Indira nodded. "Got it."

"Good. Your options will be ordered using my special dragon-driven algorithms. Swipe right if you find the faction attractive. Swipe left if you do not."

The Sorting Hate handed her the touch pad. Indira considered the first image. It was a massive chessboard. Invisible hands moved the pieces in a fast-forward sequence. Queens and rooks and bishops fell one by one. At the end of the game, only the little pieces—the pawns—remained to protect the king.

PAWN FACTION appeared, underlined and in bold. A pirate was superimposed on the right side of the screen, although he looked like the least intimidating pirate Indira had ever seen. A quote appeared next to him:

We get the job done.

(Disclosure: Please note that we only get the job done 41% of the time. We're not trying to be sued again for false advertising. The correct statement should read: We get the job done 41% of the time.)

—Mr. Smee

Indira knew enough about chess to recall that pawns were the little pieces. Most of the time, they were moved and sacrificed so that the other, bigger pieces were free to make the moves that mattered. She didn't know how Fester worked, but she could guess her mission would require her to be a little above the lowest rung on the ladder. She swiped left. *No, thanks.*

A graphic image appeared on the screen. She saw an army attempting to storm the gates of a city through brute strength, but the defenses were too strong. The graphic zoomed in on a soldier near the back of the army. The woman stroked her chin thoughtfully before raising one finger. Details of a plan emerged in a thought bubble, like one big blueprint, detailing how the army could infiltrate the city without losing more soldiers.

The woman offered an evil grin before the words MASTERMIND FACTION replaced her. Underneath that, Indira saw this faction's catchphrase: Being BAD starts with having a GOOD plan.

Indira found herself nodding. This group would consist of evil geniuses hatching extraordinary plans to destroy moons and overthrow governments. A good group to team up with, but Indira wondered if it would blow her cover. She wasn't a tech genius like her friend Gadget. She relied on instinct most of the time, and only rarely made plans before diving in headfirst. She'd stick out like a sore thumb in a faction like that. After a brief hesitation, she pressed her finger to the screen and swiped left. Better not to risk it.

A new image appeared.

This time the background looked like a 2-D video game. She watched a character leap past a few obstacles before reaching a power-up at the far end of the screen. The avatar flickered. There was a roar of noise as the character began to grow, doubling—then tripling—in size. Muscles burst through the seams of his shirt. Weapons and armor flew from off-screen, making the monstrous character look even fiercer. The words FINAL BOSS FACTION loomed overhead. A deep voice spoke what Indira assumed was the faction's catchphrase: "We are the truest test of any hero."

Indira knew that was the group she needed to infiltrate. Likely, it was the group of students who would have the most access to Brainstorm Bainrow. She wasn't sure if she qualified as a Final Boss, but she did have a magical hammer and some serious fighting skills. Maybe that was enough. She swiped right, and earned a chuckle from the Sorting Hate.

When she looked up at him, he pretended to be studying one of his massive talons. "Go on, go on. I don't have all day." And then he muttered, under his breath, so quietly that Indira barely heard him: "Final Boss. Right. I've seen more dangerous-looking lawn ornaments. . . ."

Indira tried to ignore that dig as another image appeared. It was a black-and-white photograph of a man. His back was turned to the screen, and the image cut off at the top of his collar. He held up one hand and looked to be swearing some sort of oath at court. Behind his back, however, he had the fingers of his other hand purposefully crossed. CROOKED FACTION was printed in curving, fickle letters in the right-hand corner. Once more, a slogan appeared: If you must lie, remember who you lied to. If you must cheat, make sure you win. And if you must steal, don't forget to go for the vault first.

Indira was about to swipe right when the device went blank. She tapped the screen, trying to bring it back to life, but nothing happened.

"Er . . . I think it's dead," she announced.

The Sorting Hate plucked it from her hands. He let out an exasperated noise, smoke puffing from his nostrils. "Dog! I asked you to charge the electric library! Find the power cord, you fool!" The dragon looked back to Indira. "Did you at least finish? It was taking *forever.*"

"I saw Pawn, Mastermind, Final Boss, and Crooked. But it died before I could swipe yes for Crooked Faction."

"Close enough! Besides, this process is mostly a formality. Your preferences aren't very highly valued by the algorithm. My first, uninformed opinion of you is really what counts the most."

Indira's eyes widened at that. The pet elephant stomped

around in search of a charger as the dragon dug through another pile of goodies. He turned back around, but now he had a wizard's hat planted firmly on his disproportionally large head. Indira was about to point out how ridiculous the dragon looked when he raised a single, massive claw. She was seized by powerful magic and pulled into the air like a puppet on strings.

The Sorting Hate made a thoughtful noise. "Oh, you have potential. No doubt there. You'd do well in any number of places." A twirl of the dragon's claw rotated Indira in the air. "You will be betrayed. You'll even do some betraying. But remember that the betrayer isn't as dangerous as the betrayed, yes? Oh . . . and there's something else. . . . An alliance sealed . . . by a yogurt container? Hmm. Yes. I see it so clearly now. You're going to eat yogurt at some point."

Indira's eyes darted to the ground. There was an empty bowl there, marked by traces of the yogurt that had been in it. She groaned.

"These aren't even predictions! There's yogurt on the ground right there!"

"Oh?" The Sorting Hate leaned forward, inspecting the container. "Whoops."

"Look," Indira said through gritted teeth. The magic was starting to get a little unbearable. "Is there a point to what you're doing? This spell hurts."

"I've made a decision," the dragon thundered in response. "You are as normal a person as I've seen in some time. On the verge of being a bit boring, in fact. Which means you will be —"

Another voice finished his sentence from across the room.

"A member of the Crooked Faction, of course."

12

Iago

Indira and the Sorting Hate both looked up at the interloper. Their view was slightly obscured by a tangled castle of ethernet cords. The man sat off to the right, atop a tower of DVD players. Indira was surprised she hadn't heard him enter. He wore old-fashioned pantaloons and a matching doublet, both made of black silk. A series of pearl buttons ran up his jacket, breathing at the neck to allow a high white collar to curl out over the fabric beneath. There was a sharpness to his eyes, as if he saw every tiny detail. She also noted that he was rather small for a villain. Compared to Bainrow, he looked downright puny.

"That is *not* what I was going to say," the Sorting Hate grumbled.

"What do you mean?" the stranger asked. "What *weren't* you going to say?"

"That this girl is a member of the Crooked Faction," the dragon replied.

"But you did say that. Didn't you?"

An annoyed ripple ran across the dragon's features. "You know that I didn't."

"Then who?" the man asked with a pretended curiosity. "Dog?" he called. "Dog, did you say the words 'a member of the Crooked Faction'?"

The elephant shook her massive head.

"Curious." The stranger crossed over to where they were standing. "What about you, young lady? Did you say those words?"

"No, sir," Indira replied. They all knew it had been him. What was he trying to prove?

"Fascinating," the man remarked. "Let's consider this, then. I didn't say it. Neither did Dog or our young friend. I can only conclude that those were *your* words, Hate."

Indira thought she felt magic in the air. The dragon looked unsure now.

"Iago, are you certain? It doesn't seem very likely."

"Remind me again," Iago replied. "What does your voice sound like?"

"Well," the dragon considered, "it's rather deep. I imagine a bit royal. Like a king's."

"I know what might help," Iago offered. "Why don't you say the sentence again? I'll tell you if your voice is a match for the voice that I heard."

The Sorting Hate nodded, as if that made all the sense in the world.

"All right." The dragon cleared his throat. "You will be a member of the Crooked Faction."

Iago clapped his hands. "Oh yes! Definitely. That is *exactly* how it sounded."

Indira glanced back and forth between the two, amazed that the dragon would actually believe such a lie. The Sorting Hate still looked bemused, but he shrugged those earth-colored shoulders and said, "I'm getting too old for this. Very well, Iago. Take the girl for your faction. Dog, I'm tired. Fetch a music box and one of those rotted wedding cakes, please."

Without saying goodbye, the dragon stomped off and left Indira in the company of a complete stranger. They sized each other up, but all she knew was the man's name and team: Iago of the Crooked Faction. The staring contest dragged on until Iago allowed a grin to split his face. It was sharp as any dagger Indira had ever seen.

"Hello," he said. "We have precious little time. Shall we begin?"

And with that, he led Indira through the piles of rubbish. She eyed her recruiter as they walked, curious and wary. She could just barely hear Iago muttering under his breath.

"Left of the left-footed shoes, right at the rabbits' feet . . ."

Indira followed him to a lonely corner of the great cavern. Behind them, they heard a raised voice. Iago winked at her. They caught snatches of a harsh and berating tone. Each pause was punctuated by the innocent and ponderous voice of the Sorting Hate. Indira sensed that the dragon was in trouble and that she was the reason for it. She also thought Iago had pulled a clever trick.

"Ah," Iago said. "Here we are."

She looked up to find they'd arrived at a clear dead end. Nothing but stone. No sign of doors or levers or a hidden stairwell. Iago gestured to it like it was the most beautiful thing in the world. Indira frowned.

"It's a wall," she pointed out. "Made of . . . stone."

"Indeed, but allow me to give you the first taste of what it means to be a member of the Crooked Faction." He placed his hand on the wall. Reality shivered. She saw the surface fracture and change, and where a wall had been, a door appeared. It was a pleasant shade of yellow. Iago grinned back at her before taking the handle. "The right lie, told with conviction, can become more real than the truth itself. Follow me."

Indira couldn't help marveling at the magic. She wasn't sure if it was actual magic or sleight of hand, but it was clearly very useful. Outside, she was greeted by an on-slaught of cold wind. They were standing in the cleft of a mountaintop. Patches of snow covered the dark stones, and in the valley below, she saw the huddled lights of a flickering city. It looked cozy, almost. Indira shivered, wondering if it only looked cozy because she was so cold. Iago waited with his back to the wind, holding out a fine-colored cloak like a butler.

"I can have it?" Indira asked. "Just like that."

"Just like that," Iago repeated.

She hesitated. "No strings attached?"

"Small strings attached," Iago answered. "But it's nice and warm . . . and you're so very cold."

"What small strings?" she asked, teeth chattering. A particularly nasty gust of wind nearly pinned her to the mountainside. Goose bumps were running down both arms.

"When you put the cloak on," Iago explained, "you become one of us."

One of us. That was exactly what Indira had come here to do: pretend to be one of them, infiltrate the system, gather information. All of that. She eyed the cloak. It did look *really* warm. A slender fit with a high black collar — and long enough to reach down to her knees. She saw pockets, too. Three on the outside, and she'd bet good money there were more lining the interior.

Iago shook the cloak invitingly.

"The Crooked Faction," Indira said. "Aren't you a bunch of liars and cheats?"

Iago grinned. "We're the *definitive* bunch of liars and cheats. Best in the business. No one lies or steals or cheats quite like we do."

Indira nodded. She was weighing her options. Not whether or not she should join the Crooked Faction — it actually sounded like a great starting point for her mission — but another decision. She'd noticed something, the moment Iago had stepped out of the shadows in the cavern below. Now she looked directly into his eyes again just to confirm her guess. His eyes were pearl-blue, narrow in shape. A pair she recognized. The only problem was that Indira wasn't sure if this slipup was intentional or not. Did he *want* to be recognized by her? She could either keep this knowledge to herself or ask him now and get everything out on the table.

Indira decided to roll the dice. "You were the one in the bird mask."

The leader of the Antiheroes, she remembered. Iago's face betrayed nothing. He considered her carefully, and she could tell he was running through a hundred different calculations, all in less than a breath. That brief uncertainty resolved into a smile.

"Very good. You've passed our first test," he said. "All the better. It means I can have the conversation with you here, where there aren't any other ears to listen. Bainrow's agents spy on everything at Antagonist Academy. It's best if they don't discover my place within the Antiheroes, or your mission on our behalf. Let's discuss."

Indira was piecing everything together.

"You came here to recruit me before another faction could?"

Iago nodded. "I want you well positioned. Couldn't risk having the Sorting Hate place you in Pawn Faction. You'd be starting off too low. It's possible your access would have been too limited."

That was logical enough. Indira had correctly guessed

that Pawn Faction would have left her at the mercy of the other three, more powerful factions. "What am I supposed to do now?"

"Take the cloak," he answered with a grin, "and then I'll brief you."

Indira's new "mentor" helped her into the cloak as wind whipped snow off the surrounding rocks. The effect was immediate. A barrier to the wind, another layer against the cold. There was something else, too. Indira felt a blossoming confidence. A sureness in her step. She turned up her collar, wondering what kind of magic had been woven into the fabric.

Iago nodded. "Power is power. Now you look the part. All right. Here's how it will work."

He explained everything precisely, never repeating himself, barely pausing for breath. It was clear he'd rehearsed this many times. Classes at Antagonist Academy were optional. More like workshops where characters could pick up a few tips. Bainrow apparently wasn't a big believer in books or thinking. He believed in power and strength and little else. She'd be participating in a nightly competition at Antagonist Academy called the Badlands. Her new cloak marked her as a member of the Crooked Faction. Their goal? Win the competition.

"What's the prize? For winning?"

"The better your faction does, the more likely you end up in a story," Iago answered. "Every member in the winning faction gets a Lightning Strike. It's the greatest gift our brainstorms can offer. A Lightning Strike is *the* breakthrough moment, when an Author clearly sees their character for the first time. In other words, every member of the winning team has a guaranteed role in an actual story. No questions asked."

Indira frowned. "Hate to break it to you, but I'm already *in* a story. Two stories, actually."

"I know that, but it's important that *you* understand what the members of your team care about. Each of them wants to compete and place well. You, of course, have a different goal. You're going to use our precious competition as a disguise for your true intentions."

"Stealing Bainrow's scepter?"

"Exactly," Iago replied. "The school's headmaster uses the scepter to create the setting where the competition takes place. A few years ago, we attempted to steal the one he carries around with him every day. It's a fake. The real scepter is hidden away in the Badlands. Every time you enter a new scenario, you'll have a chance to steal it. We have just twenty-eight days before Bainrow attempts his spell. If we don't stop him before then, stories change forever."

Indira was nodding. "Anything else I need to know?"

"Be careful. This isn't Fable. We don't have a Ninth Hearth." Iago's voice sounded bitter as he admitted that. Underglass had mentioned this as well. It was a shock to hear it confirmed, for some reason. She'd always assumed both cities had access to life-restoring magic. "That's why the Badlands were invented in the first place. You can die there and regenerate. But if you die in the city . . ."

"No coming back," Indira said. "Understood."

When Iago didn't give any further instructions, she eyed the city below.

"So, that's Fester?"

Iago took his place beside her. "The one and only."

"It doesn't look so bad," she said. And it didn't. She was reminded of a Christmas town, the sort of place that might have a market of handmade toys and a city center with an ice-skating rink. From way up here, she imagined little boys and girls running through the streets, throwing snowballs at each other.

"You're right. It doesn't look so bad," Iago admitted. "But that's the first lie the city tells you. Fester is the single greatest gathering of evil that has ever existed. The teachers are scoundrels. The students are the bright and budding stars of horror novels and murder mysteries. My first piece of advice to you is a simple one: trust no one."

"No one?" Indira asked, eyes fixed on the twinkling lights. "Not even you?"

"Me least of all," Iago said, grinning sarcastically. "Come on. Let's report to headquarters."

The way down was surprisingly easy. In fact, the path appeared to have been cleared beforehand. Indira trudged along, glad to have her new cloak, and surprised by how much more there was to learn about the city. Iago explained what strategies had won previous years of the Badlands competition. They descended into the valley and found their way to a mostly cleared road. It wound up to a massive, iron gate that marked the outer walls of Fester. She took note of the cruel spikes.

"Definitely good for keeping people out," she remarked.

Iago grinned at that. She almost didn't hear his response.

"Those spikes are for keeping people in."

13

Leader of the Pack

Iago slipped Indira into a back entrance of the Crooked Faction's headquarters. He instructed her to sit there and wait until the others gathered for their morning meeting. Her new mentor also left her with a small velvet bag. "For strategic purposes," he explained. "Remember, the bigger the role you earn, the more access you have. It would be nice to install you as a captain, but you have to earn that status. Use this when the time comes."

A few minutes later, Iago departed on "official school business" and left her alone for the first time in what felt like days. Indira was tracing back through all the details, making sure she was ready for her role, when voices sounded in the next room over. There was a clatter of plates, and Indira finally caught the scent of bacon and eggs. She was about to enter when she realized it was a perfect opportunity to learn a little about her new "team." Instead, she peered through a crack in the door.

A small group had arrived. There was a boy the others called Lefty. He spoke with a strange, muddled accent and laughed obnoxiously loud at everything. "Me mum says I'd steal me own head if it weren't attached," he proclaimed proudly, swiping the salt from the boy next to him.

The boy next to him was Zion Causey. He had sandy blond hair and looked the most normal of the bunch. Until Indira spotted gills just under his ears and webs between his fingers. He clearly had some underwater talents.

"I'm a middle child," Zion explained. "In a family of three hundred and fifty. It's either steal or get stolen from in our family."

Last but not least, there was a girl named Janie Judas. She looked like an outlaw. Indira found herself annoyed by the girl almost immediately. In the five minutes she listened, Janie managed to brag about pretty much *everything*. Her auditions, the stories she'd be in some day, and her dreams of becoming the student captain of Crooked Faction.

"I did my part," Janie said, holding up two stones. "Won two of my scenes. Easy as pie."

Zion shook his head in disappointment. "Only snagged one. It was a riverboat scene, perfect for my skills."

"Same," Lefty muttered. "The girl I went up against was real pretty. Kept getting distracted. She caught me lifting a Van Gogh from some museum in the last scene. Bad luck, that one."

Indira remembered that this group had just returned

from auditions. They were still in the getting-to-know-each-other stage. That meant there was room for her to step in and join the others without too many questions. Good. It wasn't hard for her to summon up the feelings and memories from her *own* rather painful audition. Peeve Meadows had beaten Indira in all three scenes. It had been an epic and embarrassing failure. Now she'd arrived too late for auditions. If all the students were comparing how they'd done, how would she explain her results?

But then she remembered the bag Iago had given her. She pulled at the purse strings and reached inside. Three stones clinked into her palm. There was a little note with them that read: *Power is power. Use these wisely.* She carefully slipped them into her pocket.

In the other room, there was more commotion. Indira glanced up in time to see the rest of the Crooked Faction students filing into the kitchen. She decided to take advantage of the distraction and slip out from her hiding place. It worked. The seated group was already eyeing the newcomers. Janie Judas, in particular, appeared to be sizing everyone up as potential rivals.

Indira got into line as quietly as she could and scooped a few eggs onto her plate. The room was pretty small, but she managed to take a seat in the corner farthest from Janie's table. Everyone was awkwardly introducing themselves, or else studying their plates like there were ancient runes carved into them. Indira was about to say something to the boy seated on her right when Janie Judas stood.

"All right. Time for our morning meeting," she said. "The Badlands competition starts tonight. It's high time we elect a captain and get this show on the road. . . ."

Her eyes swung around the room. It was clear she assumed that *she* was the right leader.

"So . . . I guess if you want to be considered for a leadership role, raise your hand."

Janie's words were inviting, but the look in her eye wasn't. It was pretty much like she was saying, *Raise your hand and you'll have a target on your back.* But Indira knew that Iago had given her the three stones for a reason. *Power is power.* He wanted her well positioned for the task of stealing the scepter. And that meant raising her hand.

Whispers echoed immediately. Janie's eyes narrowed.

"And who might you be?" she asked.

Indira smiled. "You can call me Indigo."

Janie lifted an eyebrow. "Can we? Can we *really* call you that? Are you giving us permission? It's so *nice* of you to let us. Such a doll."

Some of the other students laughed. Indira shrugged like it was nothing to her. "Call me whatever you want to, but the name is Indigo."

Janie's eyes glittered at that invitation. "Oh, now that's too much. Because if I was allowed to call you whatever I wanted to call you . . . well, based on appearances, I'd call you Shrimpy. Or Snoopy or Slowpoke or Slappy. You know, that last one sounds great. Slappy. It fits you well."

The girl held up her hands in the shape of a picture

frame. She closed one eye so that she was looking through the imagined frame at Indira.

"Wow. Yes. Everyone, this is Slappy. You can call her that now."

It was clear what Janie was doing. Indira posed a threat to her role as a leader. Which meant the girl was taking direct aim and trying to sink her chances before they ever picked up momentum. Maybe it was the dark eye shadow, or the confidence of already having been chosen for a story, but Indira decided that her best course of action was to give Janie a good, hard push back.

"And who says you get to call the shots?"

Now a true hush fell over the room. Everyone leaned forward. There were little grins and exchanged looks. Clearly, this crew enjoyed a little drama. "I say that I call the shots," Janie replied, finger poking her own chest. "And my crew backs up that opinion. Don't they?"

For a second, the two boys didn't understand that Janie was referring to them. They'd probably met at auditions. Maybe they'd ridden back in the same carriage. Lefty was the first one to figure it out. He stood, tall and gangly, cracking his knuckles to confirm he was with Janie. Zion looked a little less interested. His gills flickered nervously, but after a moment, he stood too. There were plenty of other students around the room. No one moved to join Indira.

"So . . . what's it going to be, *Slappy*?" Janie set both hands on her hips.

"Why don't we decide the leader based on auditions?"

Indira already knew how this would go. It was hard to resist smiling. "Any tiebreakers can be decided by a group vote." Janie looked ready to object to the idea, so Indira quickly added something she knew would seal the deal. "Unless you're afraid that you didn't do as well as I did in auditions."

Janie's eyes narrowed. "You're pushing the wrong person, Slappy."

"Meaning you didn't do that well?" Indira asked.

She watched the rest of the room's attention swing back and forth. Janie knew what Indira knew. If she didn't *deserve* to lead, she'd lose everyone, right here and right now.

"Have it your way," Janie replied. "Raise your hand if you won *zero* scenes."

No one put their hands up. Indira understood. It was an embarrassing thing to admit.

"I said *raise 'em*," the girl growled.

She was fierce enough that a few students finally lifted their hands. There were three members who'd failed to win a scene. "Now raise your hand if you won *one* scene," Indira said quickly.

Janie's lip curled, but the girl realized she was too late. Hands were already going up. Indira knew how to play this game. She wasn't going to just sit around and let Janie pretend to be the leader. Seven hands shot into the air. Janie tried to wrestle control back by asking the next question.

"Now raise your hand if you won *two* scenes."

Janie grinned in satisfaction as she raised her hand. Four other hands went up. Janie's face grew more and more red, though, when Indira didn't move. She looked like she was on the point of boiling when Indira offered the final option.

"Now raise your hand if you won *three* scenes."

Indira savored the moment, letting her hand rise so everyone in the room could see it. She also felt a touch of guilt. She hadn't really been to auditions. She hadn't really won anything at all. But the room filled with whispers. One boy in the back of the room threw his hand up too, but he made sure to hide it a second later, almost as if he didn't want anyone to see.

Indira's eyes fixed on Janie. She'd never seen someone look so angry. "Well . . . that's not the only thing that qualifies someone to lead. . . ."

"Oh, come on," a voice said from the crowd. "You *just* agreed to that."

"How do we even know she won three scenes?" Janie hissed. "I mean, look at her. She's just a little bit of highlighted hair and a ridiculous hammer! There's no way Slappy is telling the truth."

Indira fished through her pockets. She carefully lined up the three stones on the table in front of her. All Janie could do now was stare.

"My name is Indigo."

Janie's supporters melted back into their seats. Janie looked furious, which had Indira grinning.

"And I guess that makes *me* your new captain."

At that exact moment, the door opened with a bang. Everyone whipped around in time to see Iago come gliding forward. Indira didn't think his timing was accidental. Most likely, he'd been listening at the door and waiting to enter dramatically.

"Sorry I'm late," their mentor said. "Nefarious dealings and all that."

Iago took his position at the front of the room before looking Indira's way, an eyebrow raised. "Something amiss?"

She glanced around and noticed she was the only one still standing.

"My name is Indigo. I'm the student captain."

He raised an eyebrow. "And everyone . . . voted on that?"

When no one complained—unless you counted the dramatic arm-crossing from Janie Judas—Iago made a note to himself. "Well, that will make the meeting shorter. To other business . . ."

He shuffled through a stack of papers, then handed them to the nearest student.

"First, I have a full listing of optional workshops. In the past, I've pushed students to attend them, because some of the strategies you learn in school can help in the competition. And they definitely help in future stories. The only problem is that attending classes during the day and *then* getting pulled into the Badlands at night is exhausting. Our team has finished in third place six of the last seven years. That means we need to focus on the Badlands before everything else."

Which will make focusing on stealing the scepter more convenient, Indira thought. It was a clever start to their plan.

"You do have to attend a minimum of three workshops. If you get them out of the way, then we can focus on the real competition. Oh, and if you do attend the workshops, please don't steal from your teachers. They really hate that. Grendel almost ate one of our crew members last year over a missing stapler. . . ."

As the workshop schedules were handed around, Iago produced another velvet bag, identical to the one that Indira had been given earlier. "These are your class rings. Wear them at all times. They attune the participating students to Bainrow's scepter. This is how you will enter the Badlands each night."

Indira watched the bag make its way around the room. The girl nearest to Indira surprised her, hand-delivering a ring, even bowing slightly as she did.

"Oh. Th—" She literally had to bite her tongue to stop herself from thanking the girl. It was instinct, but bad guys didn't thank each other. Especially not the one in charge. Indira slid the ring on her finger. There was a dark whisper as it snuggled into place. She shivered at the sound.

"Every night, a bell will toll," Iago explained. "When the bell tolls, you have ten seconds to prepare yourself to enter the Badlands."

"But where are they?" Zion asked, gills fluttering nervously. "These Badlands?"

"In your head, of course," Iago answered. "The scepter directs all your dreams into one *collective* dream. Every student appears at the same time. Each night will produce a new scenario that allows you to play out different types of very real warfare. The winner of each scenario gets one point. There are bonus points for impressive performances, but most of the scoring comes down to who wins. The team with the most points at the end of the season takes first place."

There was an interrupting knock at the door. Iago called for the person to enter. A little imp, about the size of a coffee mug, stuck its head around the corner. It was a dark shade of green and had a perforated tail that trailed it into the room.

"Benefit slips!" the imp trumpeted in a high voice.

It leaped onto the table and handed Iago a folder. Their mentor flipped it open and eyed the contents. He was mumbling to himself, glancing over the notes, until he noticed that the imp was still standing there. He shooed the creature away, waiting until the door closed.

"Every imp in this castle is a bleeding spy for someone . . . ," he grumbled.

"Sir, what are benefit slips?" Zion asked.

"Pipe down with the questions, Aquaboy." Iago scanned the contents again, nodded, and held the folder up. "If you won two or three scenes in your auditions, you will receive beneficial supplies in the Badlands. Some are one-time use. Others are benefits you'll possess throughout the competition. Come grab your slips to claim your rewards."

A confusing shuffle followed. Janie let out a gleeful shout as she read her slip to the others. Apparently, she'd been gifted a special power-up that could disarm any opponent. One girl received a lock-picking kit. Another had won a supply of flash powder. Indira accepted her slip, but went back to her seat before opening it. What kind of gift would they give her for "winning" all three scenes? She read to herself:

You will receive a WALSHY.

Alarm bells went off. That was the term Everest had used to describe himself. He was a walshy. Would it look suspicious for them to be working so directly together? Indira definitely knew it might be suspicious if she *didn't* ask about the slip. It wasn't like that was a common creature that everyone knew about. She threw up a hand before Iago could continue with his speech.

"Yes, Captain Indigo?"

"What is a walshy?"

Iago looked briefly annoyed, as if he'd hoped she would keep it a secret. The expression quickly shifted to a look of surprise, however. "They're giving you a walshy?"

She held up the slip. "Yeah, but what is it?"

"A night wolf, of course."

"A night wolf?"

"You know . . . a wolf that appears at night."

"It can tuck you in!" Janie laughed to herself. "In case you're afraid of the dark."

"Not sure if they tuck people in," Iago replied. "But they do devour those who get on the wrong side of their owners."

That quieted Janie. Indira tucked her slip into an inner pocket of her cloak. At least she had a reasonable explanation for being near Everest.

Iago continued. "Keep in mind, the Badlands will change every night. Some scenarios will require you to capture a base. Others will ask you to race horses or launch spaceships. That means your benefit will only appear if it makes sense for the scenario. A night wolf—for example—won't be much use in space.

"Winning will result in more benefit slips. It's kind of like you're powering up as you go along." When no one else asked a question, he clapped his hands together, smiling wickedly around the room. "This building is our *real-world* base of operations. Take care of those workshops today if you'd like. Make sure to stay well rested during the day. Entering the Badlands doesn't exactly feel like *sleep*. You're a rotten bunch. Make me proud."

14

Antagonist Academy

Not wanting to lose her momentum as a leader, Indira addressed the rest of the crew as soon as Iago left the room.

"You heard him," Indira said. "I want everyone to get a few workshops out of the way. Take two classes today, then report back to headquarters. Let's make sure we're well rested before the bell tolls for the Badlands. Got it?"

Janie gave an eye roll, but most of the crew nodded. Indira watched the motley gathering take their feet, eyeing schedules as they did. At Protagonist Preparatory, she'd spent so much time in the classroom, learning how to be a character. It was hard to imagine a *school* that didn't care about students learning from their teachers. If she went to three classes today, she could technically get away with not attending another class for the rest of the semester.

"Kind of cool, I guess," Indira whispered to herself.

The Crooked Faction was a boardinghouse, separate from the school. Indira and the rest of the team poured out the front door and into the streets of Fester. Brooding quiet greeted them. All the charm she'd seen at a distance faded up close. Everything seemed dirty or scuffed. A black tower dominated the skyline. Indira saw figures walking the winding staircases with chains around their ankles and wrists. Was this a daily event? Prisoners being marched around?

The streets ran in a disorderly fashion between dark-roofed buildings. All the windows and doors rattled. The roads had been paved with bones of some kind. And a bell echoed in the distance like a too-late kind of warning. Indira remembered what Iago had said: the city's walls were built to keep people in. As a shiver ran down her spine, she thought she understood why.

Her crew reached the edge of a smoke-black bridge. It led across a chasm, connecting to the base of the great school tower. The bridge was wide enough for two people to walk side by side and had no protective railings at all. Indira glanced over her shoulder—double-checking that Janie Judas wasn't close enough to shove her over—and led the group across.

Below, a great canyon of fire bubbled.

"It's always a canyon of fire," Indira muttered. "So cliché."

She ignored the creaking and swaying and kept walking. Her crew was nearly to the other side when she heard a strange noise. She threw a fist up. Surprisingly, the entire crew came to a halt behind her. Janie Judas whispered a complaint, but the rest of the team waited in silence.

"Is that . . ."

A horse thundered over the rise. It was a pitch-black stallion with a pair of blood-red eyes. Fire danced across the surface of a massive silver sword in the rider's hand. Indira stared. The rider didn't have a head. Horrible laughter sounded as he cut off their access to the other side of the bridge. Indira stood her ground, one hand on her hammer, as the rider reared up.

"You're late!" he shouted, voice deep and booming and echoing from every direction. "For . . . orientation. All workshops are *downstairs*. All detention is held upstairs. The first floor is technically down in the basement. You'll find rooms arranged in a clockwise order, for your convenience. Please don't litter; we're doing our best to be a green campus this year. Recycling stations are clearly marked." The headless horseman saluted the empty air above his semi-bloody neck. "Have a good first day, rookies!"

Indira stared as the rider trotted off, happily greeting another group of students who were crossing another bridge.

"Going to stand there all day?" Janie called. "It's like she's never seen a headless horseman, geesh."

Indira ignored the girl, starting forward again. Ahead, endless staircases circled the central tower. The entryway was just a huge gaping hole where a door had once been. She walked forward and found herself in a room of stone and bone. Indira eyed her surroundings before remembering that the entire group was waiting for her to give directions.

"Pick a workshop and get moving. You know what to do."

The group dispersed, aiming for the various staircases. Taking a deep breath, she pulled out her own schedule. There were workshops listed throughout the day. Indira couldn't help noticing that each one sounded horrible in its own way:

WORKSHOP	TIME OF MEETING	LOCATION	TEACHER
Making Mountains out of Molehills	0800 hours	The Catacombs	Mr. Montresor
Safety Precautions When Using Superpowers	0800 hours	Main Lecture Hall	Emperor Palpatine
Nemesis NOW!	1000 hours	Main Lecture Hall	Grendel
Crime and Punishment	1000 hours	Detention Cell A	Miss Trunchbull
How Do I Loathe Thee? Let Me Count the Ways	1100 hours	Wailing Tower	The Stepsisters
Walking the Plank, from Bad to Worse	1100 hours	Dungeon Room 12	Captain Hook
Having a Vision	1300 hours	The Stranded Island	Dr. Moreau
He's Just Not That Into You	1300 hours	The Lonely Cabin	Annie Wilkes
You've Made a Grave Mistake—Now What?	1500 hours	The Graveyard	The Grim Reaper

"I was thinking about going to Montresor's workshop."

Indira flinched. A boy was hovering at her should

His voice sounded like it was made of rust. She glanced over to see a flop of raven-black hair stretched over delicately pale skin, and almost jumped again.

"Phoenix?"

"Keep your voice down," he whispered back. "Phobia. My name is Phobia. What's your name?"

He offered a skeletal hand. Indira shook it and jumped a third time when the entire arm detached from the rest of his body. "Ahh! Your arm! Sorry. I'm so sorry. What do I do? Is this permanent?"

Phoenix hushed her again. There were students bustling all around them, heading off to various workshops. Indira noticed that an imp nearby had stopped sweeping the floor and was watching her rather closely. She cleared her throat and handed Phoenix his arm back.

"It's easy to reattach. Come on."

She kept her voice low. "Sorry. Forgot you're a zombie."

"Undead," he corrected.

"And you raised your hand earlier." Indira remembered seeing that off-color skin tone. "Iago gave you three stones too?"

He shrugged. "No one really questioned me on it. Perks of being undead, I guess. Most people don't want to look at me for too long."

Indira thought she understood that. As they stood there, she could barely maintain eye contact with him. The magical spell for his appearance was incredibly creepy. There was a spot on his ear that she'd mistaken for a scratch but now realized was an actual spider. It was even weaving a web. Shivering, she changed the topic.

"Did you meet the Sorting Hate?"

He frowned. "Who?"

"You didn't get sorted?"

"No," he said, shaking his head. "Remember? Phobia was sorted into Crooked Faction before auditions. But they lost him somewhere in Fable and he never made it back to Fester."

Indira nodded. "Have you seen Everest yet?"

She saw the way his jaw tightened. In his undead form, that meant the bones literally clacked together loudly. "No."

"Gotcha. Want to walk to class together?"

He smiled an unfortunately rotten smile, and the two of them started down the nearest staircase. Indira couldn't help feeling a bit of déjà vu. It was the same way she'd felt that first day at Protagonist Preparatory, walking the halls with Margaret. She and Margaret had first met in Hearth Hall. They'd attended their first class together, though Indira remembered it was the first time she'd learned about the different jackets for side characters and protagonists. Her first class had been super embarrassing.

"Phobia," she said as they walked. "Pretty cool name."

"Right?! Like . . . *your deepest, darkest fears.*" Phoenix shrugged. "How'd you come up with Indigo?"

"The person who did my makeover picked it."

"I meant what I said before. The new hair really does look good."

Indira tried not to blush at that. All around them, the hallways and staircases were teeming with life. The Crooked crew had gone their separate ways, and now they ran into students from the other factions. Indira saw hulking bad guys with horns curling out of their heads. The bigger the student, the better the chance that they were in Final Boss. A few kids wore lab coats; Indira saw the initials of Mastermind Faction glittering on the front like a coat of arms. It was pretty easy to figure out which students were in Pawn Faction, too. Most of them were darting out of the way, trying not to be noticed or trampled. She also noted that they all wore necklaces, from which an actual chess-piece pawn hung. Indira thought it looked a little ridiculous.

Final Boss wore no markings. Crooked had rings and cloaks, Mastermind sported lab coats, Pawn had their necklaces, but Final Boss marked themselves simply by existing, shouldering past others like great planets that expected everyone else to orbit them. The idea of *every* single person in this building being transformed into one of them reminded Indira why she was there in the first place.

Distracted, Indira turned a corner and absolutely leveled someone. Zion stared up at them, the wind knocked out of his lungs, face red. His stuff had scattered on the floor in a circle. Indira reached down and started helping him pick it up.

"Sorry about that, Zion," she said. "Totally my fault."

He frowned at her before nodding. "No . . . no problem."

Indira offered a hand and pulled him to his feet. She was about to introduce him to Phobia when she saw movement out of the corner of one eye. She glanced that way and just caught a perforated tail whipping out of sight. Was that the same imp as before? Had it been watching her? She noted that it had left behind its cleaning supplies. Indira's stomach tightened.

What could it possibly be going to report? And to whom?

15

Mountains out of Molehills

"Montresor's workshop?" Zion asked.

Indira shook herself. "What? Oh. Yeah. We're heading there now. This is Phobia, by the way. Have you met him?"

Zion shook his head. "Cool. Didn't realize we had an undead on our team. That'll be really useful."

Indira smiled before handing Zion the last item he'd dropped. She couldn't help asking, "Why are you carrying around a spray bottle?"

Zion's cheeks went a bit red. He made a show of spraying the gills on either side of his neck. "Have to keep myself refreshed. It's easier than wearing a big diving helmet around, you know?"

"Cool," Indira replied. "Come on. We can talk on the way there. Do you really have three hundred and fifty siblings?"

"Actually, just three hundred and forty-nine . . ."

And they proceeded to the workshop, like having amphibious and undead teammates was a super-normal thing. A single room waited at the end of the hall. Desks sat beneath fluorescent lights. Indira experienced another dose of déjà vu, remembering the embarrassment of sitting on the side of the room all the golden-coated protagonists were on. But that had ended with hope. Threepwood had explained that their fates could change, if they worked hard enough.

This time she received no warm welcome from the teacher. He was kneeling at the front of the classroom, three-fourths of the way through the process of construct-ing a massive brick wall. He had olive skin and dark hair slicked back from his forehead. He was dressed fashion-ably, although Indira thought he was off by a century or two. It wasn't until they chose desks, the legs scraping against stone, that he glanced back at them.

"You're early. Very good. We'll begin when the others arrive."

Their teacher—Mr. Montresor, she assumed—turned his attention back to the brick wall. It stood five feet tall, but still had several more rows to go until it was finished. A strange way to start class, but then she'd also spent a year in the Rainy Courtyard with Professor Darcy. All the teachers at Protagonist Preparatory were a little weird too.

Indira's body hummed with nervous energy. It was fi-nally kicking in that she was on a spy mission in enemy territory. Everyone around her—except for Phoenix—was supposed to be here. Antagonists, through and through. It felt good to be stepping into an entirely new world.

Indira was so caught up in her thoughts that she didn't realize Zion was trying to get her attention until the boy tapped her shoulder. "Huh?"

"Do you hear that?"

Montresor had been patiently constructing the brick wall, one level at a time. Indira shook her head. "Hear what?"

"I keep hearing this soft, tinkling sound," Zion replied. "It's like . . . I don't know . . . like the rattle of chains."

Indira glanced at Phoenix. He was staring straight ahead, pretending to be bored and undead-like. "Not sure I hear what you're—"

But Zion quirked his head. "There it is again. It's coming from behind the wall."

Further theories were cut off by the arrival of more students. Two other members of the Crooked Faction joined them. Indira noted that none of the big baddies from Final Boss walked through the door. She was starting to get the sense that their crew did whatever they wanted to do. When no one else filed in, class finally began.

"Welcome, one and all! This workshop is entitled Making Mountains out of Molehills with Montresor."

He reached down and set a brick on his desk. Every eye danced from it to the wall behind him. There was a single space left at the very top of the wall. No more than a dark shadow. Their professor tapped the brick on his desk and smiled.

"Can anyone tell me what this is?" he asked.

A girl from Pawn Faction raised her hand. "It's a brick. Looks like burnt clay from here. Solid. Used in general construction."

"Accurate," Mr. Montresor replied. "A brick, but in the hands of an antagonist it's so much more, isn't it? For some, a weapon. For others, a distraction. For me, however, it is *revenge*."

He shook the brick for the class to see, as if that might make it appear more revenge-like. He wrote the word *REVENGE* on a lonely blackboard off to one side, then finished preparations for the final brick to go in its rightful place. As he did, Indira finally heard what Zion had been talking about. A loud rattling. A dying groan. It sounded like . . . a person. Montresor laughed as he climbed a small stepladder.

"Revenge," he repeated. "To be an antagonist, in the simplest terms, is to be *against*. There are many ways to achieve this. The first and most obvious is that you can stir the actions of the protagonist. Steal the crown, pick the lock, blow up the planet. Heroes come *running* at the sound of danger, don't they? But that's not a route every antagonist can take in a story. Not all of us have the tools to be larger than life.

"For many of you, the most natural way is to gradually become the antagonist. You have to learn to crawl before you can walk. You might not be mean enough or big enough or bad enough to steal the show at the beginning. So, what solutions are there for this issue? Anyone?"

"You could build up to it?" one boy offered.

"Maybe team up with a person who's *really* bad?" someone else said.

Mr. Montresor nodded at these, still gesturing for more answers.

"An accident," Zion suggested. "Radioactive transformation?"

"Good, good," Montresor said. "All wonderful methods; what else?"

"Misunderstanding," a voice answered, from the back of the room. "You could be misunderstood."

It was such a confident answer that Indira thought there might be another teacher in the room. She risked a glance over her shoulder and went stock-still. She recognized the person who'd spoken. She knew those blond curls. The girl's guitar case was leaning against the back wall.

Peeve Meadows.

Once upon a time, they'd been neighbors.

She'd been bright and bubbly then. Time in Fester had carved her into something else. Little flashes from the past raced through Indira's brain. They had lived next to each other in Origin. Peeve had tried to steal Indira's spot at Protagonist Preparatory. In fact, that act of thievery had been the reason she'd been sent to Fester instead of Fable. Her entire life, changed in a moment.

Peeve had also dominated Indira during their auditions. She was the reason Indira's semester had gone so awry that first year. But Indira knew that none of that mattered right now. All that mattered was that Peeve might recognize her. That would ruin everything, blow her cover. Indira faced forward, her back rigid, as Professor Montresor picked up the threads of Peeve's answer.

"Misunderstood," he repeated. "Slighted. Offended. Bamboozled. Wronged. Cast off. Denied. Overlooked. Laughed at. Ignored. *This* is the other way. In life, we suffer a thousand injuries and slights. Some people carry those burdens around forever and do nothing about them. But you, as antagonists, are the people who refuse to be ignored. You're the ones who say enough is enough."

"But how do we know how to do that in a story?" the Pawn girl asked.

"Good question," Montresor said, turning back to his board. "Let's talk about moral event horizons and breaking points. Snap too early in a story, and readers can't relate to you. Snap too late, and they won't take your anger seriously. Being a bad guy is an *art*! Let's dive in!"

From there, Mr. Montresor led them through a series of exercises. Indira thought it was all very strange. It seemed like the entire point of the class was for the students to annoy each other. Their teacher would assign them conversations to have and ask each student to imagine the insults that hid just beneath the surface of their partner's "supposedly kind" words.

It was clear, however, that the rest of the students found these drills delightful. Indira rotated through partners, carefully avoiding Peeve's corner of the classroom. Thankfully, Montresor called for the end of the workshop before she would be forced to stand face to face with her old neighbor.

She left class with a million thoughts competing for her attention. There was nervousness over Peeve's presence. Fear and excitement at Phoenix being there with her. The weight of her mission was also settling on her shoulders. Antagonist Academy was stressful.

Last but not least, there was the echoing sound of chains. Indira wasn't certain, but she thought maybe there had been someone behind the wall Professor Montresor was building.

Or was that her imagination?

Indira shivered as she headed back through the halls of the school.

16

The Gemini Scepter

Unfortunately, Zion stuck to Phoenix and Indira like glue, ignoring several cues that they wanted to be alone. The other boy's presence meant Indira could only offer Phoenix a quick and secretive smile before saying goodbye, pretending it had been "great to meet Phobia for the first time." Zion said his goodbyes as well, heading off to another workshop downstairs. It gave Indira time to walk and think. She hadn't been alone for what felt like days. She decided to stop by the cafeteria. It felt like she hadn't eaten anything in days either.

All five of the cafeteria ladies were identical. They wore hairnets, frowned if you asked a question, and, to Indira's surprise, all had the same name—MARGE—slapped on the fronts of their aprons. Indira walked the rows, unsure what she was looking at in the buffet line.

"Excuse me," she said, sniffing at a ladle full of . . . *something*. "What is this?"

The nearest Marge looked up. "Gruel."

"Gruel?" She pointed to a breaded object in the next tray. "And that?"

"Gruel pizza."

Indira gestured at some sort of cereal dispenser on the counter. "And these?"

"Gruelios, Captain Gruel, and Gruelcomb."

"So it's all gruel?" Indira asked. "Why is it all gruel?"

Marge answered, "Yes."

"Is there any, I don't know, chocolate?"

The woman pointed toward the register. "There are gruel rolls, gruel crunches, and gruel pies at the end of the line. The crunches are nice. Different gruel texture."

Indira's stomach churned uncomfortably as she set her tray down, appetite completely gone. She took a seat by the window. There was a view of bubbling magma. One lonely bridge swung in the air, threatening to throw students over the side with even the slightest gust of wind.

"This place is awful," Indira muttered.

She sat there for a while, watching bubbles form and vanish in the lava pit. She was about to pull out her schedule and pick her next workshop when a great bell tolled. It knifed through her thoughts. An unnatural feeling snaked between her body and her mind. No matter how much she fought it, Indira felt herself falling asleep . . .

. . . drifting . . .

. . . into dreams. . . .

. . . The room was full of heat and shadows.

Indira stood in a circle with three other students. The entire room was oriented around a glowing scepter. It levitated in the air between them. She'd never seen such a beautiful and alluring weapon. The shaft was slate black. It dripped with shadows, almost as if the material were on the verge of movement. The upper part of the scepter widened out into a claw that held a massive purple jewel. Glowing light pulsed from the gemstone, but the light didn't disperse outward. Instead it shaped itself like an hourglass that curled around the body of the scepter.

Indira had never wanted anything more in her life. It whispered to her.

Power is power.

"Greetings."

Beyond the weapon's glow, she saw the source of the voice approach. She recognized him, of course. From the tutorial video, and from her own audition. His skin was carved stone. His veins ran here and there like streaks of faded lava. Indira had forgotten how big he was, though. Over seven feet tall. Everything about him promised power. She understood why someone like this would be chosen to lead a school dedicated to evil and villainy. Someone like Iago could never hope to have the same effect.

"I am Brainstorm Bainrow."

He punched a fist to his chest. The others around the circle obediently did the same. Indira was a fraction of a second late, but Bainrow didn't seem to notice. She took a moment to quietly size up the others in the room.

A girl stood on her right in an old-school military uniform. She had pigtails and a face that was set permanently in a scowl. Indira noticed the necklace with the pawn hanging from her neck.

The next person over was clearly from the Mastermind Faction. He wore a pair of high-tech goggles that Indira was pretty sure Gadget would have been drooling over. The boy was a head shorter than Indira, but his wild and uncombed hair made him look a lot taller.

To his right, Indira saw the person she could only assume was the captain from Final Boss. The girl was half person, half machine. Metal implants made her look more than capable of picking any of them up and snapping them in two over her robotic knees. Oddly, the girl's name was stamped on her chest like a label:

BECKY 2000

Indira looked away when the girl's lone laser-red eye rotated in her direction. It took a moment to remember *she* was the fourth representative in the room. She was standing there on behalf of the Crooked Faction. Indira straightened her shoulders. Always better to start off looking tough.

"Welcome to the Badlands."

Bainrow swept out one hand. Indira had been so distracted by the scepter that she hadn't noticed the view. They stood at the very top of a scouting tower. Great dunes ran in every direction. It looked like an endless wasteland.

"This will be your dream home for the rest of the semester. Curfew is at dusk. Lights out after that. You will be drawn here every night. And it is in this place that you will battle for glory and honor."

Indira pretended to listen, but her eyes were lured again and again to the scepter. There was some power in it that, even now, whispered her name. This was what she had come here to steal. It was tempting to try to take it right now, but Indira knew that that was too risky. Bainrow was standing right there. Iago had said the scepter was the source of his power over the school. It was also the weapon he was planning to use to alter antagonists forever. There had to be protections in place to keep someone from just reaching out and grabbing it.

"Every night, the scenario will be different. The goal of each stage will be designed to test your team's abilities. There will be races, warfare, survival scenarios, and more. You will receive instructions at the start of each night. From that point on, the competition is in your hands. There are no limits inside the Badlands. Win at any cost. Over the last seven years, Final Boss has won this competition four times."

Becky 2000 offered a stiff salute.

"Mastermind Faction won it the other three times."

The boy with the fancy goggles nodded confidently.

"Crooked Faction and Pawn Faction . . . well, you can do the math."

Bainrow offered a smirk Indira recognized. It was the same smirk every bully she'd ever met had in their arsenal. The look had Indira's competitive blood boiling. She knew that wasn't her *real* goal here, but now she wanted to win. Indira looked around at the other captains, who would be her rivals here in the Badlands. Each of them wanted glory. They were plotting out how to win and how to earn a spot in a story. Indira reminded herself that her true goal was levitating in the air between them.

"Finally," Bainrow was saying, "a warning to you and your crews. There is only one rule in the Badlands. The device you see now is known as the Gemini Scepter. It is the engine that runs this simulation. Touching this item is forbidden. You all know the story of Teddy Two-Face. . . ."

Indira looked around at the others, who were nodding. She barely stopped herself from asking who that was, and why he sounded like some kind of mafia-involved stuffed animal.

"Teddy didn't listen to that rule. He tried to steal the scepter for himself. No one's seen Teddy since that day, but every now and again, you can hear the screams when you're in the Badlands. Approaching the scepter is punishable by expulsion, but Teddy's story is warning enough. To touch this device is to risk your own lives. Understood?"

Everyone in the room nodded again. Indira was mentally kicking herself. She'd never thought to ask Iago about the consequences of stealing the scepter. How could he have failed to mention a story like Teddy Two-Face? She was clearly on a mission to steal a powerful item, but she wasn't going to risk vanishing into some other dimension.

"The scepter will always be hidden and it will always be guarded. As such, you need not worry that your teammates will accidentally stumble upon it. Teddy's mistake was that he deliberately tried to bypass our security measures. I hope none of you will make the same error. Although, I'll admit, over the years I've grown tired of the sound of Teddy's screams. Make the same mistake, and we'll at least get to listen to a duet."

There were a few smirks at that. All the students were eyeing the scepter with clear reverence now. She remembered this was Antagonist Academy, where items that trapped people's souls *would* be celebrated.

"Very well," Bainrow said. "Now for the semester's first plot twist. Most of the time, you'll be drawn into the Badlands at night. The first competition, however, begins now."

17

The Competition

"Your crews are about to be summoned into the Badlands. Their goal? Trek through the desert and locate you. The first team that reunites with their captain is the winner." Bainrow eyed each of them. "Consider this a test of leadership. Each of you was chosen as captain. How much respect does your crew really have for you? What kind of discipline have you established? We will see in the coming hours. Good luck."

Bainrow snapped his fingers. A burst of power flung all of them back a few steps. Wind whipped cloaks and coats and garments. When Indira looked up, Bainrow had vanished. His scepter was gone too, though it left an afterimage of purple light in the air like some kind of strange lantern's glow.

Always hidden and always guarded, she thought.

Bainrow didn't realize it, but that information was a clue. No matter how much the Badlands changed from scenario to scenario, she'd be able to find the scepter by searching for the most hidden areas.

She filed that information away, but decided that now would be a bad time to start looking. It'd be a little obvious considering the four captains were all jammed into the same room together. Becky 2000 was the first to take action. She slid back a panel on her robotic arm, revealing a series of small levers and gears there. Indira watched as she flipped one of the switches. A blinking red light came on before she closed the panel.

Mastermind's captain tilted his head curiously. "What was that?"

Becky 2000's expressions weren't natural. They looked more like settings that she had to switch on and off. Her face flickered into an imitation of a smile. "Homing beacon. Don't be jealous, Eugene."

"Jealous? Not at all. That just means I can hijack your signal."

The goggled boy—Eugene, apparently—worked feverishly with some kind of handheld remote. Becky 2000 let out a programmed yawn, as if she found his efforts futile and boring. Indira was trying to figure out what she could do when she noticed the Pawn girl with the pigtails watching them.

"We should introduce ourselves," she said. "Since we'll probably be competing all semester. I'm Lizzie B. Borden. Pawn Faction."

"More like Lizzie *Boredom*," Eugene said without looking up.

Becky 2000 pressed a button and an automated laugh came out. "It's funny, because Pawns are always such boring people."

Lizzie's cheeks flushed with color. Indira noticed a pair of small axes tucked into her belt loop. The girl didn't look particularly intimidating—especially not compared to Becky—but she didn't see any reason to be mean to her.

"I'm Indigo. Crooked Faction."

Becky 2000's mechanical head swiveled in her direction, red eye scanning Indira closely. Eugene looked up from his device long enough to throw a smirk in her direction. "What's the saying about Crooked Faction? Oh yeah. You're one step up from the Pawns, but both of you are still on a staircase in the basement."

That earned another mechanical laugh from Becky 2000.

"It's funny, because basements are very low."

Indira scowled at both of them. A familiar adrenaline was pumping through her chest. She'd felt the same way during her first semester at Protagonist Preparatory. A bone-deep desire to prove the world wrong. Her real mission was to find the scepter, but it wouldn't hurt to kick things off by winning the first Badlands challenge.

The only problem was that this particular challenge depended completely on her crew. There wasn't a whole lot she could actually do. Indira crossed the room to get a look out the windows, which circled to offer a panoramic view. Every direction was sprawling desert. She spied distant figures, moving like ants. One crew in each direction.

They all started the same distance from the tower, but which one is Crooked?

Two groups were making better progress than the others. Indira didn't have to guess which ones they were. Not if Becky 2000 was using a homing beacon to send out her location. Based on Bainrow's speech, it seemed like Mastermind and Final Boss were clear favorites.

"This is annoying," Indira finally said. "All we can do is wait."

Eugene's device let out a satisfying ping.

"Looks like some of us will be waiting longer than others," he said with a grin. "And what's wrong? Don't trust your team? Guess I can't blame you, considering the recent history of Crooked Faction. . . ."

Indira knew he was just trying to get under her skin, but she couldn't resist asking. "What recent history?"

"Oh. You didn't know? Over the last seven years, Crooked Faction has *never* had the same captain for the entire Badlands competition. Why do you think your crew always loses? There's always a dramatic betrayal. It's bound to happen. The clock is ticking."

Becky 2000 laughed again.

"It's funny, because you are the one who will be betrayed."

Indira could feel the *bad* side of her begging to come out. Anger was churning in her chest like smoke. She pointed her hammer at Becky.

"Explain another joke to me and I'll be rearranging your gear boxes with this hammer."

Lizzie B. Borden gasped. Becky 2000 straightened, clearly excited by the idea of a fight. She pressed a button that made some kind of laser gun unfold from her shoulder. "Bring it on—"

A triumphant cry from Eugene cut them off. He pumped one fist, though the effect was softened by the fact that he was wearing thick laboratory gloves. "Never doubted them. Mastermind is coming in hot."

Indira saw them now too. They were riding, two per vehicle, on hovering speeders that looked straight out of a post-apocalypse movie. The crew raced over the plains, lab coats streaming behind them in the wind. For some reason, the other three crews had decided to make their way on foot instead. The team she thought was Crooked looked like they were well behind the others.

"Not so fast," Becky replied.

A great explosion cut through the air. Indira saw a pair of Final Boss students casting spells to cut off the advancing Mastermind crew. The speeders swerved, trying to avoid the blast, but the front-runner of the group was knocked sideways. Indira saw return fire from laser pistols and hi-tech weaponry. The delay gave the rest of Final Boss time to catch up with Mastermind. All the captains moved closer to the window to watch as the battle reached the base of the tower.

Indira glanced west. Crooked Faction was finally close enough for her to make out the details. Phobia and Zion were leading them. Indira squinted, but she saw no sign of

Janie Judas. Another explosion shook the foundations of the building. Below, a door spun from its frame, collapsing into the sand. Two Mastermind kids darted inside, but as their teammates turned around to defend the entryway, a crew of Final Boss students stormed forward.

It would have been exciting if Indira's crew were actually part of the action. She saw wizard battles breaking out and duels happening between winged villains. There were more explosions in two minutes than her entire first semester at Protagonist Preparatory. She couldn't help grinning at all the mayhem that was unfolding. *Being bad looks kind of fun.*

A shout at the door drowned her excitement. The Mastermind duo had arrived. The voices were faint from this side of the steel door, but they could hear snatches of conversation.

". . . vault."

"It would take five minutes at least . . ."

"Just blow it . . ."

Another shout cut off their plans, though. Indira guessed that the Final Boss team must have made it up the stairwell. There were a few loud booms. Someone shouted for backup. Indira darted back to the window. Crooked Faction had arrived on the outskirts of the action. Pawn lagged behind. Neither crew looked too eager to enter the chaos.

Indira's mind raced. She needed to think like Crooked Faction. Lie, steal, cheat. *If you must cheat, make sure you win.* There had to be some angle she hadn't considered. Indira thought about Bainrow's instructions. *The first team that reunites with their captain is the winner.* With Final Boss and Mastermind already fighting over the main entrance, it'd be impossible for her crew to reach her. But . . .

The thought had her grinning.

Bainrow never said we had to stay here.

She glanced over one shoulder. Becky 2000 and Eugene stood by the door, calling encouragement to their teams, unsure who had emerged from the duel that was happening on the other side. Lizzie B. Borden was watching Indira closely, but she was too far away to stop what happened next. The girl's eyes widened when Indira brought her hammer slamming into the glass windowpane. The whole thing shattered. Becky 2000's red eye swiveled that way. Eugene turned and shouted, "Hey. You can't—"

Too late. Indira threw her hammer out the window. The familiar tug of magic teleported her from the upper floor of the tower down into the hot sand. She ducked an incoming frost bolt from one of the wizards nearby, then looked up. Sunlight glanced off her hammer, nearly blinding. Indira lunged and caught it. There was another blast nearby, but she turned in the direction of Crooked Faction and started sprinting.

Shouts sounded from above—Eugene, most likely, warning his team about what was going to happen. No one could stop her now, though. Indira made it up the nearest dune and almost crashed right into Zion. The rest of Crooked Faction were sweating uncomfortably in their dark cloaks. Everyone looked up in surprise at Indira's sudden arrival. She reached out and touched Zion's shoulder. The world around them froze instantly.

It was like the end of a video game: avatars stuck in place, messages flashing through the air. Indira was reminded of the tutor device she'd used in Plot and how it had been able to display text in the air for them to see. The words she read now brought a satisfied grin to her face.

Simulation over.

First place: Crooked Faction.

One point awarded.

There was a brief flash of the standings. Indira couldn't turn around to look—the world was still frozen—but she imagined Eugene and Becky seeing Crooked at the top of the scoreboard, and their teams below. She couldn't resist glancing Phoenix's way. He couldn't quite summon his usual smile because of the disguise, but his eyes flashed with the briefest spark of flame. She winked at him before crowing to the rest of her team, "First place! And this won't be the last time we say that!"

There was a returning roar from Crooked Faction as the simulation winked out. Indira found herself back in the cafeteria at Antagonist Academy, blinking against the harsh light of a real day. She was still wearing the same victorious grin. She remembered the last words Becky 2000 had said to her.

Bring it on.

She planned on doing just that.

18

Spies

Back at headquarters, Crooked Faction was in a celebratory mood. Most of the team had seen Indira's stunt. It definitely earned her more respect. Having a win helped too. One win had them believing they might just steal the entire competition. Everyone was thrilled *except* for Janie Judas. Indira tried to ignore the girl's pouting as she stood to make a speech at dinner that night.

"Crooked Faction," Indira said, raising her voice, "this first win is just the beginning. I didn't come here to finish behind Final Boss and Mastermind. Year in and year out, our faction is told we should be happy with their crumbs. But I came for cake."

There were nods around the room at that. She even heard Zion say, under his breath, "I love cake."

"This year will be different. We're not just going to settle for what Final Boss and Mastermind leave us. I want us to win. Which means everyone needs to stay rested.

Get some sleep tonight. Finish attending workshops to-morrow. Be ready for whatever the next scenario in the Badlands will be. Understood?"

More nods. As expected, the only dissenting opinion came from Janie Judas. The girl stood up a little to make sure the others could see, so she'd get full credit for her joke.

"Thanks, Mom! Will you come by and tuck us each in?"

A few snickers sounded. Indira had known it was com-ing. And she also knew that actions would speak louder than words for someone like Janie Judas. She took aim. Her hammer whispered overhead, barely missing a few of the taller students in the room. Everyone ducked, and Indira felt herself being pulled across the room. She ap-peared right behind Janie, who had also ducked down instinctually. Indira caught the hammer and set her other hand on Janie's shoulder. A hard shove sat the girl force-fully back down in her chair.

"If you need me to tuck you in, I'll tuck you in."

Indira's voice had a sharp edge to it. The rest of the room fell silent now. Even Janie's cheeks went bright red with embarrassment.

"We work together. We win together. Got a problem with that?"

The rest of the crew leaned in, eager to hear Janie's answer. Her jaw tightened. "Of course not."

Indira let go of her shoulder. "Good. Eat up. Head to bed. If I see anyone in here thirty minutes from now, I'll drag them back to their room personally." She threw a final look at Janie Judas. "Let me know if you need a night-light, Janie."

And with that, she left the room.

———

Being bad offered an adrenaline rush Indira hadn't been expecting.

It had felt kind of good to put Janie in her place. It still felt good the next morning as she prowled the halls of Antagonist Academy, on her way to attend another workshop. Indira felt a thrill of danger she hadn't felt except in the most intense moments back in Fable.

You're here for the greater good.

She tried to keep that advice from Brainstorm Underglass at the forefront of her mind, but when she caught glimpses of herself in the mirror—the purple-streaked hair, the midnight cloak, the dark-painted hammer—it felt like she'd already started becoming someone else.

And she liked that feeling.

Her chosen workshop was in the Wailing Tower. It was an appropriate name: horrible cries echoed from the very stones of the building. According to the schedule, the class was named How Do I Loathe Thee? Let Me Count the Ways. Once more, she found herself in the midst of a diverse spread of villains. She spotted evil wizards, awakened mummies, and boys with acoustic guitars singing bad songs. One student had fallen asleep standing up, right in the middle of the hallway. A pair of imps were tying his shoes together and snickering.

At the front of the assigned classroom stood two women who were clearly sisters. Matching noses and the same hazel eyes. One wore her hair in a thick braid; the other had cut hers shoulder length. Both of them wore dresses. According to the schedule, these were the Stepsisters. Even though she'd spent most of her time at Fable, Indira knew who they were: the women who'd tortured poor Cinderella across a number of fairy tales.

Indira spotted an undead-looking figure in the back corner and took the seat beside him. "Hey, Phobia! How have your workshops been?"

When the person turned her way, it was very clearly not Phoenix.

"You guys think undead all look the same. We don't. Rude." And the girl gathered her things, moving up a few desks to get away from Indira. She couldn't help feeling guilty about her mistake, which was made worse by a laugh from a few rows back.

Janie Judas was there. "'How have your workshops been?' What are you supposed to be, our team mom? Geesh. It's embarrassing that we let someone like you become captain. Won't last long if I have a say."

Indira would have just ignored her, but not Indigo.

"I think it might be a little more embarrassing that the only person who can't count that win—because they didn't actually do anything—is you, don't you think?"

Janie's jaw dropped a little, but before she could respond, both sisters clapped their hands together. Attention swung to the front of the room. The workshop was set to begin.

"Welcome!" the sister with shoulder-length hair said. "My name is Clorinda. And this, of course, is my sister . . ."

"Tisbe! We are *the* Stepsisters, known the whole world round for our beauty and spite. Welcome to our introductory course: How Do I Loathe Thee? Let Me Count the Ways. After all, it's always more fun if you have a *lot* of reasons to dislike a person. Isn't that so, Clorinda?"

"Quite!" the other sister chimed in. "We'll kick things off by focusing on the qualities that you dislike in others. Do you hate when people ask too many questions? Maybe you're not a fan of certain haircuts? Good! Knowing what you don't like will help you figure out what to dislike about the protagonists in your eventual stories. Being in touch with your own negativity is very important."

The two sisters gestured like game-show hosts to the back of the room. Indira and the rest of the students turned. Hanging on the back wall was a mirror. A shiver ran the length of Indira's spine. She had a history with mirrors: Ketty had used one to start her dark spell during Indira's first year. But the true source of Indira's shiver was that this mirror looked like an exact replica of the one from her hotel room. The same one the monkey-masked woman had used to drag Indira into that first meeting with the Antiheroes.

"Now, everyone line up! The mirror will magically

summon your least favorite people. You'll need something to write *with* and something to write *on*. We want you to note the qualities of the people who appear. What is it you dislike about them? This will fuel your imagination for years to come!"

The sisters fluttered down the rows, directing traffic as they did. Indira couldn't help eyeing them more closely now. Had they been there in that masked meeting? Were both of them members of the Antiheroes? Or were mirrors like this one common in Fester?

Hesitation landed her a spot at the very back of the line. She watched as her classmates approached the mirror, took in glimpses of their least favorite people, and scribbled down feverish notes. Indira wasn't sure who would appear for her. Most of the people she disliked had been taken away permanently by the Editors for trying to ruin the world.

The line moved. Indira moved too, but the person in front of her didn't. She bowled right into his back. Her hands shot out in an effort to steady him, but the boy just swayed a little before righting himself. Indira saw something small tumble out and land on the floor. She bent to pick it up—a little black hearing aid—before peering around the boy.

"Hey, you dropped . . ."

But he was fast asleep. She realized it was the same boy she'd seen sleeping in the middle of the hallway. In fact, his shoes were still tied together. Maybe he had some kind of narcolepsy? Either that or he was overly dedicated to his nap schedule. She could hear him snoring lightly, oblivious to the line moving in front of him. Indira was sliding around him to join the others when the hearing aid let out a crackle. There was a slash of unintelligible noise. She frowned.

A quick glance showed that everyone was distracted by the exercise. Indira held the device up to her ear, making sure her movements were subtle. Those crackling sounds refined into a voice:

". . . we're a go. Our target is currently in the Wailing Tower. Eyes on the prize. We're preparing Scenario Thirteen back at the Nest. How are we doing on supplies?"

Another voice slashed in response, but Indira was too shocked to hear what they said. She was in the Wailing Tower. Were they talking about her? And was this boy a spy? She looked around nervously. At the back of the room, one of her teachers seemed to have noticed the gap in the line. She was gliding down the rows to see what was going on.

". . . something's wrong—switch channels. Code eleven—"

A sharp, piercing noise cut through Indira's ear. She yanked the device out and quickly jammed it back into the boy's jacket pocket. When she looked up, Tisbe was there beside her.

"Is there a problem? Let's keep the line moving."

Indira gestured. "Kid fell asleep. Wasn't sure if I should just skip him?"

Tisbe's response was to giggle excitedly. Indira watched

as the woman crept forward, quietly placing herself right in front of the sleeping boy. Her teacher brought both hands together in one of the *loudest* claps she'd ever heard. It startled him awake. He stumbled sideways, hip colliding painfully with the nearest desk. Tisbe roared with laughter.

"Oh, I do miss the little things. Back in line!"

Indira obeyed, but knots were tying up her stomach. What had she just heard? Was the boy in front of her a spy? And for whom? The Antiheroes? Or did Bainrow's crew have their own agents in the school? Indira remembered the imp from yesterday who'd watched her before vanishing. Was this connected to that somehow?

The boy glanced back at her a few times, even muttered an explanation for why he'd fallen asleep. Indira noticed that the other teacher—Clorinda—kept eyeing the two of them. All of it crawled under her skin.

Indira was starting to feel paranoid.

She knew that, in times of uncertainty, it was sometimes best to do the unexpected. She waited for the line to move again. Students who'd finished the activity were taking their seats. She waited and waited and waited until the moment both teachers weren't looking.

And then she darted for the classroom door.

19

Nice Is Suspicious

A full sprint down the hallway, out the exit, back into the main school tower.

She hurtled inside a back corridor, nearly colliding with an ogre bent over a water fountain. Indira wasn't sure who was spying on her, but she knew that the safest place for her was back at the Crooked Faction's main headquarters. Nothing strange or ominous pursued her as she ran breathlessly up the stairs and back to the front of the school. There were a few more startled students, some who told her to watch where she was going in grumbling voices, but no sign of spies.

Indira crossed the chasm at full speed, pausing to look back only when she'd made it safely to the other side of the bridge. No one was pursuing her, but she also noticed that the landscape was *oddly* still. This morning it had been such a busy scene: chained prisoners marching on different levels of the tower and a drum beating in the distance. Now it appeared to be mostly empty. Indira thought she saw faces in the windows, watchful and motionless, but it was hard to tell with the smoke pluming all around her.

A gust of smog passed, and the scene looked normal again. Students moving between classes. That headless horseman racing around and telling people where to go. Indira looked for signs of someone who might be following her, but no one was there.

———

Headquarters was blessedly empty.

At least Indira thought it was empty. She was rifling through a cupboard in search of a snack when a throat cleared behind her. She whipped around. Iago was lounging in one corner.

"If it isn't our fearless captain. What brings you back to headquarters, Indigo?"

She glanced toward the entrance. No one else was here.

"I need to talk to you. In class I—"

Iago cut her off with a sharp look. He stood, gestured for her to follow, and ducked into the makeshift kitchen area. There was a sink, a refrigerator, and a few drawers of essential items. Iago reached out to the light-switch panel on the wall. Indira saw reality shiver again at his touch. Originally, there had been just two light switches. Now there were three. He flicked the third. A garbage disposal turned on in a sharp whir of blades. It sputtered and spun and filled the air with its annoying grind.

Her mentor lowered his voice to a whisper. "We cannot simply *talk* about *that*. There are ears everywhere. Even in my own quarters."

Indira lowered her voice. "A boy in my class had a device in his ear. It connected to some kind of radio transmission. I'm pretty sure whoever was on that frequency is monitoring me."

Iago raised a single, knife-sharp eyebrow. "Monitoring you?"

"Yes."

"You're certain?"

Indira nodded.

"Hmm. Bainrow certainly has his own agents within the school. When did you first notice that you were being watched?"

"Yesterday? There was an imp cleaning the main hall. He was watching me for a few seconds, then abandoned his supplies."

Iago started to pace the room, a finger tapping his chin.

"What happened? Just before you saw him?"

Indira tried to remember. "I was talking with Ph — Phobia, and I accidentally pulled his arm off. . . . Then we walked to a workshop and ran right into Zion. I knocked him down by accident. Do you think that's it? I'm being too clumsy?"

Iago shook his head. "Doubtful. To an outside observer, both of those incidents would look like bullying."

"Bullying?" Indira said. "No way. I apologized to both of them. Even helped Zion pick up his stuff. There's no way that would look like bullying."

Iago raised a knowing finger. "Apologized?"

"Well, yeah . . . I said I was sorry."

He sighed. "There's your explanation. An apology might as well be an alarm bell in this place. You're attending Antagonist Academy. We do not apologize for knocking someone over in a hallway. We don't say that we're sorry about anything. We tell people to watch where they're going or next time it won't be an accident. If the imp overheard you being nice, there's a good chance it raised suspicions. Standard protocol. Bainrow's crew will monitor you for at least a week . . . which is a good thing."

Indira frowned at that. "How is that a good thing?"

"Because now we *know* they're watching you. All you have to do is put on a good show. If you play your part over the next few days—really dig into the bad-guy role—then we can swing their radar to someone else. In the next few Badlands scenarios, I want you to be a little crueler than normal. Can you do that?"

Indira thought about her interactions with Janie.

"Yeah, I can do that."

"Problem solved. They'll lose interest as soon as you prove you're not nice, and we'll be in the clear. Any updates on your actual mission?"

"Oh!" Indira remembered the scepter, and Bainrow's story about what had happened to the kid who'd tried to steal it. "You didn't tell me that the scepter traps people in other dimensions! How am I supposed to trust you if you didn't even mention Teddy Two-Face?"

Iago burst out laughing. The sound mingled with the grinding noise of the food disposal. "I didn't tell you about Teddy Two-Face because there never *was* a Teddy Two-Face. It's an urban legend spread by Bainrow himself. He says that every year. He even said it the first year! Before there was a competition for someone to disappear during! The whole point of that story is to scare students away."

"Well, if taking the scepter isn't dangerous, why haven't you just stolen it yourself? You're the head of Crooked Faction. How hard could it be?"

"Bainrow only lets students enter the Badlands," Iago answered. "Trust me, if I had access, I'd have taken the scepter years ago."

That made sense, but Indira was surprised by how much power the other teachers had allowed Bainrow. It seemed like he ran everything. When Indira didn't ask any other questions, Iago flipped the switch again. The grinding noise faded.

"That sink didn't have a disposal yesterday," Indira pointed out.

"As I've said, a deeply believed lie can be more powerful than the truth."

Iago carefully steered the conversation back to a topic that was a little less suspicious. Indira could tell from his tone that he was accounting for the possibility that spies were now listening to their conversation again.

"Ready for round two in the Badlands?" he asked.

Indira shrugged. "I'm undefeated so far."

"That victory infuriated the other factions," Iago said with a grin. "It was a good start, but don't forget why you're really here."

She imagined the scepter floating in the air before her. The faint whisper of power in the air. No way would she forget about the scepter.

"Understood."

Iago offered a bow before departing.

"Good luck, Captain."

20

Round Two

Crooked Faction trickled back into headquarters, one by one. Indira earned respectful nods from everyone at dinner. Even Janie kept the peace. They were clearly excited for round two.

Before curfew, everyone headed back to their bunks. As the captain of the team, Indira had been rewarded with slightly upgraded sleeping quarters. It offered some needed privacy, but it wasn't fancy by any means. Just a bunk with a pillow and a blanket. Nothing like her room in Mrs. Pennington's house, or her comfortable bed in the Story House.

The sun was still setting outside the window when Indira heard the promised tolling of the bell. A second later she felt herself slipping into that alternate reality. . . .

Power is power.

———

Intense cold. A snow-covered forest. It was relatively dark out, with only a bright moon coloring the landscape.

Her crew members popped to life around her, drawn into the same dream, into the Badlands. She and the rest of the crew looked around, eyeing the forest, but no one could move. The game hadn't started yet.

On her right there were three towers: an abandoned and run-down castle. After a brief wait, another bell tolled. Text appeared in midair.

Indira read:

CAPTURE THE FLAG

THE FIRST TEAM TO CAPTURE ANOTHER FACTION'S FLAG AND RETURN IT TO THEIR BASE, WHILE MAINTAINING POSSESSION OF THEIR OWN FLAG, WILL BE THE WINNER.

Indira felt her body unlock.

Let the games begin.

She didn't waste any time. "Hey! You three!" She pointed at a random group. "Pick a tower and head to the top. I want you scouting in every direction. Let's get eyes on the other bases around us."

She pointed at another group. "There's a river down there. I want two people following it west and the other two heading east. Report back. I want to know if you see bridges, castles, anything."

They all obeyed without question. A quick head count showed she still had a dozen other crewmates waiting for assignment. Janie and the pair Indira had first seen her with in headquarters were among them. Phobia stood there as well, staring at her with his lifeless eyes.

"Our best strategy is defense," Indira said. "Let's find out where our flag is hidden. I want to set as many traps around it as we can. No one comes in that front door without getting hit hard. Once we're secure, I'll send out a small team to try to steal someone else's flag."

Before they could disperse, Indira added, "Janie and Phobia, come with me."

Phoenix had been waiting for it. He was clearly eager to stay by her side. Janie, on the other hand, looked startled. Indira saw this as a big moment for solidifying their team.

"I want my best people at my side," Indira said. Janie almost rolled her eyes. "I'm serious. You're two of the best performers we had from auditions. Janie, you've got confidence. Phobia, you were skilled enough to win three scenes. I need the best with me."

Janie still looked surprised, but after a second she nodded.

Phobia croaked a response. "I'm game."

"Actually, you're dead," Indira pointed out.

Phobia cracked a grin. Janie actually laughed. Indira felt tension releasing from her shoulders. This crew could work together. She needed everyone to get along. "First step is organization. Let's figure out what resources we have."

Both of them walked with her toward the towers. It wasn't the most defensible location, but all they needed was to buy enough time for a small team to head for one of the enemy's castles. She was pretty sure their best bet was quiet infiltration.

The scout had already reached the top, about four stories up. "I know it's dark," Indira called, "but can you see anything?"

"Actually, yeah. The moon is really bright. We're mostly surrounded by forest. The closest castle is northwest of us. Looks like Final Boss to me. And then the Pawns are farther north. Can't see Mastermind."

Indira frowned. "How do you know it's Final Boss?"

"Because there's a very large Cyclops staring back at me?"

"Well, don't let him see you."

"Oh. Now he's pointing at me."

"Get down, then!"

"Yeah, still pointing."

Indira shook her head. "Wonderful."

She'd been hoping to attack Pawn Faction, but it sounded like both the other factions were in better position. She was debating what the best move would be when another scout called down from the opposite tower.

"Indigo? Found something!"

They stepped back outside. The other scout was pointing to a courtyard Indira hadn't noticed. There was a series of squat buildings inside their outer wall. "We've got horses!" the scout said. "Two of them!"

Indira glanced at Janie. "Can you ride?"

The girl was wearing a cowboy hat and boots. "What do you think?"

Indira hesitated. There were only two horses. Her preference would have been to ride off with Phoenix, but Janie was probably the strongest rider of the three of them. Going alone with Janie felt risky too. What if they infiltrated an enemy base and the girl decided to betray her? Indira was still trying to make up her mind when she heard a bone-chilling howl.

Everyone turned toward the southern forest.

Only a pair of eyes was visible at first. And then the creature wove through the trees, padding on massive, silent paws. His fur matched the surrounding snow. She watched Everest stop at a safe distance, sniffing the air. Phoenix stepped forward protectively, but Indira reached out to stop him.

"He's my benefit. From auditions. The walshy. He's a night wolf."

It's Everest, she wanted to say, but Everest had wanted to keep this part of who he was a secret, which meant it wasn't Indira's place to share. Now wasn't the time to tell him anyway. Not with Janie watching so closely.

"I'll ride the night wolf. You two get saddled up."

There was a little thrill in Indira's chest as her boots crunched over the snow. She hadn't forgotten the breathless, moonlit ride they'd had before coming to Fester.

Even in his wolf form, Everest looked at her very seriously. Like she was the only person who existed in the world. Indira glanced back at the castle, making sure no one was nearby, before turning to him.

"What do you say, Ev? Ready to run?"

He let out another wild howl. Indira laughed before climbing up his back and settling her grip into his collar. She hadn't realized how cold she was until she pressed into his back and felt the sudden warmth.

It took Janie about ten minutes to get the two horses saddled up. By then another pair of scouts had come back and reported a steep ravine to the northwest with a single bridge leading across. There was no sign of the Mastermind base anywhere.

"Everyone expects us to go after Pawn or Mastermind," Indira said. "The Final Boss castle would be impossible to break into, right?"

Janie nodded. "Right."

"Wrong," she said. "Maybe the reason they seem so tough is because no one ever tests them. Let's do the unexpected. Let's hit Final Boss."

Janie Judas didn't need convincing. One thing the girl had in full supply was the confidence to do the impossible.

Everest's lip briefly curled into a snarl when Phoenix approached on horseback. The noise spooked the horses a little, and Indira had to whisper in his ear to get him to calm down. "Come on. Let's get moving."

The trio shot through the forest, following the river. It was fun to see great bursts of snow kick up as they went.

Janie was a natural on horseback. Phoenix struggled a little, but Indira didn't count that against him. Why practice riding horses when you can transform into a dragon? The path eventually led to the bridge her scouts had seen. Even Janie—with all her confidence—pulled up short of it.

"Why didn't they mention it was old as dirt?" she asked.

As they watched, the bridge swayed and creaked. There was nothing to do but go on. Indira gave the signal, and Janie, not wanting to be shown up, plunged across. A few breathless moments and they were on the other side, moving into Final Boss territory. There were explosions well to the north. Indira wondered what kind of patrols the Final Boss team had set up, or if they'd launched one huge offensive and left their base mostly unguarded.

They dismounted near an overlook. The ice was so slippery that they had to tie up the horses before trudging up. The spot offered a view of the distant valley, as well as a glimpse of the Final Boss castle.

"Why do they get such a nice one?" Janie asked.

There was a cool drawbridge, and the walls looked pristine. She saw one guard roaming the ramparts above, but most of the action appeared to be happening well to the north. Minor skirmishes could be seen, even from here.

"It's not heavily guarded," Indira said. "What do you think?"

Another voice answered from behind them.

"I think I've caught three little mice. . . ."

They whipped around. One of Final Boss's wizards had managed to sneak in behind them somehow. She was dressed in a ridiculous outfit that made her look like an overgrown raven. There was even a beak hanging down from the hood, stretching to the upper bridge of her nose. Indira could only stare as great purple light bloomed in the girl's palms, crackling with dark energy. She was about to release the spell when the unexpected happened. The wizard—tangled in all her fancy robes—slipped like an old-fashioned cartoon character stepping on a banana.

All of them heard the resounding thunk.

21

Cruel Intentions

$\mathcal{S}$he nudged the fallen wizard with a toe. "Is she . . ."

"Knocked out," Phoenix confirmed in his rusty voice. "Bad footwork."

Indira couldn't help smiling at that. She knew Phoenix prided himself on his magical training. She wouldn't have doubted there was an entire class he'd taken on proper footwork while casting spells. Janie looked like she was considering kicking the unconscious girl for sneaking up on them.

"Deserves a good knock to the head," Janie said. "Look at that *ridiculous* bird costume. Who wears stuff like this?"

Indira nodded. It was a very distinctive look. Which gave Indira a perfect idea. "What if . . . you wore it?"

Janie scowled. "I'm an outlaw. I wouldn't be caught dead—"

"No, I mean, what if *you* wear this to sneak into their castle?" She leaned down to look closer at the fallen wizard. "You're about the right height and size. I'd bet if you put this raven suit on with the hood up, no one in Final Boss would have a clue. You sneak into the castle. You find the flag. We can wait at the bottom of the outer walls for it."

The idea had Janie nodding. "And I'm the reason we win?"

Indira wanted to roll her eyes. Instead she nodded back.

"Absolutely. You're the reason we win."

Janie required no more convincing. She switched outfits, suiting up in the raven-like cloak. They went over the plan, arranged a backup plan in case Janie was captured, then watched as she made her way to the front gates of the castle. Indira and Phoenix were alone for the first time in weeks.

Except they weren't *really* alone.

Everest curled up on Indira's other side. The wolf nuzzled into her a little, eyes flicking over briefly to Phoenix before closing. She idly petted his head, not sure what she was supposed to do or say. It had felt for months like she was trapped between the boys, but now she was literally standing between them. Phoenix made it more awkward by launching into a speech.

"Hey. I've been meaning to tell you. I was a jerk. I was more focused on Everest"—the wolf's eyes opened when he heard that name—"than I was on you. I'm really sorry for how I acted. I guess I was jealous. It's not an excuse. There is no excuse for that kind of behavior. I was jealous, though, because since the beginning it's always been the two of us. Solving mysteries. Fighting bad guys. It's always been me and you. It was hard to accept that there might be someone else who's a good fit for you. . . ."

Indira shook her head. "Phoenix, it's not—"

"You don't have to explain. I promise that I'm okay. It's just that I like you. A lot. You're the person I like the most in the world. I liked you before we were in a story together. And I'll like you long after those stories are over. But that doesn't mean I get to choose for you. If Everest is the one who makes you happiest, then I want you to pick him. I'll always be here for you. I'm with you until the end. But you were right. We don't get to choose who's right for you. That's your choice. You deserve that much."

There was an awkward silence. A light growl echoed out of Everest's throat. She shot him a warning look. In the distance, Janie was being welcomed over the draw-bridge. They all watched her vanish inside. When Indira didn't respond to the speech, Phoenix cleared his throat.

"Come on," he said. "We should get in position."

He started trudging back down the hill to untie the horses, looking like the saddest undead she'd ever seen. Indira looked at Everest again. He tried to nuzzle back into her side, but Indira pushed away and started walking after Phoenix. She didn't know what to say or do. She'd thought it would get easier, that the choice would be clearer, but she felt more confused than ever.

They left the unconscious wizard behind and headed deeper into the forest, cautiously circling. Janie had agreed to throw the flag over the southern wall if their plan worked. The path wound back around until the castle was in view, no more than a stone's throw away. They made sure to keep tight to the cover of the woods, just in case there were still scouts roaming the ramparts. Indira stopped in her tracks, though, when she heard a distant whisper.

Power is power. Power is power. Power is power.

Her eyes were drawn away from the castle, off to the west. Through the branches, she saw what looked like a bunker. It was fronted by a barbed-wire fence. There wasn't any sign of movement. And if she hadn't heard the whisper, she'd have never noticed it at all.

Always guarded and always hidden.

"The scepter is over there."

Phoenix pulled up short. Everest sniffed the air. Their horses looked unsettled.

"Should we go after it now?" Phoenix asked. "Janie's inside already."

"Bainrow said it would be guarded, which means we'd have to get around whatever security is there. Janie would probably be suspicious of us. We sent her inside and agreed to wait here if she made it out. It'll be weird if she catches us exploring some other random building. . . ."

Iago's voice echoed in her head: *Don't forget why you're really here.*

"We could go real quick?" Indira said. "Check out the defenses?"

But that plan was interrupted by a wild cry from

above. Indira and Phoenix both ducked out from beneath the forest canopy and scanned the ramparts. There were answering shouts inside the castle. Something was happening, but Indira couldn't spot Janie.

"Where is she?"

The answer flung itself out a second-story window. They watched Janie plunge straight into a snowbank. She came stumbling out, snow spewing everywhere, a tattered flag clutched in both hands. When she spotted Indira, she hefted the flag like a javelin and fired it toward them. Distracted by its flight, Indira almost missed Janie collapsing into the snow.

There were Final Boss members pointing down from the window. Another trio was rounding the front corner of the castle, all on horseback.

"Ph—Phobia. Get Janie!"

His horse was already galloping forward. Indira raced over to the flag and yanked it free of the snow. A whistle brought Everest to her side. She leaped on his back, spared a glance for Phoenix and Janie, then shouted, "Get us to the bridge!"

They bolted through the forest. Phoenix followed, but Indira could tell from the voices that Final Boss was gaining ground. Everest had a clear advantage on the tangled forest paths, but any time they reached an open straightaway, the horses would start gaining on them again.

When the bridge appeared in the distance, Indira urged him to sprint his fastest. He crossed the rickety structure in three bounding leaps. She whipped back around in time to see Phoenix, low over his mount, struggling to keep Janie upright. Great bolts of magic whistled overhead. Indira saw a flock of birds sweep through the trees—ravens, she noted—preparing to dive in an attack. The wizard they'd left behind had woken up.

Just a few lengths behind them, a crew of Final Boss members were in pursuit. The group was led by Becky 2000, who was running incredibly fast on those metal-enhanced legs. Indira's chest heaved. She knew that if they made it across, there was no way she'd hold them off long enough to get back to the castle. Iago's voice came to Indira again. His advice echoed: *I want you to be a little crueler than normal.*

Indira leaped off Everest's back. Phoenix had reached the bridge. It shook as his horse started sprinting across. His eyes locked on hers. Indira broke her gaze long enough to take aim with her hammer. A single, powerful swing knocked the right railing free of the foundations. She spun and brought her hammer around, striking the left one next.

Indira looked up in time to see Phoenix's shocked expression. The Final Boss crew was trying to turn around. Scrambling back to the other side. Too late. The entire bridge plunged.

Her stomach dropped with it, but she knew she needed to look tough. For a real member of Crooked Faction, a move like this was expected. She heard a crash below, took a deep breath, and vaulted back onto Everest.

"We need to get this flag back to base."

After a brief hesitation, he darted into the waiting forest. Indira was trying not to feel sick to her stomach. *It's the Badlands. None of this is real. Phoenix is fine.* But she kept seeing that final glimpse of pure shock on his face. Indira knew she'd done the right thing. Hadn't she?

Everest skidded to a stop. Indira realized they were back at the base.

"No, no, no . . ."

Their entire castle was in ruins. There were fallen Crooked members everywhere. She saw creepy mechanical spiders crawling all over the ruins. The entire central tower had fallen in an explosion. Mastermind had clearly been here. Indira's worst fears were confirmed when the air around her locked. She couldn't move.

A message flashed:

Simulation over.

First place: Mastermind Faction

One point awarded.

The simulation ended, but the pain was still there. Indira had betrayed Phoenix for nothing. Nothing at all.

Inside Information

The next morning, Phoenix didn't show up at breakfast. Indira felt awful, but she couldn't make things right the way she normally would. Kind gestures would just keep her on the radar of Bainrow's spies. Instead she headed over to Antagonist Academy. As she walked, she purposefully bumped shoulders with certain people and shot them dark looks if they dared to say something.

Her chosen workshop—Nemesis NOW!—was in the bigger lecture hall. She took a seat in the back and kicked her feet up on the chair in front of her, rocking it annoyingly until the Pawn boy sitting there decided to move down to the end of the row.

A professor stood at the front of the room. One look and Indira knew he wasn't an ordinary person. He was absurdly hairy, to the point that he looked like he was covered in fur. And he was gigantic. At least ten feet tall. The only thing that made him less of a monster was the sloppy suit he was wearing, complete with a colorful bow tie.

"Take your seats, take your seats," he called to the students as they entered. "Don't worry, I won't bite."

A few students snickered at that. The professor shuffled a few papers on his podium, tracing a huge, clawed finger over the words.

"In this workshop, I'll focus on teaching you the art of becoming a true nemesis. You'll learn to look for ways to be opposition. How are you different from the protagonist? How are you similar? As you may know, I have enjoyed a long and timeless career in the tale of *Beowulf*. My story was so successful that I got a rare opportunity to serve as an antihero in my own story, entitled *Grendel*. That's the kind of potential we have, but we have to focus first on being a nemesis *now*. Not tomorrow, or the next day, or the next year. We have to position ourselves properly, and we have to do it *now*. . . ."

Grendel went through several slides, always speaking in a boring monotone. Eventually he abandoned the projector and went on a winding tangent about how much he despised his own nemesis, a hero named Beowulf. Indira was pretty sure he started accidentally speaking some other language, too, because there was a five-minute section toward the end that sounded mostly like growling. His real crime, Indira thought, was being such a boring professor.

Content that any spies would think her plenty bad,

Indira headed back to Crooked headquarters, searching for Phoenix. She found Zion and a few others eating in the mess hall, but there was no sign of Phoenix anywhere. Indira decided a quick catnap might be the answer to the little headache that had been building ever since she'd left the Badlands last night.

Except that two steps into her private room, Indira felt her feet freeze to the floor. Her body was completely immobilized. At first, she thought she'd somehow slipped back into the Badlands—maybe Bainrow had another surprise competition for them—but Indira couldn't even move her head to look around.

It was like the entire world had briefly paused.

And that was when Maxi appeared.

Her friend was moving around at an unbelievable speed. Too fast for Indira to follow. She stood in one corner. Then by Indira's bed. Then right in front of her. With each movement, she blurred in and out of sight. And Indira's foot still hadn't lifted off the floor. What was happening?

Maxi appeared in front of her. She was holding a white sign with a simple message:

NO OTHER WAY TO CONTACT. USED AN ELLIPSIS BOMB.

She traded out the first sign for a second:

FREEZES TIME FOR EVERYONE BUT ME. IT'S COOL. WHATEVS.

176

Another switch:

I TRACED THE FINGERPRINTS ON THE MIRROR FROM THE RESORT. GOT A MATCH.

New sign:

INFO IS ON YOUR BED. BURN THE NOTE AFTER READING.

Maxi shuffled again:

TO ME, YOU ARE PERFECT!

Indira frowned at that one.

JK. THAT'S FROM A BAD MOVIE. OKAY. GOOD LUCK! LYLAS!

Movement. Maxi collected her signs, teleporting around the room in quick bursts. Indira was still frozen, her foot just starting to lift off the floor, when her friend vanished from sight.

Time stretched again, back into seconds that made minutes that made hours. Indira's heart was hammering in her chest as she whipped around, but there was no sign Maxi had ever been there.

Except for the letter on the bed.

"An ellipsis bomb?" she muttered to herself. "Maybe I should have been an Editor. That was awesome."

She crossed over to the bed. The letter had been typed by Maxi herself. Her friend had stamped the bottom with her signature. Indira read:

The fingerprints were a confirmed match for PEVELYN ELEANOR MEADOWS. She is a third-year student at Antagonist Academy. She was a member of the Crooked Faction during her first year. Considering her fingerprints were on the mirror in question, it's very likely that she is an active member of the Antiheroes, albeit in some kind of junior capacity. She is a solid student at Antagonist Academy, though she struggles to find a story that properly fits her abilities. During her time in Fester, she has been courted by a number of sinister organizations—chief among them the Overused Exclamation Point Society— but it's logical that she might have joined the Antiheroes instead, given her background in lying and spy work. She goes by the nickname—

Indira couldn't believe it.
"Peeve Meadows."

23

There's No *I* in Team

Indira's head was starting to spin.

Alone in her room, she walked back through all that was happening in Fester. First, the Antiheroes had hired her to infiltrate Antagonist Academy. She'd managed that much, and with the help of Iago's meddling, she had landed the captain's role in the Crooked Faction. All of that was just a cover for her efforts to steal the Gemini Scepter. Bainrow's demons were actively spying on her. And now an old rival—Peeve Meadows—was apparently in league with the people who'd hired her to come in the first place? The cherry on top was that her two love interests were also here and also undercover.

It was a tangled mess, but at least Fester wasn't boring.

—

Indira managed a little sleep before it was time to enter the Badlands again. That night marked the beginning of a dark routine. Her time in Fester started to run together. Every night, she and her crew slipped into the Badlands.

Crooked Faction's first win was a shining moment that was hard to replicate. There was a series of second-place finishes and just-missed opportunities. One scenario was an apocalypse: meteors rained down, and the team with the last survivor won. Eugene led his crew in constructing an underground bunker to steal the victory. Some of the scenarios felt like they lasted a lot longer than others, even though Indira always woke up at the exact same time each morning. Her favorite scenario featured a relay race on horses that lived for a day and burst into flames each night. Indira thought it was fun, but Janie lost her lead down the stretch against Becky 2000 after the other girl shot her in the back with that ridiculous eye laser.

The hardest nights were when the scenarios really proved the meaning behind the name *Badlands*. There were some brutal head-to-head matches. Scenarios that forced teams into siege warfare, or duels to the death. In the Badlands, there didn't seem to be any rules, and most of the students were just fine with the fact that this brought out the worst in them. Bainrow occasionally made appearances during the day, around the hallways at school. He'd stand with those massive arms crossed, a wicked smile on his face. Of course he was proud. Everyone was slipping into more and more evil territory.

Privately, Iago urged Indira to keep looking for the scepter. They were running out of time before Bainrow's scheduled ceremonial spell. Sometimes she'd get close, finding the secret location it was housed in for that particular scenario. It was hard to fully investigate, though, with her team depending on her as the captain.

Phoenix and Everest were hot and cold too. She saw Phoenix around headquarters, but he'd kept a slight distance ever since the incident with the bridge. Everest only made appearances when the Badlands scenario had an outdoor element, and he was almost always in wolf form. It felt like she'd gone from having two great friends she relied on to having no one.

It didn't help that her time at Antagonist Academy was strange. She took the occasional workshop, mostly out of boredom. The school felt completely disorganized compared to Protagonist Preparatory. Sometimes she'd find it bustling and full. But when she went exploring a new area, she'd find empty classrooms and no students at all. Indira realized that the main problem was that the school didn't feel like a home, even for true villains.

Indira made her first breakthrough on the sixth night of the competition.

Her team appeared in the desert. It was a survival scenario. Each team would take a turn inside a tower stronghold. Whichever team could hold off the other three for the longest amount of time would win, rotating through until each team had their turn. It took Indira a few seconds to realize it was the same desert with the same tower from before. The scenario had changed, but everything else was identical.

"The stages repeat . . . ," she realized. "The stages repeat!"

Final Boss won that victory easily, but Indira's heart wasn't in the competition. She was too focused on seeing if the stages rotated through in the same order. If her theory was right, the next night would take place in the forest with the castles, where she'd betrayed Phoenix.

She waited with anticipation all day until the Badlands finally summoned them again. A smile stretched across her face when she looked around. It wasn't *exactly* the same. No snow on the ground this time. It was also late afternoon instead of the middle of the night. But there was no denying that they were in the same stage as before. Those three familiar towers loomed ahead like ghosts made of stone. Text appeared, announcing this would be another round of capture the flag.

Indira knew this was her chance to steal the scepter.

Power is power.

If she set her team up to defend the castle, she could head straight for the bunker. The sun was still out, so she wouldn't have Everest to carry her there. But she could take one of the horses instead. It felt right. Now was the time to make her move. As soon as her body unlocked and the scenario began, Indira ordered the entire Crooked Faction to gather around.

"Final Boss is to the northeast, across the bridge," she

said, pointing in that direction. "If we infiltrated them once, we can do it again. Janie knows where their flag is. And we also know that Mastermind hit us with a surprise attack last time. Not this time. We're going to go full defensive mode."

Everyone agreed to that plan. A few teams went inside to discuss which entrances needed the most protection. Indira stood in the courtyard, answering questions and overseeing operations. Phobia stood with her in his usual zombie-like silence. It wasn't until everyone was out of earshot that he whispered, "You're good at this."

Indira raised an eyebrow. "At what?"

"Pretending to be bad."

Indira was a little stung at first. The incident with the bridge still wedged between them. She wasn't sure if what he was saying now was a compliment, or a confirmation that for once he'd spotted something in Indira that he didn't like. After a second, she looked him in the eye.

"Promise to bring me back? If I get too . . . bad."

He smiled a little. At first Indira thought he wasn't going to answer. Then he whispered, "Always."

There was a call from up above. Janie Judas was leaning out the third-story window.

"Indigo? There's a new set of supply crates up here. Want to take a look at them? I'm not sure what you want to keep in the castle and what should be used for offensive measures."

Indira called back, "I'll be right there."

She winked at Phoenix before jogging up the steps.

Each of the towers overlooked the river. Really, they were close enough that a good shove from one of the bigger Final Boss kids might send them splashing down into the water. Indira was a little short of breath by the time she reached the third floor. Janie was there with Lefty and Zion and a couple of others, sorting through supply crates. She was halfway to them when the door slammed shut behind her.

One of the boys—a scout whose name she hadn't bothered to learn yet—carefully locked it. Indira frowned before turning back. Janie was grinning victoriously.

"What? You really believed I was fine with all this? Did you really think I'd let you steal my crew right out from under me? Not a chance in the world, Slappy. I've been waiting for this moment since day one."

The crew was approaching, fanning out in a practiced formation. Janie had a pair of short swords. Lefty cracked his knuckles. Zion was grinning. She couldn't believe that she'd let her guard down and walked right into their trap.

"Janie. This is only going to weaken us. The Mastermind captain—Eugene—he said that this is the reason Crooked always loses. There's always a betrayal and it only helps the other teams. . . ."

Janie's eyes narrowed. "I don't take orders. I give them."

The moment came. Indira had been through so many practice rounds of combat that she knew this moment better than most. The way every muscle flexed. The way hands tightened on the grips of weapons. The nervous anticipation of possible pain. All four of her attackers paused in that moment, standing on the doorstep of violence.

Indira's arm flexed. She took aim with her hammer. On the river-facing side of the castle, there was a small balcony, backlit by the dying light outside. The angle wasn't easy, but if she could just throw the weapon through the opening . . .

But her hammer was knocked from her hand. It was impossible. Her four attackers weren't even close enough to touch her. Janie looked at her in triumph. "Forgot about my auditions reward, didn't you? One chance to disarm an opponent. Never thought I'd need to use it on *you.*"

Before Indira could lunge for the weapon, the other three were there, pinning her down. There was a small clink. Followed by another clink. And Indira found herself cuffed to a metal chair. She fought back and kicked, but Janie laughed before shoving Indira down into the seat.

"Aiming for the balcony, huh? Let us help."

Hammerless and bound, Indira could only beg them to stop as she was dragged over to the edge of the balcony. There was a tottering moment where she thought they were going to shove her over the ledge and be done with it, but Janie couldn't resist getting in a final word.

"I used to play a game when I was a little girl," she said, loud enough for the others to hear. "Float or sink. I'd throw different things in the water and see what would happen. I always liked it when they sank. When they didn't come back. I still like to think of them at the bottom of that lake. Forgotten by everyone but *me*."

Then Janie leaned closer. Her voice lowered to a whisper that even Indira could barely hear. "It'll be easier this way. Remember your mission."

And, with a wicked grin, Janie tipped Indira over the balcony. She fell fast and hit the water hard. A great smack against the back of her neck, made more painful by the fact that the chair struck her too. She tried to kick, but like everything in the Badlands, the tide was a violent thing.

It dragged her downstream and dunked her every time she tried to surface. Indira felt the weight of the chair and the manacles tugging her deeper and deeper. She'd died before, in her encounter with Brainstorm Ketty. A few times in the Badlands as well, but none of those experiences had ever felt so dark and lonely and personal. The last thing she saw—before something grabbed her around the waist—was Janie's smiling face.

Power is power.

24

The Night Wolf

It turned out that the thing grabbing her waist wasn't an underwater creature. Indira found herself gasping for air, crawling onto the bank of the river. The chair and the chains dragged behind her through the mud. Someone was helping her, pushing her along. She had no idea how far downstream she'd gone, but when she looked back to see who her rescuer was, the waiting face wasn't a surprise.

Everest. The moon wasn't out yet, which meant he was just a boy. His dark hair had grown a little longer since coming to Fester. He watched her with those sunken eyes, his sharp-featured jaw tight. It took a second for Indira to realize what she was looking at. She sputtered the words.

"Where's your shirt?"

He smirked. "Right. Sorry about that."

She watched him cross over to a nearby tree, very aware of the slight movement of muscles in his arms and chest. No one would ever accuse Everest Smith of being unattractive. Indira looked away as he shrugged back into a T-shirt. He swept locks of dark hair out of his face before smiling at her. "So," he said. "What'd you do to get yourself thrown off a balcony?"

Indira's mind was a fog. At the edges of her memory, she could hear Janie's voice. Lower than a whisper: *It'll be easier this way. Remember your mission.* Had Indira imagined that? Or was there a hidden meaning in Janie's words? How could she possibly know about Indira's mission?

"I embarrassed the wrong outlaw," she answered. Her eyes drifted back upriver. The castle wasn't in view. "Are we safe? I have no idea how far I floated downstream."

"A decent distance," Everest said. "I saw you bobbing and jumped in."

"Thanks for that. Lucky you were down here."

He nodded. "I wasn't supposed to be. They told me to hang out on the edge of the map until nighttime. I got bored, though. No one noticed. I'm more of an accessory out here, I guess."

She'd forgotten that Fester basically saw Everest as a power-up, and that that was how he'd entered the city in the first place. She had so many questions for him, but she also didn't have time to waste.

"We should get moving. . . ." But as she adjusted her wrists, the chains tightened. "Which is a little hard when tied to a chair. You didn't see my hammer floating downstream, did you?"

Everest shook his head. "No, but I think I can be of

service. My talents extend beyond howling at the moon, after all. . . ."

As he leaned down and started fiddling with her chains, Indira couldn't help noting how close he was. It shouldn't have been strange. After all, she'd ridden on his back in wolf form, felt the warmth of his fur against her skin. Somehow it felt more personal to be this close to the boy version of him. She could see water dripping down his forehead and his lips moving as he muttered to himself.

There was a shiver in the air. Indira couldn't tell if she had shivered, or if it was something Everest was doing. A second later, though, she heard two rhythmic clinks. Both chains fell away. Everest winked at her.

"Told you."

She rubbed at both of her freed wrists. "How'd you do that? You don't even have a lock-picking kit. . . ."

He waggled his fingers. "Magical hands. I mean, not *really* magical, obviously. I've just got a diverse skill set. There was a workshop the other day. Taught by a Mr. Brekker? Useful stuff, even if he kept saying something about mourners and funerals. I don't know. People are really weird here."

Indira smiled. "I didn't even realize you could attend the workshops. Come on. Let's walk, and you can tell me all about it."

The two of them fell in easily, like they'd never been apart. They skirted well clear of the castle and headed upriver, aiming for the bridge that would lead to the bunker. The sun had almost set. The moon would be out soon, and Indira felt like she was racing against the clock. She wanted to talk with Everest as much as she could before he transformed again.

". . . so yeah, they keep us all separate. We're in these apartments in the city. I've gotten to walk around Fester a little, though. I have a tail, too."

Indira laughed. "Don't all wolves have tails?"

"No, like someone following me. Haven't you ever read a spy story?"

She laughed even more at the mix-up. "How do you know you have a tail?"

"There's this little imp trailing me. Always ducks behind stuff a second too late when I glance back. Not sure *why* he's following me, but I've made sure to keep a low profile. Haven't done anything suspicious. Tried to look the part of a curious tourist. I'm sure you think I'm just being paranoid."

Indira shook her head. "No, I had the same thing happen to me. Bainrow apparently keeps an eye on anyone who doesn't come here the normal way. It was kind of like the shoe scene in our book, remember? Where we found out the old man was actually a spy?"

The annoying back-and-forth with Everest and Phoenix had distracted Indira from the fact that her sequel was actually a *lot* of fun. The story had involved several plot twists, and Everest's arrival had been one of them.

"Right," he said. "I remember that. You were amazing, by the way. I was always bumbling my way through scenes. You never missed a beat."

Indira felt her cheeks warm. It was easy with him, almost natural. But all it took was a pause in the conversation for Indira's warring emotions to float back to the surface. Phoenix or Everest?

Time for a subject change. She was trying to think of something else to talk about when Everest nodded upward. "Moon is coming out. What's the plan? Are you going to take control of Crooked Faction back from Janie?"

Indira shook her head. "No. I'm not sure how much longer this scenario will last. We might not have much time. Remember the bunker? Across the bridge?"

Everest nodded uncertainly. "I think so, yeah."

"We're heading there. Time to focus on the real prize."

When Everest transformed, Indira climbed his fur-lined back. It was the warmest she could hope to be after Janie's betrayal had dumped her in the cold river. She hadn't realized how slowly they'd been moving until Everest started darting down forest trails with that same breathless speed as before.

The bridge had been restored for the new scenario. She eyed the opposite bank for signs of Final Boss, but there wasn't any movement.

"It's across, then to the left."

As they glided along forest paths, Indira's guess was confirmed. A whisper in the air. *Power is power.* The scepter was hidden in the same spot. Everest padded to the edge of the fence. The top was barbed. The bunker door looked fairly solid, and there was some kind of statue to the right of it. Was this really the only defense Bainrow's organization had installed?

"Keep an eye out for traps," she whispered.

Everest sniffed around the border until he found a good spot. There was already a slight gap between the fence and the ground. He started digging and she couldn't help grinning. One love interest had been reduced to an undead. The other one was happily digging holes with his claws to get behind enemy lines. At least they were both proving themselves.

Everest backed away, nudging her with his muddy nose. She laughed before eyeing his work. "Nice. Let's go."

But as Indira lowered herself, the world around them froze. She had that familiar sensation of being locked in place. The whispers coming from inside the bunker grew louder and more urgent. *Power is power is . . .*

Text appeared, and Indira knew she'd taken too long. Final Boss had won the game. She glanced at Everest and caught a fleeting glimpse of those lovely, sky-speckled eyes. And then she was back in headquarters.

The opportunity had slipped through her fingers.

25

Detention

Morning brought out all the feelings.

Indira felt some embarrassment about having been suckered in by Janie's act. That feeling mixed with confusion over the words the girl had spoken before throwing Indira into the river. It had been really nice to walk and talk with Everest, but that was overshadowed by her failure to locate the scepter. All those thoughts were leading to the beginnings of a plan, though.

In the hallway, Indira could hear a few of her crewmates filing down for breakfast. A part of her considered challenging Janie. Taking control of Crooked Faction, here and now. But something about Janie's words wasn't sitting right in her mind. *Remember your mission.* She waited for the footsteps to stop, then headed to campus instead.

At the school cafeteria, she sat alone, eating Gruelios.

Definitely a new low point.

As she walked the halls, other members of Crooked

Faction avoided her like the plague. Even Phoenix glanced her way before heading down the opposite hallway—likely on Janie's orders. It was a smart move for Phoenix to fall in line and keep his cover. It still stung a little to not get one of his usual smiles.

Indira realized a workshop would be useless right now. Her best path forward was Iago.

She found his assigned room, deep in the bowels of the school, but it was empty. A note on his schedule directed her up to the "gardens," where Iago was apparently holding detention. Indira ducked back into the hallway and slammed right into someone. She barely kept her feet. The other girl stumbled back a few steps before righting herself.

"Watch where you're going, rookie."

Indira's heart leaped right into her throat. It was Peeve Meadows. Her old neighbor adjusted the strap on her massive guitar case before catching Indira staring. Indira mumbled a quick apology and was trying to slip past the girl, but Peeve caught her by an arm.

"You know, you look familiar. Have I seen you somewhere?"

Indira nodded. "Montresor's workshop. You were . . . I was there."

Peeve's eyes narrowed. "That's right. Mountains out of Molehills. Useless workshops. Let that be a lesson to you, rookie. Get placed in a story, or else they'll just keep making you attend the same stuff every year. I've seen

Montresor do that bit with the wall three times now. It's a real treat. You're Crooked Faction?"

Indira nodded again. They were so close. She couldn't believe Peeve didn't recognize her. A shrill bell rang overhead. Indira thought it was a little early for workshops to end, but she hadn't been paying attention as she walked around the school. Peeve finally let go of Indira's arm as a stream of students came pouring down the hall toward them, released from class.

"I was Crooked my first year," Peeve said quietly. "Not a bad faction, but factions don't matter much after you finish the Badlands competition. You should consider *broadening your horizons.* Maybe think about what you want to do after school."

The girl brushed past Indira, catching her with a lowered shoulder as she did. Indira was jostled a bit as other students rushed past in an effort to make it to their next classes. Broaden her horizons? What did that mean? Why did it sound so familiar?

Indira made a note to contact Maxi. She wasn't sure *how* she would do that, but maybe her friend could look up that phrase and try to trace any connections. After all, Peeve's fingerprints had been found on that mirror. She had to be involved with the Antiheroes somehow. Was this some kind of secret guidance? Or did Iago's team not give all the information to all their agents? The encounter had her heart beating double as she headed up to the gardens.

Annoyingly, the area where Iago was hosting detention was up at the very top of the building. Indira climbed countless staircases before finally reaching it. Iago sat at a fancy table in the middle of a courtyard. He was surrounded by students working silently, on hands and knees, carefully tending the flowers of one of the most beautiful gardens Indira had ever seen. There were some flower species she didn't even recognize. Butterflies fluttered in the air. It was strange to see anything so lovely in a place like Antagonist Academy.

Iago looked up as she approached. "Ah. My former captain."

Indira ignored the sarcasm. "What is this place? The note said you were holding detention up here?"

Her mentor smiled. "I am. Is this not what you imagined detention would be like?"

"Not really. I pictured a dungeon."

"This whole place *is* a dungeon. Most antagonists find it far more excruciating to be quiet and still in a peaceful place. Tending to flower beds? It's torture for a lot of them." Iago gestured. "Besides, some of these flowers are highly poisonous."

A boy in one corner dropped to the ground, clearly unconscious.

"Did he . . . You said there's no Ninth Hearth—should we . . ."

Iago nodded. "Help him? No. He will recover in a few hours. Should have worn his gloves. You're only supposed to break the rules that are smart to break."

Indira watched the boy twitch a few times before set-tling. It felt wrong not to help, but helping in this place wasn't the norm. She took a deep breath, remembering why she'd come. "Janie betrayed me."

"What did you expect her to do?"

Indira shrugged. "Work with me? Our team was doing well."

"Aha. What is the saying? You have to learn to crawl before you can walk? You're still crawling, it seems. Be-trayal is the name of the game here. It's who we are."

"Janie also said something. Right before she betrayed me. Is she . . ."

Iago raised a finger to silence her, then reached for a pen on the table. At a touch from his hand, it shivered into a new form. Indira could feel the magic this time. He was trading a lie for the truth. It was a clever trick, and a part of her wanted him to teach her how to do it.

The pen transformed into some kind of old-school grinder. Iago started turning the handle of the device, crushing leaves and nuts inside. A thump-thumping noise of turning gears filled the courtyard. Iago's lips barely moved, and Indira had to strain to hear each word.

"She is one of our agents. We find this new posi-tion beneficial for our cause. Honestly, it couldn't have worked out any better. You no longer have to stick with your crew. No one expects Janie to involve you in her plans. You can search for the scepter as soon as you enter the Badlands now. Janie's maneuver frees you up. No one will be watching you, because no one cares about you anymore. You have twenty more days. Get the job done."

Iago stopped turning the little handle, unlocked the device, and dumped a mushy green powder into a bowl. He added a liquid she didn't recognize and swirled them slowly together.

"What is that?" she asked.

Iago smiled. "Oh, this? It's pesto."

She stared at him.

"It goes great with pasta."

That brought out a scowl. "Any other advice?"

Iago looked thoughtful for a moment. He sat back in his chair before speaking in a voice that was far more poetic than anything he'd used until now. It rang like an ancient warning. "'Tis in ourselves that we are thus or thus. Our bodies are our gardens, to the which our wills are gardeners."

"Right. And what's that mean?"

"What happens to us is up to us. You can do this. I believe in you."

Indira left the gardens, trying to take that encouragement to heart. Iago was not quite as uplifting as Brainstorm Underglass. He didn't have any of Deus's optimism, either. But at least she was walking away with a plan that she could actually put into action.

Go to the bunker.

Find the scepter.

Job complete.

26

A New Technique

The next five days were painfully boring. Janie made a point of isolating Indira. It helped to know that the girl wasn't just doing it out of spite. She was doing it to give Indira a clear path to search the Badlands, but still. Indira quickly discovered just how boring it can be to be alone.

This was made worse by the fact that Everest didn't appear in the next few Badlands scenarios. One was a repeat of a water stage, only this time the competition was playing a game of Sharks and Minnows, but with *actual* sharks. An apocalypse stage had Crooked Faction trying to survive a mutant uprising. Indira made vague searches for the scepter, but in reality she was biding her time for the best possible opportunity.

She was waiting for the stage with the bunker. It was the one stage where she knew exactly where the scepter was hidden, and she knew she had more than enough time to actually get to that location before the game of capture the flag could end.

The desert stage came first. Another scorching landscape with a central tower. Explosions everywhere. Crooked Faction scored a surprise victory that had everyone in good spirits. That actually worked in her favor. It felt like everyone was distracted going into the next night.

As usual, she carefully avoided the rest of the crew. There was a ruckus down near the kitchens. She could hear Janie's voice echoing from her room. Really, she was surprised the girl hadn't demanded she move out of the so-called captain's quarters. It would have been exactly the kind of spiteful maneuver she'd expect from Janie.

Eventually, the noise died down. She could hear the others returning to their bunks to get ready for the Badlands.

Indira was absently turning the ring on her finger — with the engraved Crooked Faction emblem — when a bang sounded at her door. She sat up straight, one hand reaching for the grip of her hammer. There was a grunt. Someone tried to turn the handle. She frowned.

"What on earth . . ."

Indira stood upright as the door slammed open. Phoenix was there. Still in his undead disguise, of course, but clearly breaking his cover. Both his eyes were bright with flame. He looked at her in desperation as three other Crooked Faction students struggled to pin him down.

It was all chaos and tangled limbs.

". . . Indigo . . . it's not . . . everything . . . one big . . ."

Lefty yanked him by the hair, cutting off his sentence.

Indira was moving to help him when the world vanished.

—

Breathless cold filled the air.

It was dusk inside the Badlands. Indira saw the familiar towers. Her crew was on the right. Another capture-the-flag game was announced. As soon as the air around her body unlocked, she broke into a sprint away from the castle. Straight into the woods. She didn't know what had gone down, but there was no way she was risking a power move from someone else in Crooked Faction.

As she wove under branches and down paths, boots soaked from the melting snow, she almost ran smack into Everest. He grinned, clearly thrilled to see her again, but frowned when he saw her expression.

"Hey. Ind—Indigo. What's wrong?"

Indira shook her head. "Phobia. One of the people who betrayed me figured out that Phobia was with me somehow. He was trying to tell me something. Then the Badlands snatched us away."

Everest considered that. She saw the briefest twinge of jealousy cross his face. The two boys had been against each other since they'd first met.

"I'm still in my apartment," Everest confirmed. "No one escorted me on campus tonight before the bells tolled. Which means they started the Badlands early, I guess?"

Indira frowned. What had Phoenix wanted to tell her? She could still see the glowing flames in his eyes. She hated that she hadn't thought to find him here, in the Badlands. She could have easily brought him along on this mission. At least they couldn't hurt him in the simulation. Indira vowed that the second they returned to Fester, she'd put her hammer to good use. Everest was watching her closely.

"What do you want to do? Should we go back for him?" he asked.

Indira shook her head, remembering the plan.

"No. We can't waste time. Let's get to the bunker."

———

The two of them forged ahead as the sun began to set. Indira knew they'd make far better time when the moon came out and Everest could shift into his wolf form. Twice they saw Final Boss scouts. One was roaming the opposite riverbank. All they had to do was steer inland, though, to avoid him.

The second scout came riding over the bridge on some kind of large goat. Indira heard the creature bleating as they whipped by, a war horn bouncing in rhythm against the boy's back. Little by little, they made their way toward the destination. They were across the bridge before encountering more movement. There was a small Final Boss crew roaming the adjacent valley.

Indira crouched with Everest, eyeing the best path forward.

"How about there?"

He pointed to a path on their left. It wasn't the most direct route, but the path had a hundred trees and hollows for them to hide in if any scouts appeared. It'd be their best bet for getting through the area without earning unwanted attention. Before she could agree, a branch snapped.

Indira and Everest whipped around.

There were three figures closing in on their location, all fifteen paces away, crouching as they snuck forward. The central one was Becky 2000. Her foot still hovered above the freshly snapped branch and her laser-red eye was swiveling.

"Run," Indira hissed.

They darted in the opposite direction. Down the hill and toward a snow-packed road. There were whoops and shouts. She didn't have to look to know their enemies were in pursuit. She heard their footfalls. The eager breathing. Indira wasn't sure how long she could run at a full sprint, but that didn't end up mattering.

Two more Final Boss scouts appeared ahead of them, cutting off any chance of escape. The foot soldiers chasing them fanned out in a circle. It was a trap. Indira and Everest came to a stop in the middle of a dirt road. Five fighters against just two of them. Indira couldn't believe their bad luck.

She locked eyes with Everest.

"Well," she said. "We were going to have to fight eventually."

He was grinning at her. They'd spent *hours* practicing this. It was a big reason why Indira had been so torn. She had something special with Phoenix, of course, but there was also something special about the fact that Everest was the only other person who could use Indira's hammer.

They took up their stances, standing back to back, as their enemies closed in around them. It looked like Everest was weaponless, but he and Indira knew better. The first attacker lunged. Indira sidestepped him, shoving the boy toward Everest. She landed a blow on the second attacker. Then the hammer vanished, as expected, from her hand. It appeared in Everest's, and he landed his own blow, before Indira pulled it to herself again.

Each time the hammer teleported between them, a shock wave of power knocked their opponents back. Their movements became a dance. Whenever Everest had the weapon, Indira was bending and dodging and avoiding blows. But when she pulled the weapon back to herself, she went on the offensive again. A quick jab, a second swipe. Then Everest had the weapon and was barreling into the person from the opposite side. It was a rhythm they'd carefully honed. One by one, their opponents dropped.

The last one standing was Becky 2000. She'd been waiting to enter the fray, which felt like a true Final Boss move from a video game. Her metal arms transformed into blades, and then she advanced with a series of sweeping strikes. Indira had to admit the robotic girl's blows were brutally strong. There was also an efficiency to the way she fought. Everything was tight; no motion was wasted.

But robotic creations fight in patterns. It didn't take long for both Indira and Everest to get a sense of her style: what kind of strike would follow the next, and so on. Indira waited for a weakness in the pattern, then shouldered into Becky to knock her off balance. Everest was ready, sweeping the girl's legs from under her. And as Becky fell, Indira drew the hammer back into her hand and drove her down even harder with an overhead slam to the stomach.

Becky hit the ground hard, circuits overloading, and didn't make an effort to get back up. Everest's chest was pumping. Indira grinned at him. "You looked a little rusty."

He laughed. "I've still got it."

They high-stepped through the fallen attackers. Indira led Everest on through the forest. There was no reason for subtlety or hiding now. She doubted Final Boss would pursue them after what had just happened. If they could beat them that badly once, she knew they could win again.

As they reached the curtain of trees, she glanced back just to make sure there was no pursuit. And the sight sent a chill down her spine. All the fallen soldiers had taken their feet. They weren't giving chase. Instead they were staring. Whispering to one another. She frowned at the final glimpse of Becky's watchful laser eye before picking up the pace to catch up with Everest. The forest path was growing darker. She tried to shrug off the bad vibes. The group's stare felt like a warning. It was like they knew that something bigger and badder was waiting ahead. Indira locked eyes with Everest.

Bring it on, she thought.

27

Primary Objective

Everest transformed again in the moonlight, but this time they were positioned right outside the bunker. He quickly sniffed out the location from the last time and started digging. The snow made it slightly more difficult, but after a few minutes, they were through. Indira had spent a lot of time wondering what kind of safeguards Bainrow and his crew might use.

There were no massive walls. No locked gates to pick. It was just the bunker door, guarded by a creature who Indira initially mistook for a looming statue. The way she unfolded from her crouched pose was like poetry—or like a sword coming out of a sheath. Indira only knew that it was a woman because the creature had a human head and human shoulders. Dark hair swept down to meet her lower half, which was shaped like a winged lioness. She licked her lips at the sight of Indira dismounting from Everest's back. Her tail swung hypnotically from side to side.

"Approach, mortal."

Indira definitely would *not* obey that command. Not before she knew who she was dealing with. There was something familiar about the creature. Had she encountered something like her in one of her stories? Or back in Fable? It was at the edge of her memory, on the tip of her tongue.

"Who are you?" Indira asked.

"I am the one who asks the questions."

Indira bristled. "Kind of rude."

The creature stared. "No, that's who I am."

"Huh?"

"I am the one who asks the questions."

"I know. You just said that."

"No . . . I mean that is my identity . . . You know, never mind. I am the Sphinx."

And that word brought the memory back to life. She'd met a sphinx once. During her first year, when she'd been considering quitting. She'd gone to Quiver to visit David. On her way back to Fable, she'd encountered a creature like this. Half lion and half man. Only it had been reversed: a lion's head attached to a man in a suit. And he had not been a very effective guardian.

"I need to enter the bunker."

The Sphinx smirked. "None may enter unless they answer my riddle."

Indira glanced sideways at Everest. She was weighing whether or not the two of them could take on a creature like this one. But all the stories about guardians echoed in her mind. No one just forced their way through. They had to play the game they were being offered.

"And what if I get it wrong?"

Another smirk. "I will devour you — soul and all."

Everest let out a growl. Indira appreciated his reaction. She'd been expecting to have to leave and come back, something like that. She wasn't even quite sure *how* someone devoured a soul. But she also thought it unlikely that she could *actually* die. Fester didn't have a Ninth Hearth, but Iago had mentioned earlier that the Badlands was a simulation. Dying here wasn't like dying in the real world. It was the whole reason they practiced warfare in a big simulation like this one.

Indira raised her chin boldly. "Ask your question."

Everest growled again, but too late. The Sphinx spoke, sharp teeth glittering.

"What walks on four feet in the morning, two in the afternoon, and three at night?"

Indira rolled the clue around in her mind. At first, she thought the answer connected back to Everest. He walked with four feet at night and two by day, but three? That didn't make sense. The creature was clearly using his presence as a distraction from the real answer. Indira realized that she was pacing. She also realized that the Sphinx was mirroring her steps, slinking back and forth, a predatory expression on her face.

"Four feet in the morning . . ."

Indira was thinking and thinking when a voice echoed in her mind. It sounded dreamlike and distant, but Indira had no doubt that it was Iago. It was a sentence from memory, but she felt like Iago was saying it directly to her now, whispering the words in some secret corner of her mind.

You have to learn to crawl before you can walk.

Of course.

That was the answer.

"A human," Indira said. "A person. We crawl as babies. Four legs in the morning. We walk as adults. Two legs in the afternoon. And . . ." Three legs? Her brain scrambled. Why three legs? She frowned before figuring it out. "And we use a cane in old age! Three legs! The answer is a person."

The Sphinx's eyes narrowed. She let out a dissatisfied growl before taking flight. Her great wings swept the snow in circles around their feet. Indira shielded her eyes, but when the wind swirls stopped, she found the bunker entry open and the Sphinx winging in the sky above.

"Come on, Ev."

The interior was like the inside of an inverted lighthouse. Just a single, winding staircase leading around, but instead of going up, it descended into darkness. Indira took it. Everest padded along silently behind her. A tingling excitement ran down her spine. Her goal was in reach. The whole reason she'd come here. She just had to get to the scepter *before* this scenario ended. On and on they went in an endless, tiring circle.

Finally, she reached something besides stairs. A much smaller door—like the kind that might lead to an attic or basement—was stationed there, already half open. Indira pushed it the rest of the way and was ducking inside when she heard a slight whimper from Everest. She looked back.

"What? Oh . . ."

The entry was too small for him. He paced back and forth, unsettled.

"It's all right. I'll grab the scepter. It will pull us back to Fester. The Antiheroes will be ready. Down goes Bainrow. Got it?"

The noise he made didn't quite sound like agreement, but Indira knew they needed to act quickly. If Bainrow somehow found out she'd passed the Sphinx, it was possible he'd send in reinforcements. It was also possible that someone would win the scenario. Resolved, she turned her back on Everest and entered. There were three more steps down into the basement. A circular walkway oriented around the glowing scepter, which was the only light in the entire room. She could hear it whispering to her again.

Power is power is power is power . . .

A final obstacle presented itself.

The scepter was levitating out of reach, beyond the railing. Indira eyed the drop. It looked like an endless black pit. The kind you might fall in and then never stop falling. She took a deep breath and climbed on top of the rickety barrier. Once she felt balanced, she swiped for it. Her fingertips brushed the scepter. Her arms pinwheeled as she almost fell.

But the weapon kept whispering to her, beckoning her . . .

Indira reached out again. This time she decided to fall. It would be worth it. Her feet left the railing. She snatched the scepter, and purple light flashed in an arcane blast of power. She hovered there in midair and felt the weapon's magic pouring into her veins. It pulsed through her, racing like a river along waiting paths. Filling every empty part of her. Racing and racing and racing.

It felt really good. Until it didn't.

When the power reached the very tips of her toes and fingers, she felt the magic *twist*. There was a sequence of painful triggers. First the collar of her gifted cloak tightened. She felt as if she was choking. But she couldn't lift her hand to tug it free. Both hands were stuck in a death grip on the scepter.

She couldn't imagine ever letting it go.

Power is power is power . . .

At the same time, the ring Indira had been given tightened. It squeezed and squeezed until Indira thought her finger might fall off. But the worst pain came when the power inside her began to tighten as well. She felt it curling around her bones, suffocating her veins, dancing through her mind and heart. Like an unwelcome guest.

It gathered everything that made her Indira Story, shoved those qualities into a dark corner of her mind, and slammed the door shut.

28

Hubris

Her eyes opened.

She was no longer in the Badlands. Now she stood on a stage. It was the same classroom she'd attended for Grendel's boring lecture. A massive crowd had gathered. All of them were there to watch *her.* In the front row, she spied teachers she recognized — Montresor and the Stepsisters and Grendel — along with other members of the Antagonist Academy faculty.

In the second row, members of the Crooked Faction were seated: Janie Judas and Zion and the others. Farther down, she saw Becky 2000 and Eugene and Lizzie B. Borden. Every prominent person she'd encountered since she'd arrived in Fester. Indira's vision of the room flickered in and out. The power was still flooding her veins. There was applause. Indira stood motionless as Iago and Bainrow walked out on the stage to take their places on either side of her. The two looked like opposites standing together. Bainrow towering and powerful, Iago small and secretive. Watching them now, Indira couldn't help noticing they looked like . . . partners.

"It actually worked," Bainrow said.

Iago circled. "Seven years in the making, my friend."

Indira's confusion must have shown on her face, because Iago shot her a look of false sympathy. "Allow us to explain, *Indigo*." He smiled his cruelty, and it was as if Indira finally saw him for the first time. Not just a small-time crook or liar. This man was every lie ever told. He was an ancient kind of evil. She could only watch as he slid on a pair of black gloves. "You are now our puppet."

He lifted a finger. Indira's body moved involuntarily. She raised the scepter up into the air. Another twitch of Iago's finger brought her arm back down. It was like someone was pulling the strings of her mind, carefully controlling every function. She had that same feeling she'd had in the Badlands, of being stuck, paused. Only she wasn't sure if this feeling would ever fade. And this wasn't a simulation.

"Heroes," Iago said with disdain. "If we can count on one thing, it's that they are always eager to come to the rescue. *Hubris* is the name for it. A pride that whispers they need to be in the middle of everything. Thank you, Indira, for coming to rescue us from wicked Bainrow."

There was laughter from those seated. Bainrow gave a theatrical roar before joining in on the laughter. There were whistles from the audience as the massive demon bowed his way offstage like a trained actor.

"You see, this is the true art of being a magician," Iago continued, speaking to both her and his captivated audience. "You must have a bright ribbon in one hand. It must draw the eye. Lure in the victim. So that they do not see the magic you're doing in the other hand.

"We brought you here with great purpose, Indira. The Antiheroes? Fake. Bainrow's Final Boss Protocol? Fake. All just bright ribbons to lure the eye and hide our true purpose."

Indira gritted her teeth. Her voice was a growl. "Why?"

Iago looked a little surprised that she could speak at all. He curled his fingers and her body went rigid again. Indira realized the gloves were controlling the power inside her. The scepter's stone gleamed. Iago eyed her for a moment, then answered the question.

"Fable is *our* land. It was taken from us. It is the true epicenter of Imagination. Authors center their tales on people like *you*. The supposed *heroes*. Why? Because of the city that once belonged to us. A city that *will* belong to us again. And when we take Fable as our own, we will be the new center of the universe. Stories will revolve around *us*."

There was a roar of excitement from the crowd.

"But Fable has always been very well protected. We are permitted entry once a year for auditions, but there are powerful spells that have kept us from launching a large-scale attack for centuries. Those same spells have also kept us from enjoying the benefits that you have always enjoyed. No Ninth Hearth, remember? Until now. *Every cage has a key.*"

Iago looked her in the eye. Those were Indira's First Words. The very first line of her very first story. Now he was using them against her.

"And you shall be *our* key. We started with Bainrow, seven years ago. He was tasked with making the school look like it was being run by a truly evil faction. Someone big and bad prepared to make everything worse. Gave you little *heroes* something to feel heroic about.

"Then we created the Antiheroes. Good guys with a bad side, right?" Iago winked at her. "Our fake missions put us on Fable's radar. And then all we needed was the right hero for the job. You were perfect, Indira. An in-world hero. Someone who had saved Imagination before, because if you didn't know, Imagination rewards its favorites. And you've done that twice. Bravo. All it means for us is that you have even more access to Fable than most. Now all the permissions you have been granted will be gifted to us."

Indira's chest kept rising and falling. It was the only reason she knew she was still alive. Her mind felt like an elaborate trap. Every thought she had hit a wall. *Move your hand. Grab your hammer. Fight back. Tell him he's got no chance.* Each time, however, the thoughts rebounded back to her. It was like she'd been pushed back into a tiny corner of her own mind. Helpless.

"Let's take a moment to thank the folks who put on such a convincing show." Iago turned to the audience. A spotlight roamed. "Janie and the Crooked Faction, of course! A brilliant job with all the distractions. Nothing like a little fake rivalry to take your eyes off what's truly happening!"

Their crew whooped and hollered and bowed. Indira didn't see Phoenix with them.

"A shout-out to the other factions as well. Becky and Eugene and Lizzie. All very well done. Utterly convincing work." He gestured. "And our next award goes to the Antiheroes for a brilliant opening scene!"

Indira watched some of the teachers stand, sliding masks over their faces. The Stepsisters were both snakes; Grendel was the bear and Montresor the lion. Peeve Meadows was there too, and she pulled the monkey mask over her face briefly before winking at Indira. She was the one who'd pulled her through the mirror in the first place.

Indira couldn't believe it.

"How about a round of applause for all our extras? After all, the best lies are in the details!"

The rest of the audience stood now. Indira spied the undead girl she'd confused for Phoenix in class. There was the boy who'd fallen asleep in line in front of her. Other students too, whom she'd encountered in her classes or detention. Every single one of them had been in on the pretend show.

It was all a lie.

Indira's mind traced painfully back through the details. Her best clue had been the earpiece. How many other students had one? All of them? It was clear they'd been using them to monitor her status and keep everyone up to date. That probably explained the school, too. How sometimes it would be full of students who looked busy, but other areas would be completely silent. They'd been putting on a show wherever *she* went. Maybe they didn't have enough actors to cover the entire school.

Then there were the gifts she'd been given. The ring and the cloak. There were the workshops, which had all been fake. All her interactions with Janie. Maybe even Phoenix's and Everest's presence there. What better way to distract her than including the two boys she liked most? There'd also been Zion, interrupting her conversations with Phoenix.

Every single thing had been a distraction. All of it was a trap.

Anger roared to life in Indira's chest.

It was less of a thought. More of a feeling. Maybe that was why it broke briefly through the great barricade in her mind. She felt like setting the entire city on fire.

Her hand defied Iago's command to remain still. She reached for the hammer at her hip. They'd left it there, maybe assuming she had no power to grab it. In one smooth motion, she lunged for him. But the great liar turned just in time. Those gloved hands went up, and Indira froze mid-swing.

"Oh, no, no, no . . . ," he chided. "We are only just beginning."

The walls in her mind doubled in strength, circling around her awareness. The scepter's power surged. She watched helplessly as Iago flicked his wrist. Indira's hand opened involuntarily. The hammer she'd had from the very beginning, all the way back in the little town of Origin, dropped to the floor with a dull thud.

It was like watching a limb be cut away.

"Now . . ." Iago stood directly in front of her. "Take us to Fable."

Indira's last vision was of that room, filled with antagonists, all rising to their feet. And then her vision of the world faded. She could feel her body moving. She could tell she was marching. There was a thunderous herd of footsteps following behind her, swirling like a dark cloak.

An army was on its way, aimed like a spear, to Fable.

29

Prison Is Awkward

PHOENIX

Phoenix was chained to a wall in the bottom of a rather
dark cell.

The light outside flickered, the way it always did in
bad prison movies. He'd been dragged down here by the
Crooked Faction crew a few hours ago. He still couldn't
believe his bad luck.

He wasn't sure where things had gone wrong. Brainstorm Underglass had filed his paperwork, transformed
him into an undead, and sent him north. It had felt like
a fun undercover adventure. The first clue that something was off came after he'd parted ways with Indira and
Everest. He'd been expecting moments when his identity would be questioned. Why had the character he was
replacing vanished? Where had he been? Surely they'd
be suspicious. No one had looked at him twice, though.
He'd thought it was a credit to his zombie-like appear-

ance. Maybe people just didn't think too much about the undead being spies.

Everything had changed today when he'd grabbed the wrong notebook in class.

It was an honest mistake. After an acting exercise, he'd returned to the wrong desk, snatched the notebook, and headed on to another workshop. When he'd opened it up to take notes, he'd been shocked to find that the journal was already writing itself. Words were being scrawled by an invisible hand.

> Target is moving to third floor.
> Team A on alert.
> Let's get Team C in position for Scenario 23. Extras at the ready, please.

Phoenix was smart enough not to panic. He'd simply turned to another page, listened to his professor, and pretended to take notes. But every time he glanced back at that first page, the truth became more and more obvious. All these notes were about Indira. Someone was keeping tabs on her every move.

And then he'd finally noticed the journals. Everyone had one like this. Not just a few potential spies. All the students. All the teachers. Only Phoenix hadn't been given one. He left class feeling paranoid. Were people watching him? Did they know he'd been sent from Protagonist Preparatory? He went back to Crooked Faction's headquarters, determined to tell Indira. But she hadn't shown up at dinner.

Phoenix had delayed, eyeing the door, hoping she'd come. Finally, the crew had started yawning their way back to their bunks. He'd pretended to fill up his plate again, even though he'd barely touched anything his first go-around. Janie's crew was still there.

"Phobia! Join us! Don't be such a loner!"

Not wanting to look suspicious, he had. It was clear Janie was trying to extract more information out of him. She asked a ton of questions. When all he did was answer in undead groans, she finally got bored. Phoenix eventually stood and announced he was going to sleep. He made it to the hallway before pulling out the stolen journal.

He turned to the first page and read: *Get him!*

That was his only warning. Lefty barreled into his back, and he barely slid free of the boy's grasp. He darted up the stairs and down the hall, all three of them on his tail. As he slammed into Indira's door, he missed the handle. Lefty lunged for him. The others piled on. He'd managed to rip open the door, but he couldn't get a proper sentence out while getting elbowed and tugged and pinched.

Indira had looked so confused.

And then they'd been snatched into the Badlands.

But just for a few minutes. When he'd blinked back to life, Bainrow had been standing over him. The demon had no problem hauling Phoenix to his feet. He was incredibly strong. As they dragged Phoenix away, he'd caught a glimpse of Indira sitting upright in bed, her eyes snapped shut, muttering as she navigated the Badlands. His desperation to warn her hadn't worked. They escorted him to the same jail cell that he was currently sitting in.

He still had no idea what had happened to Indira. Hopefully, he hadn't blown her cover or anything. Phoenix was thinking about his next move when footsteps sounded. The guards made their rounds down here just so they could offer a few extra insults to the prisoners. He was determined to show no weakness. He stood tall as the shadow became a person.

"Phoenix?"

He made his eyes look lifeless. "I told you, my name is Phobia."

But the light flickered bright enough for him to see who was there. A dark-haired boy with an annoyingly handsome face. Where Phoenix was thin as a rail, Everest was more athletic and muscled. His jealousy really spiked at the sight of Indira's hammer tucked into Everest's belt. This was the special bond that Phoenix could never claim. Seeing her weapon in Everest's hands now made one thing clear, however. His rival must have somehow helped the antagonists.

"It was you," he accused. "You betrayed her. So . . . what . . . you're her antagonist in book three or something? How could you do this to her? She trusted you."

Everest turned away. In one smooth motion, he shattered the overhead light with Indira's hammer. The row of cells went dark. Phoenix could only see fitful shadows, but he heard metal against metal. The scraping sound became a groan, and Everest was there, just a few feet away.

"Seriously? You think I'd help them? How about keeping your voice down? You're not exactly making our escape any easier."

Phoenix found himself annoyed by the British accent. As if that was really all that *charming*. But his mind caught on the most important word his rival had spoken. "Escape?"

"Yes, escape. Unless you plan on helping Indira from this disgusting prison basement."

Phoenix straightened. "I don't need your help. I was about to escape by myself."

Everest took a step back and folded his arms. "Sure. By all means, escape."

He waited. The moment stretched out awkwardly. Phoenix's attempts to transform into his dragon form had not gone well. There was some kind of anti-magic metal running through his chains. After a second, he bowed his head.

"Fine. Help me."

Everest immediately started working on picking his locks. Phoenix couldn't help feeling his annoyance surge. There was nothing worse than having to be saved by the *other* boy that Indira liked. But thinking about her was a good reminder. What would she do? Phoenix knew, deep down, that Indira Story would do whatever it took to save the day. She didn't care about little rivalries. She didn't have time to be petty. She'd always been too busy being a hero. His right chain fell with a clank. Everest started working on the left.

Phoenix cleared his throat. "Thanks. For rescuing me."

"It's at least partially selfish," Everest replied. "Indira's been captured."

"Captured?"

The second chain fell to the ground. "Yeah, I'll explain. Come on."

And the two of them slipped off into the shadows, together.

30

Escaping Is Awkward

EVEREST

Everest led Phoenix through an underground tunnel. "Can you change your appearance?" he asked, unsure how the other boy's magic worked. "Everyone will be looking for a zombie."

Phoenix muttered a few magic words under his breath. There was a strange shiver of light, and then the decaying features melted away. He was back to the long red hair and patterned freckles across his nose. As they reached the end of the tunnel, Everest couldn't help glancing at him again. He'd never really liked him. They were competitors, after all. But he'd come for Phoenix because he *knew* Indira cared about him.

Thinking about her reminded him of his current mission. Inside the Badlands, he'd seen a great flash of light from the scepter. Indira had vanished. A few seconds later he'd blinked back to life in his own bed. Outside, the entire town was buzzing with news: all talk about "the plan finally working" and that this was "the beginning of a new order." He'd carefully made his way back to Antagonist Academy.

He snuck into the back of the main lecture hall and watched as they paraded Indira around like a puppet. As the rest of the crowd followed Indira out of the great hall, Everest backtracked to the stage area. A few students had taken turns trying to steal Indira's hammer. When they gave up their attempts, he'd used his power to summon the hammer into his hand. Holding the weapon had helped him settle his thoughts. His next step had been to find Phoenix.

Now they were escaping together.

"I turn into a wolf."

Phoenix stared at him in surprise. "Huh?"

"When we walk out there . . . The moon is out. I'll turn into a wolf."

There was a little spark of emotion on Phoenix's face that he tried to hide. Everest thought he knew what the other boy was feeling. Transforming into a dragon had been his leg up. The one clear advantage he had in the competition for Indira's affections. Now they were on even footing.

Everest went on awkwardly, "I think I've got a plan for how to get us out."

Five minutes later, they were about ready.

"Are you sure about the one-strap thing?"

Everest nodded. "Looks authentic."

"Fine. Let's go."

They'd taken mud—at least he *hoped* it was mud—and decorated Phoenix's face and chest. A slight adjustment to his robe made it look more like a kilt. With the red hair, he was a dead ringer for some kind of Scottish warrior. The final touch was Everest himself.

He stepped out into the moonlight. The transformation was immediate. He felt his bones stretching. Felt the wildness in his chest. He shook his whole body before turning around, loping up to Phoenix. There was a spike of emotion there that almost curled back his lips, almost had him baring his teeth. This was an enemy. This was a rival . . .

. . . this is Indira's friend. It's one of the people, he remembered, *that she cares the most about in the world.*

That human voice echoed. Phoenix was Indira's pack. Instinct didn't want to accept that truth, but when Phoenix held out his hand, Everest did not snap at it with his sharp teeth. Instead he lowered his nose, nuzzled Phoenix briefly, and then turned to let him mount. The other boy pulled himself up and slid his hands into the collar's grooves, and then they started trotting down the alley. It was easy to slip into the packed streets and join the streaming army as it headed through Fester's southern gates. They were too far back to see Indira at the front.

Everest didn't panic. He let out a growl, reminding himself to stay focused on his mission.

Phoenix gripped his collar a little tighter and leaned down to whisper.

"Don't worry. We're going to save her."

The growing army continued to march.

31

Information

MAXI

Maxi hadn't signed up for *this*.

The streets of Fester were flooded with grinning goblins and brooding villains. Her earpiece was a stream of constant chatter from the Editors in the area. Something had gone wrong. All the reports said Indira was marching back to Fable and there was an army following her. There was no way Indira would have actually joined forces with them. There had to be more to the story.

Maxi knew it wasn't their place to intervene. The Editors were supposed to let stories like this unfold, stepping in only in the direst of circumstances. But she had one clue to follow, and she was going to pursue it no matter what her bosses' orders were.

After all, Indira's life might depend on it or whatever.

She followed the directions she'd been given. The address led her down a back alley, which wasn't surprising. The entire city of Fester felt like one big back alley. She promised herself she'd have a long spa day after this, just to get the grime off her skin.

Maxi found the front desk of the apartment building abandoned. Most of the hallways were empty too, except for the occasional straggler. She passed a pair of vampires who were in the middle of an argument.

"I don't *know* if it's cold there, Levi. I've never *been* to Fable."

"Well, I'm not going to carry your jacket around when you realize it's too hot out."

Maxi slipped by them, heading deeper into the poorly lit apartment complex. At the very end of the hall she found the address she'd researched. The numbers on the door were correct, although the 9 of 109 had fallen off the nail and looked like it was attempting to escape.

Usually, she'd have knocked, but the person who lived here was no doubt marching at the front of the army outside. This was the longtime apartment of Peeve Meadows.

Maxi had found the girl's prints in their system. Something about the name sounded familiar, but she honestly didn't remember until seeing the girl's photo in one of the record books. It had all come back to her then. Peeve had been there on the day Maxi, Indira, and Phoenix first met. Back in Origin. It was strange to think of all that had happened since. And stranger to think that Peeve had lived such a different life—in such a different place—from the rest of them.

Maxi pulled her precious Editor's pen out of a jacket pocket. A squiggle of red ink in the air changed the locked door to an unlocked one. She entered. The place was dingy. A bowl had been abandoned on the table and cereal had all but cemented itself to the bottom. The living room consisted of a single chair and a stack of books in one corner.

Maxi eyed the cover of Peeve's most recent read: *The History of Imagination.*

"How studious," she whispered.

The living room led to a bare-bones kitchen. She saw another door leading to a bedroom. Maxi was just following a hunch. She'd found Peeve's fingerprints on the mirror. Not strange, really, to think that Peeve was a member of the Antiheroes. That lined up. The strange part was that there had been *any* fingerprints at all. In all her research, she hadn't found any slipups like that from the Antiheroes. All the information about them was tightly controlled. They covered their tracks.

So.

Why had Peeve made such a simple, unexpected error?

There was a high-pitched scream. Maxi jumped a little before locating the source of the noise. There was a kettle on the stovetop. Steam hissed out. Someone was making . . .

"Tea?"

Peeve Meadows slipped out of her bedroom, calm as you like. The girl had wild curly blond hair that was shoulder-length and tied off by a patterned bandana. Her checkered top was tucked into a high-waisted skirt that

Maxi would have gladly borrowed if they were friends. Even at a glance, Maxi could tell that life in Fester had changed her. This was not the sputtering girl she'd first met in Origin. Peeve pulled two mugs out of a cabinet, as well as a couple of tea packets.

"I've got wild orange."

Maxi's head tilted just slightly. "That's my favorite."

Peeve nodded. "I know."

As she watched, the girl poured two cups. She ripped open the little packets and let the teabags drop into steaming water. Peeve turned and set Maxi's cup on the table between them.

"We should talk," she said. "Since you conveniently broke into my apartment."

Maxi didn't move to grab the tea. She still had her Editor's sunglasses on. It was their organization's policy to always play it cool. Never make a scene. And they most certainly would *never* admit to wrongdoing.

"The door was unlocked."

Peeve snorted. "Right. I'm sure it was. Don't you want to know why I'm still here? I was supposed to be out there, marching at the front of the army. So why am I here instead, Maxi?"

Maxi shrugged, like it wasn't all that interesting to her. Peeve snorted again before ducking briefly back into her room. She returned with a black guitar case. Maxi's mind dug back through buried memories. She had a glimpse of another version of Peeve standing in line with them in

Origin, holding the same guitar case in hand. There'd also been a note in Peeve's file. The dossier claimed the girl could lull someone to sleep with a few strums.

"Indira was tricked. The Antiheroes are fake. It was all a carefully designed trap to lure her here. Iago's controlling her now. He plans to march south to Fable. Indira will give the antagonists full access to the city for the first time in centuries. His main target is Protagonist Preparatory. I need you to take me there before they arrive. I read that Editors have ways of traveling quickly."

Maxi glanced over at the stack of books. "You shouldn't believe everything you read."

There was a brief flicker of concern on the girl's face. She'd been depending on this. Which meant she'd known that Maxi would come. "You left your fingerprint on the mirror on purpose."

Peeve nodded. "Iago has eyes and ears on everything. It was the only way that I thought I could guarantee a meeting with you. Clearly it worked. So, can you take us to Fable or not?"

Of course she could. Maxi had a hundred tricks up her sleeve. Editors had abilities that other characters in Imagination could only dream about. Maxi asked the question that actually mattered.

"Why should I trust you?"

Peeve shouldered her guitar case.

"Because I'm the only one who knows how to save Indira."

The girl walked past her and headed for the door. Maxi

still hadn't made up her mind. Should she help Peeve? Or get back to headquarters? There'd be a mile of red tape to get through if she took this to her bosses. Before she could turn around, Peeve called over one shoulder.

"Don't forget your tea."

Maxi had been trying to ignore the lovely scent. Wild orange had been her favorite flavor for months now. She took a few sips, annoyed at not having a proper travel mug, and followed Peeve.

32

Flip of the Coin
DEUS EX MACHINA

Deus Ex Machina sat at a table in a mostly empty tavern. There were a few retired booksellers in one corner, discussing their favorite stories. The rest of the place was unoccupied. He was sitting with one of his favorite librarians. He'd consulted her on how the rest of this story would go.

You might already know this, dear reader, but librarians are invaluable resources. Founts of knowledge. Some might say they are the truest heroes we have left in the world. Others might say that they're simply a group of folks who love to read. Either way, it should be no surprise that even someone as powerful as Deus might go to one, seeking advice.

"What do you say we flip a coin?" Deus asked. "If it lands heads, I'll make some last-minute tweaks. If it lands tails, I'll stay here and not change anything."

Mrs. Ruby grinned at him. "Do you really think you

could resist trying to help? It's not like you resisted in 'Red Riding Hood.'"

"Well, the woodsman was a compelling character."

"How about the Great Eagles in *Lord of the Rings*? They were barely mentioned!"

Deus shrugged. "Birds saving the day—who doesn't love that age-old tale?"

"And that sword in Harry Potter randomly teleporting everywhere?"

"It wasn't random!"

The librarian laughed. "Oh, Deus. Fine. Go ahead. Flip your coin."

Deus Ex Machina—provider of convenient solutions—reached into a special pocket. Out of that special pocket, he produced a special coin. The two of them locked eyes as he flicked the silver high into the air. And as the spinning coin reached the height of its arc, Deus was moving.

———

Blink.

———

He stood outside Protagonist Preparatory. There, on the ground, he produced a single muddy puddle. It was almost cartoonishly perfect. He tested it with his foot and heard the flawless squelch of mud and water. He eyed the angles once more and smiled. It would do just fine.

—

Blink.

—

He was in the head office of Brainstorm Underglass. His fingers drummed on the desk as he walked across the room. There was a series of rather well-ordered cabinets on one wall. He located the fifth drawer up, third on the left. With a careful tug, he left that particular drawer open.

—

Blink.

—

He was in the home of Detective Malaprop. The bumbling inspector was sound asleep. Deus paused a moment, confused. The detective's bed was the strangest he'd ever seen. It was bright orange, shaped in an oval. The pillows looked like green leaves, and Malaprop wore distinctly brown pajamas. It was the strangest decoration he'd ever seen. . . .

And then it hit him. Deus held up a hand to stifle his laughter.

"Apricot. He's sleeping in an apricot. Good heavens."

Deus produced a wrapped gift and birthday card. He

set them on the kitchen table. He was about to leave, but for good measure he decided to underline the name on the front of the card. Just in case Malaprop somehow thought the gift was for him.

———

Blink.

———

He was on the back terrace of a new Story Condominium. He double-checked that he had the right address before leaning down and loosening the screws of the railing. He gave it a testing shove. The wood groaned. Any more weight and it would likely snap off. He glanced over the edge and made sure he had the angles just right.

———

Blink.

———

He was in the dorm room of David Story. Deus froze at first. In spite of the late hour, the television was still on. David sat on the couch with a video-game controller in hand. Deus frowned. If he made the tweak he'd intended, it might echo the wrong way now. What to do?

But as he edged forward, he realized that David's hands on the controller were slack. His chin dipped down to his chest. Asleep. How convenient.

He adjusted the time on David's digital clock by two hours, then turned on the alarm.

———

Blink.

———

He stood in a tinkerer's room, busy with tools. It looked more like a garage than a bedroom. There was someone curled up in a rolling chair, burrowed into a big jacket like a squirrel. Deus produced a single hex-head bolt and left it standing upright on the desk.

———

Blink.

———

The final room was lovely. There were amateur paintings on the walls. Each one showed a different weather pattern. A storm out to sea. A light rain. Gusts of wind, which were not particularly easy to capture. They'd all been created for meditative purposes, he knew. Deus walked over to the nearest table and set a peanut-butter-scented candle out. He reached into an interior pocket of his jacket and produced a matchbook. With a flick of his wrist, the flame caught. He held that to the wick. A familiar lunch-box scent wafted into the air.

He left the matchbook there, just in case.

———

Blink.

———

He was back in his seat at the tavern. The coin was falling. Deus reached out and caught it in his palm. He brought that palm back, slamming it on top of his opposite hand. He sat there for a moment, his chest heaving. The librarian rolled her eyes.

"I've known you for too long, Deus. I saw you moving. It's subtle, but I saw you moving."

He revealed the coin. It had landed heads.

Deus smiled at her. "Just a few polite shoves. Now we'll see if that is enough to save them."

33

The City's Favorite Daughter

BRAINSTORM UNDERGLASS

Brainstorm Underglass woke at five a.m., as always. She went downstairs to exercise in her personal gym, as always. That was followed by a balanced breakfast, but her normal reading of the morning paper—*Aesop's Fables*—was interrupted by a knock at the door. One of her assistants had arrived, bearing an urgent message.

"We have word of an approaching army."

Underglass lifted a single eyebrow. "Did you say *army?*"

She slipped quickly into a black power suit with pearl buttons. Normally, she'd have changed out the cuffs and picked shoes to match, but alas, there were worlds to keep in order. As they walked across the courtyard to Protagonist Preparatory, she was briefed on the situation. Indira Story was leading every villain from Fester to their doorstep. An army would soon reach the outer perimeter that had long separated good from evil. It was an unbreakable spell that had stood for centuries.

"Bainrow knows about the barrier. So what is his play? A workers' strike, maybe?"

About seventy years ago, the antagonists had boycotted for better contracts. It was the closest they'd ever come to creating full-on chaos in the world of Imagination. Not an actual war—the magical barrier had long protected Fable from outright attack. But it had still been profoundly damaging to have all those antagonists not accepting their roles in stories. She hadn't imagined Bainrow capable of that kind of organization. He was more brawn than brains. It was an odd move on his part.

More disturbing was Indira's presence at the head of the army. It was that particular detail that left her feeling out of sorts as she took a seat in her office, distractedly listening to the ongoing reports from her flustered assistants.

"Our contacts say Fester is a ghost town. Everyone has mobilized."

"Indira's got some kind of new weapon."

"She almost went to Fester. Years ago. Can we pull up the report on that?"

Underglass was still thinking through all the details as the assistants continued their string of updates. Could the Antiheroes really have convinced Indira to join them? Or was something else going on? Brainstorm Vesulias stood at the back of the room, brooding. Underglass was pacing behind her desk when she noticed the open cabinet. All those neat rows were in order. Having anything out of place bothered her. And she always made a sweep of the room before leaving for the night. Why was this drawer open?

She walked over to shut it, but the light of the room caught on an object inside. Underglass carefully pulled the cabinet open. A great horn rested within. She'd placed it in this spot nearly a decade ago. Her predecessor had liked to show it off to guests. That wasn't her style.

It was the Horn of Heroes.

Underglass picked up the ancient tool. There was a leather strap strung through a small loop at its base. She slid the strap around her neck and felt the ivory beneath her fingers. It was unlikely she'd need the horn, but being organized meant having backup plans. She'd said that very thing to Indira Story before sending her north. After a moment of consideration, she turned back to the assistants. All their theories and chatter fell quiet.

"No point in guessing. Let's go see what they want. Parley."

———

Fable was still in the clutches of autumn. It felt strange to walk past babbling brooks and charming farmhouses, especially knowing what waited in the valley beyond. The great army of Fester had gathered on the outskirts of the city. It was no small company of soldiers; it was a truly massive gathering, an army. There was some slight organization to their waiting rows, but Underglass could see—even at a distance—what separated Fable from Fester, good from evil. There was no desire in their ranks to truly be a team. Each antagonist was just waiting for their own moment in the spotlight.

It was unfortunate that Fable wasn't in a better costume. A sci-fi setting would have given her access to launch codes and hi-tech defenses. Other versions might have gifted her with great castles or militarized forts. All they had to defend them now were apple orchards.

And the magical barrier.

The hairs on the back of her neck stood as she approached its edge. There were not many people in their world who could have sensed the magic. It hung there, invisible to the eye, but no less meaningful for being unseen. The spell had been cast centuries ago. It circled the entire city, promising protection from exactly what stood at their doorstep at this moment. No force of evil had ever passed it, not without express permission from Protagonist Preparatory.

She promised herself they would not pass it now.

Underglass paused at its edge. There was movement along the ranks, and she saw their champions striding forward. Bainrow was there, stone-muscled and vain. Iago strode beside him, those devious eyes drinking in the details. Grendel loomed in the background, all fur and teeth. It was a motley crew. The only person who didn't belong with them was Indira Story.

She'd been made over, as they had planned. A purple streak colored her raven-dark hair. The hammer she'd made famous was missing, though, replaced by a dark scepter that pulsed with arcane purple light. Underglass knew it was not right to have favorites, but Indira had been hers for some time now.

"Indira? What's all this about?"

The girl didn't respond. She stared straight ahead, as if the city of Fable was the only prize she could see. That detail brought several pieces of the larger puzzle together in one fell swoop. Underglass had expected a conversation or a debate. Maybe Indira had learned how poor the conditions were in their neighboring city. Perhaps someone had pulled on her sympathetic strings. Indira had always had a soft spot for injustice; it was a rather large part of the girl's charm. But she didn't argue for better working conditions. She didn't accuse Underglass—and the generations of brainstorms before her—of cutting Fester off from valuable resources. She didn't even blink.

This wasn't actually Indira. She was under some kind of spell.

"Ah yes." It was Iago who stepped forward, that reptilian smile spreading across his face. "Indira is indisposed at the moment. She's a bit busy leading our revolution."

Underglass resisted rolling her eyes. Iago had a gloating look. It was clear that he was relishing this moment. Clearly, he had tricked them. She wasn't sure about all the details of what had unfolded, but as she watched Bainrow defer to Iago, she knew she'd gotten something wrong about the Antiheroes. It was clear that Indira was in their control, and it was Underglass's fault for sending her to Fester in the first place.

Was this why they'd come? To ransom the city's favorite daughter?

"Enough with the theatrics," Underglass said. "What do you want, Iago?"

"Oh, just a small request," he replied. "We simply want what was once ours: Fable."

Now she did roll her eyes.

"It was never yours."

Iago looked up and down the rows. Underglass followed his gaze. There were villains of every sort gathered. Every single character was watching attentively. They knew—whether from stories or instinct—that this moment was as important as what came next.

"Once, we lived here. It was our land first. There were *real* heroes in stories, and the first Authors made up villains to match them. We were Imagination's first guests. Protagonists came after. Settling into the town we'd already built. And then, one day, you forced us out."

Underglass threw her words back at him. "That's not true."

"Forced us out," Iago repeated, voice rising. "Removed our access to the Ninth Hearth. Drove us into the mountains. Treated us like dogs. We should have been equals. You made sure that protagonists were always at the center of stories. Isn't that how the gears of the Great Exchange are programmed to turn? For centuries, it has been set so that Authors think of *you* first. You are their North Star. Their guiding light. The natural beginning point. Not anymore."

Underglass could not hide her shock. Which of the brainstorms before her would have allowed him access to the Great Exchange? It was their prized secret. A priceless treasure on which their entire foundation had been built. The idea that Iago knew of it frightened her more than any revelation thus far. She answered him firmly.

"Our protections still hold, Iago. Do you see where your army has stopped? No evil can pass this place . . ."

". . . unless invited by good. That is how the quote goes." Iago looked triumphant. "And we've been invited to the party. Haven't we, Indira?"

Underglass's eyes fell on her favorite student. Before she could say something, try to break through whatever spell they had placed on her, Indira lifted the scepter. Purple light thundered out. It hit the invisible wall of protection like a detonated bomb. Underglass watched ripples of light and shadow chase down its length, running in both directions, dissolving their outer wall like it was no more than a fancy bubble.

"No . . ." Underglass was stumbling backward. "This isn't possible."

"Get Indira's other contacts," she heard Iago command Bainrow. "You have the addresses. I don't want to risk her seeing any of them before we secure the school."

A thousand different spells ran through Underglass's mind. She'd always been a capable wizard. And there were powers that she could call upon as a brainstorm. Her mind couldn't hold any one thought, however, as the evils of Fester streamed forward to invade her beloved city.

Instead of a spell, her hands fumbled on instinct for the horn. It dangled against her chest. Before the swarm could reach her, she put that great horn to her lips and let out a single, mighty blast. She was overtaken an instant later. Villains crowded around her, hungry for their first taste of true victory in centuries. At least she'd sounded the horn. It was her last hope.

That sound would echo through the city.

A call to heroes. *Come. Save us.*

Breaking Ranks

PHOENIX

"W hat's the plan?" Everest hissed under his breath.

The sun had risen and Phoenix's accomplice had transformed back into a boy. They were positioned about ten rows back from Indira. Riding a wolf had made catching up to the front lines of the army quite easy. It had also earned them a lot of cool points with the other villains. Getting any closer to Indira was far more difficult. There was a tight-knit crew of guards and professors circling her at all times.

It was also impossible to see what was happening now. They'd stopped along the outskirts of Fable. Their view was blocked. Too many ogres standing at the front. Bad organization, really.

"Get Indira," Phoenix whispered back. "If we can stop her, we can stop the army."

"Right," Everest replied. "But how do we actually get to her?"

Before Phoenix could answer his question, there was a burst of magic in the sky. Both boys looked up—just above the mountain-like shoulders of the ogres—and saw magic racing out from the center of the blast. Phoenix could *feel* something break. Something magical and ancient. It was like watching a great redwood fall after centuries of being alive. He held a hand to his mouth as a war cry sounded. The entire crowd started shoving forward. Their footsteps shook the ground. Everest and Phoenix stumbled along with them.

"Hey! Over there! Look!"

Phoenix spotted Janie Judas, pointing in his direction. He hadn't noticed her running a few rows behind them. She'd stopped dead in her tracks. Lefty and Zion flanked her. Even though there were herds of villains rushing past, Janie started making her slow and deliberate way over to them. She clearly recognized Phoenix, even with his zombie disguise gone. But he had no intention of being captured again. He could already feel the burning sensation at the backs of his eyes.

Enough was enough.

"Everest. Get ready to climb on my back."

"Phoenix, I really think we need to—"

"Just do it!"

Phoenix let the fire chase through his veins. It was smoke and fury and freedom. He gave in to that feeling and felt the magic surge through him. Everest backed up a few steps.

When the smoke cleared, Phoenix was looking down

at Janie and her crew. They looked afraid. *You should be afraid,* he thought. Roaring, he released a stream of fire. It caught the edge of Janie's sleeve as she leaped to one side. The nearest antagonists all changed course. It gave Phoenix the opening that he needed. He set his right shoulder lower and felt Everest scramble up, searching for a place to hold on. When Phoenix was sure he was settled, they took flight.

Three wing flaps brought them up to the tops of the trees.

Phoenix's enhanced dragon eyes spied Indira instantly. She was walking with deliberate intention up the hill, aiming straight for the heart of Fable. Figures were gathering in the city, but still too far away for direct warfare. Some of the more eager antagonists were running ahead in their excitement to shed first blood. Phoenix saw Iago walking with Indira. Several other professors and baddies surrounded her like an entourage.

One thought pulsed in his mind: *I have to rescue her.*

Three more wingbeats drew him even higher into the sky. Everest was trying to shout something, but Phoenix had already decided. He had no way of telling his rival to hang on for dear life, so he hoped Everest was smart enough to figure out they were about to dive. Phoenix waited until he was gliding directly above Indira to make the descent.

It was the usual rush. Air and cold and exhilaration. Everest let out a noise of surprise as they came spiraling down toward their target. The villains protecting Indira all looked up, but if he moved fast enough, there was no way they could stop him. Phoenix's wings swept out to slow his momentum. He was reaching with his right claw to grab Indira when she turned, pointing her scepter directly at him. A great bolt struck his right wing.

Pain lanced through that half of his body. Phoenix went spinning away and barely managed to keep them airborne. Another bolt sizzled through the air above them, crisping his shoulder as it went. Waves of pain crashed through him. He could feel his body slumping. Everest shouted again, but before Phoenix could crash, an unexpected updraft carried them higher. Phoenix thought maybe it was adrenaline or instinct, but a glance showed that his wings weren't even working. The right wing was shredded to pieces.

It wasn't until he completely lost control of his limbs that he saw the responsible party. On the balcony of a nearby building was a blond wizard with glowing eyes. A good friend.

"Squalls," Phoenix whispered, before losing consciousness.

35

How to Catch a Dragon

ALLEN SQUALLS

Allen woke up that morning to an unexpected scent.

He moved sluggishly through the motions of getting dressed. The entire time, the smell of fresh peanut butter wafted through the air like a promise. Allen normally set out candles. It was part of his therapy. Ever since the adventures in Ordinary—and his reenrollment at Protagonist Preparatory—he'd been learning to control his powers. It was not long ago that he'd only been able to summon storms by falling asleep. The artwork on his walls, the calming candles, even some wizard's yoga—all of it helped Allen in becoming a true master of his own magic.

But as he walked into the living room, he frowned.

"Is that peanut butter?"

He didn't remember lighting this particular candle. Really, he didn't remember buying a candle of that scent. Not remembering small details wasn't entirely unusual, though. He still sleepwalked from time to time. There was a matchbook beside the candle too. He picked it up, eyeing the elaborately drawn letter *D* on the front. Maybe he had gone somewhere in his sleep?

Before his mind could follow any of those strange details, however, his stomach rumbled loudly. The scent reminded him of his favorite breakfast spot in Fable: Cratchit's Crepes.

It was a family-owned diner on the south end of town. He usually just ate cereal for breakfast, but every now and again he'd make the morning trek to their locale. The food was unbelievable, and the scent of peanut butter had him remembering their special smoked peanut-butter crepe. He glanced in the mirror, combed his hair a little, and headed out the door.

Mrs. Cratchit ran the place with her son Timmy. It was early, but Allen was a bit surprised by how few customers there were today. He put in his order and settled into a seat by the window. It overlooked a courtyard with a charming little fountain. It was a pleasant and quiet way to start the day, especially given how much training he had waiting for him this afternoon.

A few minutes later, Mrs. Cratchit came bustling out with his order. She wore a blooming dress, as always, that puffed out like a great balloon. Her sleeves matched the shape, waving like sails as she set the plate down. She always offered a smile as warm and welcoming as her food.

"Doing a little carb-loading before the big showdown?" she asked.

Allen blinked. "Showdown?"

"I doubt those are houseguests out there," she laughed. "I figured it must be some kind of contest or something? Didn't see anything in the papers about it, though."

Mrs. Cratchit gestured to her balcony. Cratchit's Crepes was on the third floor and overlooked the southern half of the city. Allen wasn't sure what she was talking about, but curiosity had him setting down his fork and knife. He might as well check. As he stood, he heard a great horn blast. It rang like a bell, echoing louder, the sound sweeping past and through him like an invitation.

Come. Save us.

It felt like someone was whispering directly to him. It was strange, but strange things happened all the time in Fable. Odd noises and epic quests came and went every day. Characters were always practicing for their stories, often using rather bizarre methods.

But as he pushed open the shuttered door and walked out onto the balcony, Allen's jaw dropped. There was an actual army running up the hill toward the city. This didn't look like a practice drill. He saw confusion. Great giants bounding forward with their massive, muscled legs. Witches gliding on brooms. All of them aiming at the heart of Fable.

Were they under attack? Why hadn't anyone told him?

A burst of color caught his eye. It was a burnt clay, made more magnificent by a sweep of wings. He recognized the form as it swept higher into the air. Allen stumbled to the railing.

"Phoenix?"

His friend swept up to the clouds before diving down. Allen watched, cheering his friend on, even though he had no idea what Phoenix was doing. At the very last moment, there was a blast of purple light. Phoenix swerved to one side. He looked like a plane that had lost a wing. Turning end over end, on the verge of smashing into the ground.

Allen Squalls summoned his magic.

Storm clouds rumbled overhead. He'd been practicing, though. It was not enough to throw out some random thunderbolts; this required finesse. He drew on the wind. He swept all his power into those gusts. He experienced a slight shock when the magic caught Phoenix. He guided the blowing gale, slowly drawing his friend out of harm's way. It was like yanking on a heavy rope to pull an anchor out of the sea. Allen dug his feet in and pulled, hand over hand.

It took most of his strength to pull Phoenix safely up to the building's balcony. Thankfully, his friend had shrunk out of his dragon form halfway there, which made it a little easier. Squalls was surprised to find another boy clutching the unconscious Phoenix tightly. They both landed in an unceremonious heap. Mrs. Cratchit stood by the door, a little surprised by the arrival of new guests.

"Should I get some crepes ready for them as well?"

The dark-haired boy with Phoenix grinned.

"We're going to need more than crepes to fight them off."

36

The Birthday Party
DETECTIVE MALAPROP

It was such a pheasant mourning.

Detective Malaprop had woken up with every intention to continue investing in his newest case, but then he'd remembered the birthday party. There was a card on the table for little Patch Pennington. A birthday present too. Sometimes he was surprisingly well prepared for life's curveballs. He tucked the gift under one arm and headed out the door.

Everyone seemed a bit busy this morning. He waved to an ogre who was setting a nearby building on fire with a torch. "Best of luck with your renovation!"

He knew a lot of buildings in downtown Fable were being remodeled, but hadn't realized that the ogre community had gotten those contracts. A very superstitious turn of events. He wrote a note to himself. Another potential investigation!

Malaprop whistled the tune to "Wheels on the Bush" as he rounded the corner. There was a single road leading out into the vast neighborhoods of Story Houses. Last year, the Penningtons had moved into a brand-new apartment complex. They were one of twelve stories in their book, which meant they had a rather lovely third-floor condominium.

The detective passed a pack of wolves. He politely tipped his cap to them.

"Good morning! Rise and swine, as I always say!"

The wolves looked at each other in confusion before trotting past him. Malaprop found the roads surprisingly packed for such an early hour. He was halfway to the Penningtons' when he spied a friend. Indira Story was striding at the front of a rather odd group. She'd dyed her hair and put on darker makeup. By pure coincidence, Malaprop's path had him intercepting their crew at the crossroads.

"Indira!" He waved. "Really liking the new haircut! Very stylus!"

His old friend didn't offer her typically warm smile. He did see the corner of her mouth tug upward, just a fraction. Malaprop supposed she was trying to remain businesslike in front of her colleagues. One of them — a man in a frumpy-looking tunic — scowled at him.

"Don't you mean *stylish*?"

Malaprop frowned. "Pretty sure I know what is stylus and what is not, sir. I minored in Fashionable Crimes back at university, after all. Plus, I'm not the one wearing something from the fifteenth centurion, am I? All the same, a good day to you!"

His mother had taught him to always be kind, even when others were rude. Malaprop tipped his cap one more time to Indira and continued on his way. From the looks on the faces of her entourage, he was pretty sure he'd successfully gotten in the final word. They all looked completely baffled. He didn't want to be too prideful, but he knew his improvement was a credit to all the pronunciation classes he'd been taking.

"Practice makes permits!"

As he arrived at the edge of Mrs. Pennington's neighborhood, he looked back. There really was an odd assortment of people out today. And everywhere he looked, they were fighting, rolling around on the ground or running into some kind of pretend battle.

"Hmm. Must be Random Wrestling Day. Thought that was next week. . . ."

He reached the Penningtons' building without any other strange encounters and knocked politely at the door. His detective senses kicked in, however, when the door creaked open on its own. It hadn't been shut properly. And a glance showed that the wooden frame was shattered.

"Forced entry!"

Malaprop's instincts were rarely wrong. His mind quickly linked the broken frame to another case he'd spent the last two months working on. There'd been a string of burglaries, and his investigation had indisputably proven that the most likely culprit was a band of robotic bears.

He took a deep breath and shouldered inside.

"Stop in the name of the lawn!"

37

An Uninvited Guest

MRS. PENNINGTON

It was not the best morning for Mrs. Pennington to have slept in.

Her fiancé—Jack—was downstairs with Patch. The two were in the middle of a game of checkers when their uninvited guest arrived. He did not knock. He did not politely ring the doorbell. He simply shouldered through their front door like a linebacker. A snarl unleashed spittle across the room. Mrs. Pennington woke up immediately upstairs. Motherly instinct roared to life. She barely paused to throw on her robe before taking the stairs two at a time.

Jack was cornered. His only defense was a rolling pin she'd left on the kitchen counter last night. Patch stood behind him, peeking out to make *pew-pew* noises as he shot their intruder with imagined lasers. A great monster approached. He stood three times as tall as Jack. If not for the lovely vaulted ceilings in their living room, he wouldn't have fit. Jack waved the rolling pin, trying to look threatening.

"Seriously?" the intruder laughed. "I fought the mighty Beowulf. Do you truly think that I fear a man who wields baking implements? I am Grendel, the terror of Heorot."

Mrs. Pennington snatched a plate of cookies from the kitchen table.

"And I am a *mother* and you should be *ashamed* of yourself!"

She started flinging the cookies at the intruder like missiles. Grendel stumbled, taken off guard by the surprise attack. It allowed Jack to herd Patch to the back of their apartment, near the sliding glass doors. Mrs. Pennington saw that he'd left them open to let in the crisp morning air. When she'd finished launching cookies, she snatched up her current knitting project. Grendel lunged, but a mother protecting her children has adrenaline that even ancient monsters can't hope to match.

She dodged his first strike, wrapping her unfinished scarf around one of his arms. Ducking right, she tied his other arm to the first, effectively handcuffing him. The monster let out a furious roar, but Mrs. Pennington had spent months sparring with Indira. She knew how to face an opponent. She matched his steps, shifting her body, always stepping just out of reach of his claws.

It was an unexpected dance for a villain like Grendel. Even though his own mother had been a force to be reckoned with, he hadn't expected this much opposition from someone in a bathrobe.

Their tussling brought them closer to the open screen door. Mrs. Pennington was pulling with all her might to keep him away from Jack and Patch. Grendel was about to break free of her tangling scarf when a shout echoed from the front of their apartment. She looked up in time to see Detective Malaprop streaking across the room. He leaped through the air and performed a surprisingly nimble jump-kick.

The blow struck Grendel right in the chest.

The monster went sprawling back, and Mrs. Pennington barely had the presence of mind to let go of her scarf. He crashed into the back railing of their balcony. Mrs. Pennington expected him to rebound, but the wood snapped as he hit it. He let out a roar before vanishing from sight. Jack made sure Patch was safe before peeking out over the spot where the railing had been. He called back to them, "He's tangled in the pool tarp!"

Mrs. Pennington was breathing heavily. What on earth was this all about? And where had Detective Malaprop come from? Just to put a cherry on the top of her confusion, the detective stood up and brushed off his jacket.

"Happy birthday, little Patch! Next time, though, I suggest not inviting any robo-bears. They are dangerous creatures, and also notoriously bad gift givers."

Mrs. Pennington burst out laughing, in spite of the thunderous beat of her heart.

38

The Missing Piece
GADGET

Gadget didn't really believe in *sleep*.

She believed in tinkering. She believed in ripping apart car engines and putting them back together again. She believed in blueprints and mechanics and having the right tool. And if sleep occasionally swept her off in its current, it was most likely to happen in the arms of her comfortable work chair. Which was exactly where she woke up that morning.

Light was slipping through the cracks in her blinds. Gadget yawned. Her current projects were all a lot of fun, but also a lot of work. She cracked her neck, eyeing the workshop space.

And her vision landed on a particular object.

"What are *you* from?"

There was a hex-head bolt sitting upright on her desk. Her mind traced back through her list of projects. When had she used hex-head bolts? And why would this one *random* bolt be here? All alone? She had a flashback to the incident last year on her adventure with Indira. She'd taken apart the group portal before their tutorial. And she'd forgotten a single piece of the device. It had caused chaos. The rogue Author had been able to enter their world because of her error.

So, what was this one for?

It hit her like a strike of lightning.

Indira's surprise. She'd been commissioned by a friend of Indira's. It had taken weeks to get it just right, especially with the Grammar Police constantly asking to see her building license. Early on in the project, she'd even run into Indira right in the middle of working on it. She was lucky she hadn't spoiled the surprise. After a ton of delays, she'd managed to finish the job.

Now she was worried that she'd left out one crucial piece.

Gadget was out the door and on her electric scooter in no time. There was a lot of noise and bustle this morning, but she was laser-focused on her task. She'd taken this route so often lately that she knew it better than the back of her hand. Down the road, a sharp left, and then under the bridge. She popped off the sewage grate and switched on her headlamp. She'd been a little nervous about going underground the first time she'd visited the location, but most of the rats and mice in the city were either pastry chefs or adventurous detectives.

It was Fable, after all.

Three left turns, up a rather grimy ladder, and through

one more sewage grate. She wasn't sure how Indira's friend had known about this place, but Indira was one of the few people Gadget liked, so she hadn't asked any questions when she'd been approached about helping with a surprise for her. Besides, it was a fun test of her skills to get the device to work.

The room had once been a ballroom. It had a dance floor and a high ceiling and dusty chandeliers. She supposed it had gotten much more use when Protagonist Preparatory had needed to train all its characters in an endless variety of nineteenth-century dances. Now it played host to the underbelly of the surprise Gadget had been hired to pull off. She double-checked the massive cushion she'd tied to the floor. It had deflated a bit over the weeks, but it was still more than ready for its task.

Satisfied with that part of her design, Gadget started climbing the rope ladder she'd installed. Heights weren't her favorite thing in the world, but when you labeled yourself a tech guru, you had to go wherever the tech was needed. Sometimes that meant climbing a rickety ladder with a hex-head bolt clinched between your teeth.

About two minutes later, she'd reached the bottom of her installation. It was an intricate design of gears and springs, wedged against the right angle of the wall and the ceiling. The most difficult work had been making sure she had the weight and countermeasures just right. Her efforts were also complicated by the fact that Fable's magic had resisted her alterations at first. Sometimes she'd come back to the site and find that the digging she'd done the day before had been completely restored. But eventually Gadget had been able to bend this particular section of land to her will.

Now she searched for the place where her missing hex-head bolt should go. Her fingers combed the different joints. Her headlamp roamed. "There you are."

One of the joists was empty. She carefully inserted the missing bolt and smiled with satisfaction. "Always have to double-check the details."

Carefully, Gadget lowered herself back down the ladder. She was admiring the finished project when footsteps sounded. In that empty ballroom, they echoed like the ghosts of dancers. Gadget aimed her headlamp that way. Two figures were approaching. Both shielded their eyes until she realized she was blinding them. She flicked off the light and frowned.

"Maxi?"

The girl wore her Editor's sunglasses as usual. She walked stride for stride with another person Gadget recognized. The same person who'd hired her to do this job in the first place. It was such an odd coincidence, though. Almost as if placing the last bolt had summoned them.

"Good timing," Gadget said. "It's finished."

Maxi frowned at that. "You know each other?"

Peeve nodded. "I hired Gadget a few months ago."

"She's Indira's friend," Gadget added, as if that might clarify something. "This is all for her big birthday surprise or whatever, right? It's going to be hilarious."

There was an exchange of looks between Peeve and

Maxi. Gadget tried to read the subtle communication going on between them, but she'd always been bad with people. It was easier to assess buoyancy or balance something with a level. People were far more complicated.

"It won't be that kind of party," Maxi finally said.

"We should gather the others," Peeve added. "You've got their locations?"

Maxi let out a sigh. "Duh! Of course I have their locations."

Satisfied, Peeve turned to Gadget. "You're sure it will work? That balloon looks a little flimsy."

Gadget grinned at her. "Oh, it will work."

39

Big Brother

DAVID

David arrived at Protagonist Preparatory exactly two hours early.

He didn't *know* that he was two hours early. He was just going through his normal routine. He woke up. He eyed the (incorrect) time and got ready. He made his way to the school without noticing that the sun was only just starting to rise. Nor did he notice that all the coffee shops and breakfast spots were filled with different Marks from those he normally saw.

David had been this way for months now. He was focused, because he had a secret.

At the end of Indira's second book, David had discovered something. There was a small shed on the back side of the Story House. No one else had noticed it. When he walked inside, he discovered it was a new scene. A scene just for him. After acting out what had been written by the Author, David discovered the shield.

It was made from the same material as Indira's hammer, except it was attuned to him. At first he thought this simply meant he'd have a cool new ability in the third book. But then he realized the shield was an invitation from their story's Author.

You can play a bigger role in all of this.

David had taken the shield to Brainstorm Underglass, who'd confirmed the possibility. Ever since that discovery, he'd done nothing but practice.

Now, down in the Arena, Odysseus greeted him.

David ran through the normal exercises. Surprisingly, none of the usual gym rats were there today. They all worked out on similar schedules, so it was odd for so many of them to be missing. David ignored that, practicing new techniques, until a bell tolled. It wasn't the one they used between classes at Protagonist Preparatory. This bell sounded more ancient, more ominous.

He looked to Odysseus for guidance.

"Report to the Ninth Hearth," Odysseus said. "The school is surrounded. We're under siege." The former king of Ithaca was no stranger to sieges. David had been listening to his stories for weeks, in between practice sessions. Odysseus had been present for the famous battle of Troy. He was a legend.

They walked to the Ninth Hearth together. All the teachers were gathered. New students sat by the various fires. Word was spreading. Something bad had happened.

Professor Darcy approached them, offering that winning smile.

"Can you come with us, David? There's something you should see."

David followed, shield bouncing along the straps of his back. A few of the other professors were standing with Brainstorm Vesulias at the front doors of the school. He did not smile when he saw David, only gestured out the entrance and into the courtyard. When David saw what was waiting for them, his jaw dropped. It couldn't be.

"Is that . . ."

"An army. Led here by your sister. Do you know anything about this?"

David shook his head. "She was on a secret mission in Fester. That's all I was told."

The army formed a circle. Their view only showed the front of the school, but David guessed they'd been cut off in every direction. He had to squint to find Indira standing at the front of the army. She definitely looked different. Her hair colored, her eyes darkened. The army's front line had formed up ranks about five hundred paces away. Vesulias looked like he was on the verge of hyperventilating.

"Underglass was overrun by them this morning," he explained. "This army shouldn't even *be* here. There are spells in place that protect us from attack. None of this makes any sense."

The brainstorm kept muttering to himself, sentences running together. It was clear that he was a nervous wreck without Brainstorm Underglass there to guide him.

Dr. Montague—one of Indira's least favorite teachers, David remembered—was the first to step forward.

"We need to consider closing the front doors."

Odysseus concurred. "It is our last defense. It will buy us time."

But David shook his head. "The front doors are always open. Isn't that the whole point? Isn't that what Protagonist Preparatory is supposed to be? If we close them now, what about all the students who are still out there somewhere? They'll get picked off one by one."

"Sometimes you lose the battle," Odysseus replied, "in order to win the war."

David shook his head again but said nothing, and the others moved the conversation on without him. Indira was the one who'd told David about the front entrance, years ago. She'd explained that the doors never closed. They were always open, always ready to greet every good character. Heroes or sidekicks, it didn't matter. All were welcome.

David felt helpless as Brainstorm Vesulias gave the order.

It took several people, shoving with all their might, to get those ancient doors to budge. There was a scrape of wood against stone as they began swinging shut. David's eyes swung to Indira out on that distant plain. *What is happening, baby sister?*

Instinct tugged at his chest. Indira would never close the gates and leave him out there, no matter what. Before the doors could fully close, David ran. Odysseus shouted something. Other teachers reached for him. But all his training had given him speed. Every morning he'd learned to be more agile and nimble. It was easy to leap over their arms, through the sliver of an opening, and land with a roll. He came up on one knee as the great doors slammed shut behind him.

And that's when he realized he was alone. Staring down hundreds of villains.

David was Indira's brother, though. How many times had she taken on the rest of the world and won? It was his turn. David pulled the shield from his back. He settled into his stance and started bravely forward. The distant army crowed. Some laughed. Others banged their shields threateningly. His eyes were locked on his sister.

She walked out to meet him. David had never negotiated with an army before, but he'd read about the basics of how it should work in stories. They always walked to the center and paused. There was some kind of clever back-and-forth. He couldn't find the words to speak, though, when he saw Indira up close. There was the dark makeup and the dyed hair and the glowing scepter. He didn't mind any of that. It was her eyes that startled him. Indira wasn't even seeing him. It was like she was looking right through him, to the distant school. There was no hint of recognition.

This wasn't his sister.

His eyes swung to the entourage that came forward

with her. It was easy to find their leader. Always the person with the most annoying smile. "What did you do to her?"

The man shrugged. "We simply unlocked who she really is."

"Liar."

That made the man smile wider. "Well, of that I am certainly guilty. You are in our way."

David settled deeper into his stance. "I will not move."

"Then she will move you."

He snapped his fingers. Indira jerked her scepter up into the air. David's eyes met hers. He saw the darkness and the shadows, but buried deep inside he saw Indira, too. The bolt of power she unleashed wasn't anywhere close to the maximum power. She was holding back, because of him.

David held up his shield and the magic rebounded into the sky. A second later, war horns sounded in the distance. He craned his neck to get a look at the back lines of their army. Heroes were pouring into the streets. They were cut off from the school, but he could already see them doing damage along the back lines.

Their leader's eyes narrowed on David. He realized he was the only thing that stood between them and the school. The man started walking forward, but there was a loud squelch.

It was hard to resist laughing. It was kind of hilarious to see someone who looked so polished step in a random mud puddle. David heard him mutter something about new shoes before carefully skirting around to one side. As he circled, he raised his gloved hands.

Indira unleashed another bolt.

David raised his shield, but now she pressed forward, pushing the power with all her might. He tried to shout to her over the noise of the spell.

"This isn't you, Indira! You were meant for more than this, baby sister!"

But she was there in front of him. The army's leader had been forced a few steps to one side by the muddy puddle, though he looked no less gleeful about what was happening. David's hands shook as his shield started to crack. He was forced to a knee. The purple light washed overhead.

Indira's spell slammed against the front doors of the school. They were pulverized instantly. Crumbling to ash and dust. David stared up as Indira readied another spell.

"Finish him!" the man shouted.

But as she moved to obey, David heard another noise. A light scrape of stone. It sounded like laughter. David's stomach clenched as the ground beneath him gave way. He caught a glimpse of bolts and metal and springs, and then he and Indira were falling.

Together.

40

Broaden Your Horizons

PEEVE

Maxi escorted the last guest into the ballroom.

Nearly everyone Indira loved was there. Peeve knew they'd gotten incredibly lucky. No one they'd tracked down had been captured or taken. No one had even been engaged in battle. It was almost as if someone had been keeping an eye on them all.

Peeve had been hoping for a few familiar faces, but looking around, she knew this was a gathering of some of Indira's closest friends. And they were her best bet for breaking the hold of Iago's spell. It was a little awkward to see all the affection they had for one another. How friendly they all were. Peeve knew that this crowd of people might have become her friends, in some other life.

Maxi nudged her. "Are we ready?"

Peeve ran back through her checklist, thinking over all the details. *Gather the friends. Ready the spell. The scepter . . .*

"Ahh! I almost forgot!"

Peeve scrambled to open her guitar case. It had not carried a musical instrument for months now. Instead she pulled out the scepter she'd asked the skeletons to find for her in the Land of Forgotten Stories. The Gemini Scepter. No one had ever thought to ask why it was called that. *Gemini* meant "twin." Which meant that the scepter Bainrow had been using was one of two.

Peeve hefted hers up, testing its weight, and realized she'd forgotten another minor, but rather important, detail. "Fire. We need fire."

Everyone looked to Phoenix. He was struggling to stay on his feet. Most of his power had been drained in some earlier battle. He started to limp forward, a hand outstretched, before Allen Squalls cut him off. "Don't waste it," he said. "We'll need your strength for later. I've got a match."

He pulled out a surprisingly fancy matchbook, struck the light, and held the flame out in Peeve's direction. She tilted the scepter's gemstone to him and was surprised by how quickly it caught. Golden light poured out from the stone. It speckled their faces and colored the floor like a disco ball. Even Peeve could not help admiring its beauty.

"Now we're ready."

Almost on cue, there was a noise. Everyone looked up.

Gadget's trapdoor worked. Peeve stared as the girl who'd changed her entire life plummeted from the sky. She wasn't alone. David Story hit the balloon first. He came rolling down the side as Indira struck it. The force of the impact didn't shake her grip on the scepter. Peeve had hoped that it might. Instead, Indira rolled three times and came to her feet. Those lifeless eyes scanned the room. She lifted her scepter, intent on destroying them all, but then she finally saw who she was aiming at.

Mrs. Pennington stood with an arm around Patch. Detective Malaprop was writing notes on the back of his hand in permanent marker. Phoenix and Everest stood shoulder to shoulder, begrudging friends for the moment. Allen Squalls was behind them, a smidge of peanut butter still at the corner of his mouth. Maxi and Gadget framed the other side of the group. The tinkerer threw up both hands excitedly. She was the only one who shouted, "Surprise!"

Peeve only knew their names, but she could see the impact each one of them had on Indira now. Iago's control over her faltered for a precious moment. These were the people Indira had allowed to shape her heart and mind over the years. It was no simple thing to destroy something so precious, even if the scepter demanded she do just that.

Her hand was shaking. The scepter was begging for her to finish them all. The bright tip was already filling with purple light. Peeve stepped forward.

She raised her own scepter. The two were twins. Light and dark. Good and evil. There was no hesitation in her. She'd been planning this from the start. She blasted Indira with golden light. The opposite magics struck each other with enough force to shove everyone back a few steps. Peeve gritted her teeth. The light wasn't fading. A great ball of swirling color formed in the air between them. With a final burst of strength, Peeve completed the spell she'd been planning.

Let's go back to the beginning, Indira. Broaden your horizons.

Light and shadow tangled.

The two girls disappeared.

41

Good versus Evil

INDIRA

Peeve Meadows was playing the guitar. Again.

Indira curled beneath a blanket, one house over, trying her best to not allow the strangled music to steal her precious sleep. Life in Origin offered very little comfort. Each of the characters-in-waiting assigned to the coastal town enjoyed the following: a private room, a comfortable bed, and a view of the sea. And right now, Peeve Meadows was ruining Indira's favorite of the three.

Indira rolled out of bed with a groan. She did the same thing she did *every* morning that she wasn't visiting David, the same thing that every character in Origin would do as soon as they woke up: she looked out the window.

Her shack offered a porthole view of the sea. Great crashing waves, a rocky shoreline, and the town's rustic harbor. But Indira looked out past those things. They were just background noise. Every character set their eyes on the distant sky, hoping beyond hope to see the arrival of the Author Borealis.

"Just clouds," Indira said, rubbing her window with a sleeve. "Almost always clouds."

She sighed before heading outside, eager for breakfast. Her door opened on rusting hinges. She let it swing hard into the side of her shack, hoping the noise would give Peeve an idea of just how loud *she* was being. Indira walked out to the mailbox that was assigned to her decrepit shack. She popped the back of it with a fist, and the broken front came snapping open. Inside, she found a wrapped biscuit smothered in honey.

A glance showed Peeve Meadows striding over from her identical shack with a serious look on her face. Indira thought it was a little too early in the day for a serious conversation.

"Good morning!" Peeve said. "I think we need to talk."

Indira gestured. "I was about to do some exercises."

"We need to talk."

The tone of her neighbor's voice was different. Peeve had always been bright and cheery. Indira hadn't ever paid much attention to her, because why make friends in Origin? Characters got chosen and shipped off to Protagonist Preparatory. Or they'd go to places like Quiver for hired work. She'd never thought twice about Peeve until now. The girl sounded almost dangerous.

"Okay. Let's talk."

Peeve led her to a set of chairs. Indira took the seat

across from her, hoping she'd still have time for her run after this conversation was over.

"We're visiting your memory right now, Indira."

It was the strangest opening line she'd ever heard. Indira stared.

"Okay. Right. Did you get enough sleep last night, Peeve? Do you have a fever?"

"You go for a run," Peeve went on, ignoring her. "While you're gone, the Author Borealis lights the beacons of chosen students. Your beacon? It lights up. That beautiful green. But you're not here. I know it's wrong. I know I shouldn't do it. I know it's a lie. But I'm desperate, because I've started hearing from other kids in Origin that sometimes people *never* get chosen for a story. Do you remember what I do next?"

The answer echoed back to Indira from another corner of her mind.

"You stand in front of my house."

Peeve nodded. "And then you return just in time and catch me lying, right in front of the rep from Fable. It was the biggest mistake of my life, Indira. Do you remember what happened next?"

Indira's mind was racing.

"We traveled by dragoneye. Dexter said you'd be going by a different route. None of us knew then, but you were transferred. Antagonist Academy. I found out during our auditions."

Peeve didn't smile or gloat, even though she'd wiped

the floor with Indira during those auditions. "One moment. One decision. One mistake. And I was an antagonist. Just like that."

Indira could hear the bitterness in the girl's voice. This memory was a big part of Indira's life as well, but for completely different reasons. It was the first time she'd been chosen. The first time she'd stood up for herself. It was the beginning of her journey to becoming a hero.

"But . . . you did lie, Peeve."

The girl's eyes flashed. "I know I did. I know it was wrong. But don't you see? We were neighbors. We weren't all that different, Indira. In fact, I'd say I was a lot nicer than you were. I made you tea some mornings. I always tried to make conversation. You just ignored me.

"But after that one moment, you got to go play the hero. Do you have any idea what I went through? What life in Fester is really like? It isn't the show they put on for you these past few weeks. I'm talking about actually living there. The classes are awful. The teachers are worse than the students. But the worst part is how the *good* guys treat us. Like we're dirt under their feet. I decided to help you because I thought you—of all people—would understand."

Indira frowned. "Understand what?"

"Good and evil," Peeve said. "It's not as simple as everyone pretends it is. There's not this clear line separating the two. We've been doing it all wrong for centuries. Do you really think that I was evil?"

Indira slowly shook her head. "No."

"And do you think *all* the other kids at Fester are evil?"

"Probably not."

"And do you think *all* the heroes in Fable are really good?"

Indira remembered Chem, the girl who'd bullied her during her first year. There were other examples too, of kids who were haughty or spiteful. No one was perfect. That was the point Peeve was trying to make.

"No."

"Good. Now we're getting somewhere."

Peeve snapped her fingers.

———

Indira stood in Underglass's office. The light in the room was a little off. Peeve was standing in front of Indira's long-time mentor. She felt a sharp twinge of pain: Underglass.

"This is *my* memory." Peeve glanced over at Indira. "I never told anyone else about this moment. I was sent to Fester and went through orientation. Then we were brought back to Fable for auditions. I lied about going to the bathroom, and I snuck into Underglass's office instead. Right before our auditions. I begged her to take me as a student. I told her there'd been a huge mistake. I wasn't antagonist material. It was just one little lie."

Indira watched the past version of Underglass shake

her head sadly, gesturing to a file on the desk. "She told me the line between good and evil is a firm one. My fate had been decided."

Peeve walked deliberately around the desk. She moved past where Underglass sat and approached the painting Indira had first noticed just a few weeks before. Peeve swiped her hand the same way that Underglass had and the painting vanished. A door into the dark.

"Come with me."

The lock clicked. Indira couldn't resist. Nothing about this conversation made her comfortable, but at least it was better than being trapped in a distant corner of her own mind, forced to watch her favorite place in the world slowly burn to the ground. She walked into the shadows. And then her eyes adjusted and she saw the great iron wheel, turning its inevitable course. All the individual gears moved around it like constellations. On the right, Fable glinted like the North Star that it was.

"This is Iago's plan."

At the sound of his name, Indira's throat tightened. She could feel the collar digging into her neck and the ring choking her finger. All that power running through her veins.

"He wants Protagonist Preparatory, but he *really* wants the Great Exchange. His plan is to reverse the gears of the wheel. If he can get it turning in the other direction, antagonists will become the center of every story. Not just the occasional antihero, but the true centerpiece of Imagination. Protagonists will be demoted. It will change forever how stories are told. And as a bonus, the antagonists get access to the Ninth Hearth and all of Fable's other resources. He will take everything he can from you."

Indira watched the wheel turn. The mechanical stars fluttered in their orbits. Her attention swung to the smaller star that she knew represented Fester.

"What do you want me to do?"

Peeve replied, "I want you to answer a question for me. If I'm so bad—if I'm meant to be an antagonist forever—then why am I the only one who can save you?"

Indira thought about that for a moment, then answered with her own question. "If you're so good, then why'd you let me get all the way to Fable before using the other scepter?"

Peeve cracked a smile. "I thought you'd figure that part out. You're right. I could have stopped you back in Fester. I've had the other scepter this whole time. That's where we're different. I'm not trying to rescue *this* world. I'm trying to make a better one."

"A world where Fable is under attack?" Indira challenged.

"A world where Fester doesn't need to attack Fable, because they're actually equal."

Indira's eyes swung to the upper right corner again. The bright star of Fable winked at her. Fester was not nearly as eye-catching, and how could it be? Everyone favored the city of good. Authors and readers and all of Imagination. Indira felt the same unfairness that she'd felt during her first year, when she'd been treated as second-class just because she was a side character. That was an injustice she'd never forget. Now she saw the same anger written on Peeve's face. These weren't just empty words. Peeve had lived through the pain of such things.

Indira understood. "You wanted me to destroy the barrier first."

Peeve nodded. "If I failed at everything else, at least the barrier would be down. That's why I waited until you reached the city. Plus, the spell Iago cast over you is hard to break without friendly faces. It was a lot of work gathering your loved ones. Maxi helped. But yes, I wanted you to break the barrier, because it's not just a shield protecting Fable. It's also a weapon. One that's been used *against* Fester."

Indira knew that was partially true, even if she didn't want it to be.

"So what do we do now?"

"First, we negotiate." Peeve grinned. "I'm the only one who can break the spell that Iago has over you, which means my help comes at a cost."

"Charging a fee to save the world? Not exactly proving your heroic qualities."

"You haven't heard my terms."

Indira bit her lip. "Fine. Let's hear them."

Peeve held up three fingers.

"First, no more barriers. Never again. Everyone gets access to the Ninth Hearth."

Indira nodded. That seemed fair enough.

"Second, no more Protagonist Preparatory—"

Indira's jaw tightened. "You can't ask for that, Peeve. This place is my home. You have no idea how much it means to me, how much it means to—"

"I wasn't finished. No more Antagonist Academy, either. At least not the way it is now, separated and unfair. Make them one school that works together. Everyone comes and tries things out for a year. Students get placed where they're comfortable. Both sides equal. Stopping Iago isn't enough. We have to break the wheel and make a new world."

Indira considered that. It was hard to imagine Protagonist Preparatory any other way, but maybe Peeve had a point. Their system had taken one look at a girl like her and shipped her to the wrong place, over one mistake. The same was true of her friend Cavern, who she'd partnered with the year before in Plot. Maybe that did need to change. Indira offered a begrudging nod.

"What's the last thing?"

Peeve smiled. "We save the day. Together."

Her confidence had Indira grinning. Peeve offered a hand.

"Deal?"

"You realize this depends on us actually beating Iago, right?"

Peeve nodded. "I already have a plan for that, too. I was in Crooked Faction. I spent time around Iago too. He never thought much of me as a student, but that doesn't mean I didn't learn some of his tricks. You want to know how to beat a liar?" She grinned. "You beat him at his own game. I know exactly what to do when we face him."

Indira shook the girl's hand. "Then let's beat him. Together."

—

Light fractured, blinding.

Indira blinked back to life in an old, cobwebbed ballroom. Peeve Meadows stood right in front of her, arms trembling as she tried to keep a massive scepter in the air. Indira noticed that her own scepter was gone. The two weapons had combined into one. Darkness and light wove together in the newly formed gemstone. Indira took it as a good omen.

And she finally remembered that they weren't alone. Peeve was flanked by most of the people Indira held dear. She drank in their faces, like someone who'd been stumbling through the desert.

Everest Smith was the first to step forward. He tossed the familiar hammer into the air. Indira caught it on instinct. Light shivered down its length. She smiled as everyone else crowded forward for an awkward group hug.

"Well, come on. We've got a school to save."

42

The Battle for Protagonist Preparatory

Indira and Peeve led the crew out of the ballroom.

Every now and again she'd hear a whisper of Iago's voice in her mind, trying to regain power over her. It would shiver down her spine and she'd look back, thinking he was there with them. Peeve had quietly explained this to her before they started moving. When the two scepters joined together, Iago's control over her vanished. It had freed her from the larger spell, but Peeve also said that Iago's influence would still be there. Like an echo that needed time to fade.

She was already working on separating little parts of her mind. Making sure the part that knew their plan was hidden, so that if Iago did try to access her thoughts, he'd see only what she *wanted* him to see. It helped that every time she looked back over her shoulder, the people she loved most in the world were walking step for step with her. They gave her a new confidence.

Let the battle begin.

"I'm pretty sure I blasted the front entrance," Indira said. "Iago is making his way to Underglass's office. That's where I'm heading; the rest of you . . ."

Indira realized the rest of the crew had stopped walking. She turned around.

"What?"

Phoenix was grinning. "You're not really going to try that whole 'the rest of you stay here' speech, are you? After all of this? It's a little cliché."

Mrs. Pennington hefted a rolling pin. "We came here to fight for the city we love."

"We're with you," Everest added. "To the end."

Indira caught Peeve smirking at her. "Friends," the girl said. "I've heard they're stubborn creatures."

There were nods from around the group, although Indira distinctly heard Detective Malaprop ask someone if this was still the case of the missing robo-bears. She had no idea what that meant, but as she turned again, she couldn't help smiling. No matter what happened, they'd be together.

Only Patch and Mrs. Pennington's fiancé—Jack— decided to stay behind. Patch gave Indira a huge hug before heading back to the safety of the ballroom, humming a song about baby sharks.

Peeve and Maxi directed Indira down another hallway. Someone had excavated the lone entryway, which apparently had been sealed. Indira shouldered into a narrow underground. The walls were filled with familiar decorations. "We're in the Sepulcher."

The rest of her crew followed her through the entry. The covers of unfinished books stared down at them. Indira had never liked this part of the school. It was where one of her least favorite classes had taken place. It was also the source of Brainstorm Ketty's plot against her. Ketty had been an unfinished character, which was why she'd sabotaged Indira's efforts in the first place. She shook away those memories and kept moving.

They didn't have to go far to find the first echoes of battle. Steel sung against steel. They rounded the corner to find Dr. Montague locked in a duel. Another young man, dressed the same way, was bearing down on him with every swing.

"You've gotten *lazy*, Romeo!" The stranger lunged. "Haven't been practicing?"

Montague swung back. "You were always so jealous of my success, Tybalt!"

"My name is cooler! I should've been the star!"

He swung at Dr. Montague's head.

Before Indira could step in, Juliet came storming out of another hallway, a sword in hand. "I've had quite enough of *both* of you," she said, leaping between them with a flurry of blows.

Indira wasn't sure either of the boys would survive, but she could tell that Juliet had this room under control. She gave the signal and her tight-knit crew took the stairs up to the first floor.

In the main hall, chaos was king.

Indira's team stumbled to a halt as they tried to process

everything that was going on. Apparently, Underglass's horn blast had worked. The old heroes had come. There were individual battles happening everywhere. Down one hallway, ogres were on their hands and knees, trying to reach through classroom doors to grab whoever was hiding inside. They looked like a bunch of giant children reaching their hands into giant cookie jars.

A pack of wolves had been cornered in the opposite hallway by a recognizable flash of gold. The statues from the Librarian Hall of Fame had come to life and formed an impenetrable front line. It looked as if they were taking their call to defend the school rather seriously. She even saw one of the librarians wielding a golden sword made of books.

Several familiar rivals had found each other in the chaos. She saw Robin Hood shooting arrows at the Sheriff of Nottingham. His Merry Men were locked in a battle with a band of pirates. Captain Hook and Peter Pan tangled in another corner, with Peter attempting to use some kind of futuristic watch as intimidation. Odysseus was circling the giant Cyclops Polyphemus, who kept calling him a nobody. Indira actually had to back up a step when a fashionably dressed man came racing past, followed by some kind of police captain.

"Once a thief, always a thief, Valjean!"

Maybe the most absurd participant in the fight was a glowing tower on her right. It was a dark and wandering eye. Its bright beam of firelight roamed the scene. Whenever it landed on a protagonist, a creepy voice would whisper: "Right here! On your left! Get him!"

A woman Indira knew from Antagonist Academy—Miss Trunchbull—chastised the eye as she ran past into yet another battle. "Are you going to do any *actual* fighting, Sauron?"

It was tempting to join the chaos and help, but Indira knew that their battle was at the opposite end of this hallway. Every second they wasted gave Iago a better chance at infiltrating Underglass's office and reversing the wheel of the Great Exchange. Her crew tightened its formation before forging on through the makeshift battlefield.

Halfway across, Indira was forced to stop when a great monster was thrown through the air, sliding to a halt right in front of them. The hero who'd thrown him was dressed in armor, but looked like he was from a much older time period. Indira recognized the monster: Professor Grendel. He was climbing back to his feet when Mrs. Pennington started toward him, rolling pin in hand. Grendel actually yelped. He scrambled back in the direction of the muscled hero.

"Not again! I'd rather fight him!"

Indira raised an eyebrow. Mrs. Pennington gave a *What did you expect?* kind of shrug. It took a second for Indira to stop laughing and refocus. "Okay. This way. We need to get to the front hallway."

Their progress was halted again, however, by a menacing football team. Each player looked capable of fighting a bear. Their coach called from the imagined sideline, "Bring 'em back in body bags!"

Indira saw them settling into formation, putting hands to the floor in preparation to rush. They were joined by a pack of skeletons on one flank. Indira knew her team would be wasting precious minutes if they were forced to fight their way through all of this.

"Everyone, lock arms."

Indira offered Peeve her left arm. The others linked up with the two of them. A series of explosions shook the room. The football team took that as their cue to sprint forward. The skeletons were right behind them. Indira waited for them to get closer. Then she took aim and threw.

Her hammer's magic tugged them through the air. Indira had never tried to teleport so many people, but she knew it would work. These were some of her favorite people in the world. How could any of them be a burden to her now? Together, they blinked across the room; Indira caught the spinning weapon. There were a few gasps. The football team looked around, dumbfounded.

"Come on!" Indira called.

They took the same hallway she'd taken a hundred times. Past the school's entrance. Her heart sank a little to see the shattered doors there. It was her magical blast that had wrecked them. Indira jogged past the entrance to Hearth Hall, but pulled up short when she reached the corridor that had always led to the brainstorms' offices.

"It isn't—it should be right here?"

There was a solid wall. Indira gave the stones a testing shove and was amazed to find that they weren't an illusion. It was as if there'd never been offices this way. She knew exactly what had happened. Pecve came forward and confirmed it. "This is Iago's work. This wall is a lie. A lie with enough power behind it that it becomes reality."

Indira remembered all the moments Iago had done the same in front of her. The door he'd created after talking to the Sorting Hate. The third light switch in their headquarters, which controlled the garbage disposal. Even turning a pen into a grinding mechanism. He'd used the power so casually, but she'd never thought a lie would be what undid all their plans.

She kept her voice low. "Can you undo it?"

Peeve shook her head. "I'm not strong enough. Iago is the best at it. I didn't think he'd be clever enough to cut us off from the entire hallway. There has to be some way around, right?"

Indira worried there wasn't.

"Back to Hearth Hall," she announced. "Maybe Vesulias is in there. He'd know a way."

Their crew cautiously turned back down the hall. A glance inside Hearth Hall showed that the fighting was even fiercer here. Indira saw this was where all the students and teachers had gathered. The protagonists had barricaded one half of the room and were warding off attacks from a much larger group of antagonists. Indira spied Janie Judas leading the students of Antagonist Academy. Every few seconds, the villains would send soldiers forward to test the lines.

But the students of Protagonist Preparatory weren't alone. The front lines of their army were full of soldiers as thin as spears. Each one stood tall and fought poorly, but their numbers were clearly helping ward off the attacks. The Marks of Fable had been through plenty of war novels, and now they were using that knowledge to hold their own.

Indira's eyes moved past the two armies to the Ninth Hearth. Its magical fire was roaring. It was sad to see hundreds of ghosts already flickering in its glow. At least they'd recover, she thought. Indira's crew gathered themselves and sprinted across to the Protagonist Preparatory side of the room.

Arrows soared overhead, barely missing as they reached the safety of the protagonist army. Her eyes scanned the ranks. She didn't see Brainstorm Vesulias anywhere.

"Indira?"

Alice strode the back lines like a general. Indira's favorite teacher was bleeding from a sharp cut above one eyebrow. That didn't stop her from grinning mischievously.

"No escaping this fight," her teacher said. "Not with the Queen of Hearts over there."

She gestured. On the other side of the room, Indira saw a rather diminutive woman seated on a stack of ten chairs. It looked like an absurd throne. From that height, she commanded her army over and over with a simple and horrible line: "Off with their heads!"

Alice rolled her eyes. "Such a drama queen. Have you come to join us? We could use the help."

Indira nodded, then remembered her true task.

"No, actually, I'm sorry. I need to talk with Brainstorm Vesulias. The way to Underglass's office is blocked by a lie. Iago can create lies that become reality. We just need to know if there's some other way to access their offices. A back entrance? That kind of thing."

"Made from a lie?" Alice grinned. "Well, you just need a little bit of the truth, then."

Indira resisted pointing out that now was not the time for riddles. Desperate, she started searching the room again for Vesulias. Alice had to snap her fingers to get Indira's attention.

"Did you hear me? That's your answer. You need the *truth*."

Her former teacher reached into the pockets of her robin's-egg blue dress. Indira stared as she produced a vial for each of the ten members of their group.

"You just keep a bunch of random vials in your pockets like that?"

Alice shrugged. "I have all sorts of secrets in here."

There was another push from the opposing army. A few antagonists broke through the front lines before getting shoved back. Indira helped pass out the vials as Alice gave instructions.

"You must think of something you know is true. It cannot be a half-truth or a small truth. It must be something that—deep down in your core—is true beyond all else. The vial will fill with your words. Drink them. If the thing you spoke is true, you'll be able to walk right through his lie."

Indira knew better than to question Alice. She was the master of escaping and infiltrating. Instead, she looked to her vial and spoke the first, desperate truth that came to mind.

"I want to save the school."

The empty glass colored with bright gold liquid. Everyone else followed suit, whispering their own core truths. She saw Phoenix blush a little as he whispered his. It colored with a liquid that looked like molten lava. Everest's looked like a night sky speckled by moonlight. One by one, they whispered their truths and filled their vials.

"Botanists up!" Malaprop said.

Everyone drank. Indira thought her draft tasted like bravery. Encouragement rushed through her veins. The others drained their final sips before handing the vials back to Alice. "I'm going to stay with the students," she told Indira. "Go. The school's fate rides with you. We'll do our best to provide some cover."

Her former teacher turned and let out a roaring command. Their ranks formed up. Indira watched as a team of Marks went charging across the hall. Janie's crew held their ground, swiping past shields with their swords, but the distraction provided the opening Indira's crew needed.

They sprinted back to the entrance. Down the corridor, the lie wall looked as solid as ever. Indira wasn't feeling any special tingling that confirmed this would work. She looked around at the others, trying to keep the momentum of her confidence going.

"Everyone ready?"

Nods all around. Indira held up her hammer. Everest signaled that he was ready to fight. Phoenix and Squalls stood side by side, one with fire in his eyes and the other as calm as a waiting storm. Maxi and Gadget looked like some kind of FBI team, each wielding specialized tools the functions of which Indira wasn't even sure she could guess. Mrs. Pennington had her rolling pin. Detective Malaprop had a frying pan. Peeve hefted the massive new scepter. It swirled with golden light and shadows.

Indira's eyes fell on David last. "What's that? New shield, big brother?"

He grinned at her. "It was supposed to be a secret."

"I think spoilers are allowed in emergencies," she replied. "All right. I have no idea what's waiting for us behind this wall, but I can't think of anyone I'd rather go to battle with."

There were nods of agreement. No one was debating whether or not this was the right decision. Every single one of them was set. They would fight until the end. Their fortitude reminded Indira of the words she'd learned in this very school. Words she'd spoken before. Words she spoke now.

"Loyalty leads to bravery. Bravery plants the seed of

self-sacrifice. And self-sacrifice is the highest call of every character in every story. It's time to live those words. Everyone, with me."

Taking a deep breath, Indira charged. She could feel the others sprinting straight at the wall with her. There was a brief moment when she feared Alice's idea wouldn't work and they were all about to do something really embarrassing. But Iago's wall vanished at the exact moment her shoulder collided with it. They came stumbling into the hallway she remembered, with the three brainstorms' offices up ahead.

And the place was full of antagonists.

Except none of them were expecting company. Brainstorm Bainrow was on a couch at the end of the hall, his feet kicked up comfortably. The Stepsisters were drawing on the walls with crayons, like a pair of children. Montresor was humming the tune to a song. There were three students Indira recognized. Becky 2000 stood with Eugene and Lizzie B. Borden, and all three captains were laughing about something. The door leading into Underglass's office was open.

Indira saw speckled light pouring out. Iago was in there.

"Charge!"

43

The Final Exchange

Montresor swung a brick at her. Indira ducked down and hit his exposed stomach with a blow from her shoulder. He went sprawling to one side before being trampled by the rest of their oncoming crew. The Stepsisters were a step quicker. They slid together instinctively and deflected the incoming wave to the other half of the hallway. Indira saw Mrs. Pennington and Detective Malaprop peel off from their group to engage the evil duo. She pushed forward, eyes fixed on what was ahead.

Eugene adjusted his goggles before flinging three steel balls into the air. They rolled down the hall and then sprouted eight legs each. Robotic spiders. Indira saw front fangs that looked like hypodermic needles. She hesitated until a sharp buzz filled the air behind her. A small swarm of metallic bees took out the lead spider. Indira didn't have to look over her shoulder to know these were Gadget's inventions.

Lizzie B. Borden was next. She came sprinting forward, axes raised, while Becky 2000 glided into motion behind her. This time a bolt of fire swept over Indira's shoulder. The blast forced Lizzie to leap to one side. Indira blocked Becky's first swing with her hammer before ducking past her and leaving that fight to someone else. Bainrow was on his feet. Indira knew he'd be their toughest battle. He was made of stone and rippled muscle. The demon lord grinned.

"Finally, a worthy opponent."

David and Everest had slipped past Becky 2000 as well. They kept pace with Indira as Bainrow struck. Indira dodged the first blow. Everest tried to take advantage of her distraction, but the demon backhanded him away. Indira realized the demon didn't need weapons. That diamond skin made his entire body impenetrable, and dangerous.

The three of them circled Bainrow in the tight hallway. He lashed out with a thunderous kick that David barely managed to block with his shield. It was forceful enough to send her brother sliding back a few steps. Indira swung desperately, but Bainrow caught her wrist. His grip tightened as he flung her over one shoulder like a rag doll. She hit the back wall hard.

As she slumped down, she got a full vision of their narrow battlefield. Phoenix and Squalls were pressing Becky 2000 with their spells—machine versus magic—ducking and casting in unison. One of the Stepsisters was down; Malaprop and Mrs. Pennington were battering the defenses of the second. It wasn't an artful brawl, but at least they were winning.

Gadget and Eugene were still locked in battle, which was really just the two of them standing at opposite ends of the room and sending various mechanisms whizzing through the air, like a couple of kids in some kind of violent science fair. Lizzie B. Borden was swinging wildly at Maxi, who blocked each blow with a pair of daggers that had been carved in the shape of commas.

Only Bainrow was too powerful for them. He blocked a weak swing from Everest before landing a blow of his own. Everest let out a sharp cry as he struck the side wall. David's shield work was beautiful; he moved his feet flawlessly. But that wasn't enough to take on a demon lord this powerful. Bainrow pressed him back each blow. It looked hopeless.

Until Peeve shouldered forward.

When they'd discussed the plan, Peeve had been hoping to save as much of the scepter's magic as possible for their showdown with Iago, but they clearly needed help. Blinding light filled the hallway. Peeve's bolt hit Bainrow square in the chest. Indira had to scramble out of the way as he struck the wall just above her.

"Indira!"

It was Phoenix. He'd slipped away from his battle, leaving Squalls locked in the duel with a weakened Becky 2000. She'd never seen Phoenix look so ragged. The flame in his palm kept flickering out, and his entire right side looked bruised and bloodied.

"We need to get to Iago, don't we?" he asked.

He reached out to help Everest to his feet. Peeve ran to join them, chest heaving from the power of the spell she'd just used. Bainrow was struggling back up. He let out a menacing growl. The other fights were still raging, but Indira knew Phoenix was right. There was no telling how much damage Iago had already done. Speed mattered now.

David was there. "I'll hold off Bainrow. Go. I won't let him through, baby sister. Promise."

Indira wanted to tell him to be safe, not to do anything foolish, but this was what her brother had always wanted: a chance to be the hero. She gave him a tight nod.

Everest, Phoenix, and Peeve ran into Underglass's office. Indira caught a final glimpse of Mrs. Pennington tackling Becky in an effort to help Squalls; then she was ducking into the office after her friends. David took up his stance by the door. Indira actually gasped when he manipulated the metal of his shield into a new form, carefully wedging it in the doorway.

"Whoa! Really cool shield, David!" she called.

"Get moving," he shouted back. "I'll buy you as much time as I can."

Underglass's office was a mess. Cabinets had been ransacked. Closet doors had been opened. Items were scattered. The insult to her mentor was the final straw. At the back of the room, that dark doorway waited, open. There were brief flashes within.

"Be ready for anything," Indira warned. "Ev and Phoenix. You go first."

She was hoping they'd be a good distraction. She wanted Iago distracted. Indira glanced over at Peeve and gave a nod. They'd planned for this kind of showdown. Peeve searched the closet before flashing a thumbs-up. There was a shiver of magic in the air. Indira let the spell settle into place before following the boys into the room.

Once more, Indira worked to divide her mind. Hide the plan from Iago at all costs. She forced the rest of her mind to focus on what was right in front of her. Indira liked their odds. Even if Iago had tricked her before, now that it came down to combat, he didn't stand a chance.

Above, there was the endless night sky; ahead, the turning wheel. Now, however, it was turning in the opposite direction.

The gears were trying to find their place in the new system, unsure when to rotate. She'd barely noticed the first time, but there'd been a rhythmic noise that was pleasing to the ear, almost like music. The wheel had learned its rhythm over centuries. Now the gears stuttered and clogged and fought to find their way. Iago was standing before the great wheel, awash in the strange new patterns that were developing because of what he'd done. Indira hoped it wasn't too late.

"Iago!" she called.

He turned, offering that dagger of a smile. "Miss Story. Fancy seeing you here."

She scanned the shadows for traps. Did he have a hidden army in here? A fleet of bad guys that might come flooding into the room at the last minute? As they approached, Iago didn't signal anyone. He didn't look hopefully to the entrance. Instead his eyes glittered with satisfaction.

It was like he thought he'd already won.

"Have you come to admire my greatest work?"

The four of them fanned out, stopping about ten paces away. Peeve was on Indira's right, Everest stood on her left, and Phoenix stood on his left. A glance showed that Phoenix was truly on his last legs. There was no way he'd be able to transform into a dragon. She hoped he had a little fire left. It would have to be enough.

"We came to stop you," Indira answered. "You know you don't stand a chance against the four of us. No more tricks. No more lies. This is over, Iago."

Iago nodded. "Four against one is rather unfair. But you haven't figured out who my protégé is yet, have you?"

Instinctually, Indira looked in Peeve's direction. Her old neighbor stood there without smiling. There was no reaction on the girl's face at all. Indira's heart pounded a little, but Iago didn't glance her way. She wasn't the person he was talking about.

"Oh? You didn't know?" Iago laughed. "Sometimes our lies become the truth. We're that good. I've been training him for years now. . . ."

Movement on her left. Indira was expecting someone to come out of the shadows for some final revelation. Instead, Everest Smith slid smoothly behind Phoenix. He wrapped an arm around his neck. Phoenix struggled, but Indira already knew he didn't have the energy to resist. She could only stare as Everest summoned her hammer into his hand and held it out threateningly.

"Do not come closer."

She tried to reach for it and found the connection between them closed off. He'd stolen *her* weapon. Indira's mind struggled to properly translate the action. Why was he holding Phoenix like that? Why was he shifting to face Indira instead of Iago? *What was happening?*

"Everest Smith. My best student. My most talented liar. Honestly, he's the best since . . ." Iago paused to think, then smiled. "Well, since me."

Phoenix's eyes looked like dying sparks. Everest dragged him, step by step, over to where Iago stood. Her eyes found Everest's. She tried to put as much loathing into the look as possible. How could she have ever compared the two of them? How could she have been so easily fooled by his charm? Everest was flash and Phoenix was fire. She should have known better.

"Sorry, love," he said. "Nothing personal."

Even his accent sounded annoying now. She could see Phoenix still making an effort to resist, but his magic had run out. Anger pulsed in her chest. As she watched the tides of their battle change, the wheel shuddered. It was starting to pick up momentum. Smaller gears were shifting and falling into place with the new orders Iago had given. Her eyes went to the two gears she knew represented Fable and Fester. They were starting to cross paths, like an eclipse.

It was almost time.

Her eyes flicked back to Iago, the person who'd orchestrated all of this.

"You won't win."

"Already have," he replied. "The wheel is adapting. And, truly, this is just the first step. We'll reverse course. Once the change is complete, and Fester is accepted as the new core in the world of Imagination, I can do the same thing to your kind that was done to us. All it will take is a single spell to cast every hero out of the city. We don't have to win those battles raging around the school. We just needed to win in here. Besides . . ."

Iago raised his gloved hands.

"Scepter or not, you are still within my power."

Indira heard his voice whispering in her head. It wasn't nearly as powerful as it had been when she was holding the scepter, but with all his effort behind the words, it finally broke through. *Serve me now.* She turned like a puppet on strings.

"The Badlands were *my* design," Iago explained. "A backup option, so to speak. We studied your mind, Indira. Each night was an opportunity to learn how you tick. Each night was an opportunity to do some tweaking. And now you are mine." He pointed. "Destroy Peeve."

Peeve's eyes went wide. She struggled to raise the scepter. Indira was too fast. She darted across the room and had Peeve by the throat. Her hands tightened in a stranglehold. Peeve choked out a gasp. She dropped the scepter. Iago looked delighted as he watched Peeve struggle. Indira kept tightening her grip. She let Iago feel the anger inside her. She let him think that his plan was working.

Tighter and tighter and tighter.

Until Peeve's head popped off. Indira burst out laughing. "Whoops!"

Indira turned and waved the detached body part at Iago. He looked truly shocked for the first time since they'd met. "Oh. Did you not know?" Indira asked, channeling his own sarcasm. "Our lies can become the truth. It's really a clever trick. Did you think a former student of yours couldn't learn how to do it on her own?"

The illusion that Peeve had created finally gave way to the reality. Indira wasn't choking Peeve at all. Her hands were tightly gripping a broom they'd found in Underglass's closet. She tossed it to the floor, allowing Iago to see the fullness of his failure. It was a satisfying moment.

"But . . ." He spun, eyes searching. "Where . . ."

Golden light lit the back corner of the room. The real Peeve Meadows was standing behind the wheel, her spell at the ready. This had been Peeve's plan. She'd studied under Iago. She'd learned how to create lies, even if Iago had never seen talent in her. Now he would know just how big a mistake that was. Peeve had waited for the illusion to settle into place before slipping through the shadows, circling the room. Iago had been so distracted by their approach that he hadn't seen her getting in position.

Indira smiled as she spoke. "We're good guys with a dark side."

"Bad guys with a soft spot," Peeve added.

"Not all dark. Not all light."

"We're something in the middle."

Overhead, the gears representing Fable and Fester overlapped. It was the moment they'd been waiting for. Indira gave the signal. "Now, Peeve!"

A blast of force shook the entire room. The light from Peeve's scepter struck the back of the great wheel like a gold-plated punch. Everything shattered at the same time. Iago was standing too close. The pieces became shrapnel, hissing out like arrows. One pinned his fancy cloak to the floor. He was still trying to pull it free when the main section of the great wheel fell, crushing him beneath it.

Everest was forced to dive to one side. Phoenix stumbled into Indira's arms the moment he let go, and she caught him, dragging him away from the crash radius. Before Everest could make a run for the door, Peeve cut him off, pointing the still-glowing scepter with menace.

The two girls locked eyes, and understanding passed between them.

They'd just changed the entire world.

44

Negotiations

The moment the wheel shattered, every character felt it. Good or bad. Protagonist or antagonist. The secret magic that had guided their lives until now was suddenly gone. Indira and Peeve were the only ones who understood that something wonderful might grow up in its place.

David dropped to his knees the moment Indira told him what had happened. Bainrow looked defeated, until Peeve explained what this might mean for antagonists. The news echoed out like that. Great rivals paused in the middle of battles, their chests heaving, as they listened to whispers of a new world. Begrudgingly, most of the characters started setting their weapons down.

Not everyone fell in step right away.

Everest Smith was locked up for what he'd done to Phoenix. Indira considered giving him a second chance, and a third, but he kept trying to lie his way out of trouble. Protagonist Preparatory didn't have actual dungeons, so Maxi relocated him temporarily to the Editors' head-quarters. Their crew of dark suits and sunglasses was now moving through the crowd, taking account of everyone who'd been injured during the battle.

Thankfully, the Ninth Hearth was restoring everyone—protagonist or antagonist—who'd been mortally wounded. Rumor was that it would take a while, given there were so many characters to restore this time around.

Indira stopped there to visit Brainstorm Underglass, the battle's first victim. Her mentor beamed a little and offered a nod that promised they'd talk when all this was over. A team from Daedalus Construction arrived long after the dust had settled to begin repairs on the front doors of the school. Indira saw them taking measurements as she walked past.

The first step of negotiations was brutal, mostly because Indira and Peeve each had to negotiate with their own people first. There were a lot of snobby heroes who turned up their noses at the thought of working so closely with Antagonist Academy. They expressed many of the same concerns Indira had had in the beginning. Could bad guys ever *really* be good?

Peeve had similar difficulty calming down the antagonists. After risking everything to invade Fable, they felt like it would be a failure if they simply agreed to terms with the protagonists. Many felt certain that they'd be cast back out again at the first chance. This was where Peeve's heroics came in handy. The fact that she'd been the one to destroy the wheel—and orchestrate a master plan that had been even more devious than Iago's master plan—won over a number of villains.

It took all their efforts to bring both sides to an official meeting.

Alice stood on behalf of Protagonist Preparatory. Fester had a more difficult time electing a representative. Choosing someone from the old regime felt like a step backward to Peeve. Thus it was the Sorting Hate who took a seat at the table. The contrasting pair made for quite an image. Alice was like a willow tree, slight and graceful. By comparison, the old dragon looked like a building that had been brought to life. Both of them sipped tea, freshly fetched for them by none other than Dog the elephant. Alice was wise enough to thank the creature profusely, which earned an approving nod from the Sorting Hate.

When they finally settled in, Indira and Peeve sat down as arbitrators, hoping to help the deal along. "Our proposal is pretty straightforward," Peeve said, sliding them each a tourist map of Fable. It was similar to the one Maxi had brought that first day, when she'd led Indira around the city. "Protagonist Preparatory will maintain most of its current building. Very few changes, except here."

She noted a new hallway on the blueprint. Maxi had been tasked with editing the document so that everyone could envision the new concept.

"That hallway," Indira explained, "will lead into an adjacent building. See this property over here? It's barely in use. It's where they used to do all those Choose Your Own Adventure books. Most of the building is free space. We want to convert the whole thing into Antagonist Academy."

Alice looked thoughtful. "Which means both schools will be in Fable?"

"Actually, they'll be on the same street," Peeve answered. "Neighbors."

The Sorting Hate sniffed. "It's rather odd to think of us being so close."

Indira picked up that thread. "It's important to improve communications and work together more. There have been several transfers in the past. Students who started as protagonists, but ended up finding a better fit in Fester. And some students—like my friend Cavern—who transferred here. The schools never wanted to discuss them, because they were each too proud to believe any student would ever want to go to the other school.

"Working together will improve everything. Most of the problems with our old system began when Fable forced the antagonists out of the city." Indira had read up in preparation for the meeting. Initially, she'd assumed it was just propaganda that Fester taught its students, but then she saw records in Underglass's office that confirmed the school's decision to "remove all villainy" from the city. "That decision created distrust on both sides. The antagonists felt—rightfully—that they'd been tricked. And protagonists were suspicious of what was happening in Fester. That decision created an unnecessary and vicious cycle."

"Until now," Peeve added. "We can break that cycle by having the two schools side by side. We really do think it will change everything."

Alice nodded. The Sorting Hate looked deep in thought until Dog poked the dragon's side with her trunk. He blinked a little before leaning down. The elephant trumpeted.

"Oh! Very interesting. Dog informs me that there is a *suspicious* building in place between Protagonist Preparatory and the proposed site of Antagonist Academy. She wonders—and so do I—why there is a barrier between them, if this decision is intended to unite us all?"

Finally they'd arrived at Indira's favorite part.

"It isn't a barrier. It's a third school."

Alice grinned. She'd been wanting to ask the same question. The Sorting Hate reached out and affectionately scratched Dog behind one ear. "Is it for training pets?"

Indira shook her head. "We still have the Menagerie for that."

"A school for geriatrics?" the dragon guessed next. "I've been meaning to bring up the distinct lack of elderly characters in the last few decades. As someone who is over three thousand years old, I feel like this bias toward—"

"You know, we can just *tell* you what it's for," Indira suggested.

The Sorting Hate bristled before gesturing with one of his membranous wings. "Oh, go on, then."

"It's a starting point. We learned our lesson with Peeve. She made one mistake and was shipped off to Fester. But everything she did to save Fable? She should have had the option to be a protagonist if she'd wanted to be one. And then there are students like Everest Smith." Indira still didn't enjoy saying his name out loud. "Clearly an antagonist, but he was initially chosen for Protagonist Preparatory. Iago watched his auditions and saw potential there. Apparently, he started recruiting him years ago. But both these characters were sorted too soon, before they could learn more about who they really were. Peeve and I both believe it would benefit characters to have a neutral place to train. Somewhere that allows them to test the waters before deciding if they want to be good or evil."

Alice looked satisfied. "It's genius."

"What will you call it?" the Sorting Hate asked. "It's a grand idea, and it deserves a grand name. How about . . . the School for Good and Evil?"

Peeve shook her head. "That one's been done before."

"Bayside?"

"We're not even by the water."

"Hill Valley High School?"

"Sounds old."

"Starfleet Academy."

"Too limited to sci-fi."

"Unseen University?"

"Hmm. Can't really visualize it."

"Yale?"

"Isn't that a *real* school?"

"You'd be surprised. Hogwarts?"

"Is that a school or a disease?"

Indira listened patiently as the dragon kept rattling off absurd suggestions. When he finally fell silent, scratching his scaled chin in thought, she spoke.

"If you agree to this new setup, I think I have an idea for the school's name."

It took a little more discussion, but both parties eventually signed the agreement.

45

Origin

Indira walked down a dirt road with Peeve Meadows.

Whispers followed them. Everywhere she looked, characters-in-waiting were peeking out through windows or staring openly from their front stoops, all of them curious about the official visitors sent from Fable. Each shack had a mailbox. Indira remembered the little honeyed biscuits that were delivered to them each morning. The sound of characters practicing monologues.

Indira and Peeve walked until they reached a pair of recognizable houses. They eyed the unlit beacons, the slanted roofs, the rusting door frames. Both stood in silence for a while.

"Can't believe how small they are," Indira finally said.

Peeve nodded. "That was our whole life once. A little room and a lot of hope."

"Don't get too sappy on me," Indira said, nudging Peeve's shoulder.

Curious characters had slowly gathered in a crowd while they talked. Stragglers were still making their way, but most of the characters-in-waiting were in earshot. Peeve raised her voice.

"By order of Fable, these houses are to be evacuated. Your new home will be in Origin—"

A boy just a few rows back snorted. "This *is* Origin."

"—Institute. You'll be going to Origin Institute."

There was a shuffling of feet. Whispers ran through the crowd. The same boy spoke again.

"Never heard of it."

Indira smiled. "You have now. It will be the new starting point for every character, good or evil. From now on, you won't have to wait for the borealis to come. Whether or not you're chosen for a story will depend on *you*. On your skill level. Your ability to grow and learn and adapt. Every person here has a guaranteed spot waiting for them at the new Origin Institute. After a year of intensive training, you'll have the *choice* to attend Protagonist Preparatory or Antagonist Academy. Now, just to be clear, that doesn't mean everyone ends up in a story. I've learned that you don't have to be in a story to live a purposeful life in our world. There are a hundred different roads to take and each one is as worthy as the next. But we created Origin Institute so that everyone at least has a chance. You don't have to sit here hoping you get your shot. In the new system, you're guaranteed a chance. But what you do with it? That's up to you."

There were more whispers. Indira knew this was just

the beginning, but something about it felt so right that she couldn't stop smiling. There was a stretch of silence; then a girl at the back raised her hand. Indira pointed to her. "Do you have a question?"

"Uhh . . . sorry . . . I was just . . . Are you Indira Story?"

More whispers. She could hear some heated debate happening. The outspoken boy snorted again. "No way! Indira Story is like six feet tall and can shoot lightning bolts with her eyes."

Indira laughed at that. She reached back and unhooked the hammer from its new strap on her back. Sunlight glistened down the length of metal. She twirled it once and caught the boy's eye.

"Want to see one of those lightning bolts firsthand?"

He blushed a little at that. Peeve elbowed Indira.

"Okay, that's enough. We're here to introduce the new school, not walk you around on some kind of celebrity—"

Another hand at the back.

"And aren't you Peeve Meadows? The girl who defeated Iago?"

It was Peeve's turn to blush. She fumbled for a moment, surprised that her name had already spread this far. Indira nodded encouragingly.

"Yes," Peeve answered. "I'm Peeve Meadows. . . . Uh . . . did you know these were our shacks? Indira lived right there. I lived there. We were neighbors once. There's—well, there's no telling what you might do. If a couple of misfits like us could save the world, the sky is the limit for you."

There were a lot more questions after that. Editors were arriving to sort out travel back to the city. Indira slipped away from the crowd, allowing herself to be swept back into memory. Peeve was right. Once upon a time, she'd been a young girl in a little shack. She'd been on the verge of never being chosen for a story. She'd even been given an eviction notice. But here she was, three years later, already having saved the world three times.

None of it felt real, but she supposed that was the way Imagination always felt. Now she walked the same path she'd taken back then: down the road and into the city center of Origin, aiming for the place where she'd used a dragoneye for the first time.

And she turned that corner to a fine surprise.

Phoenix was there, all dressed up. For him that meant a nice pair of jeans and a fashionable maroon cardigan. He'd even combed his normally unruly hair. His eyes sparked at the sight of Indira rounding that familiar corner. She couldn't help grinning in return. This was where they'd first met. Phoenix was standing there like he'd been waiting for a while.

"Thought you'd never come," he said, smiling. "I was starting to sweat."

"Oh yeah? The boy who sets himself on fire and turns into a dragon can't stand a little sunlight?"

He smiled at that. "I have a surprise for you."

Indira watched as he stepped to one side. Behind him, there was a square tile of flawless glass. Phoenix had set a dragoneye in the *exact* spot where Dexter DuBrow had once placed it. She crossed over and stood there with him, watching the glass fill with a gorgeous and memorable turquoise. A dark slit opened in the square's center. That great marble eye stared out at them. Patterns of gold wove like bright rivers through a backdrop of forest green.

It was the same dragoneye they'd taken then.

"The Sorting Hate felt bad," Phoenix explained, "for the minor role he played in your captivity. I told him a way that he might make it up to you, and he was happy to help."

A voice spoke from somewhere deeper than stone or bone.

"Come now. I don't have all day!"

Phoenix and Indira laughed. She thought she remembered the dragon saying something similar to that the first time around. Phoenix held out his hand. Indira took it. The two of them stepped onto the dragoneye at the same time. Indira was struck by déjà vu again.

"Why are you sweating?" it asked.

Phoenix caught her eye. "I'm nervous, I guess."

Indira heard the quietest whisper, saw a flash of blue, and just like that they were *elsewhere.*

———

A familiar entryway.

Indira's fingers were still laced through Phoenix's.

"The doors!" she exclaimed. "They look just like they did before. It's perfect."

Phoenix nodded. "I knew you'd want to see them in pristine condition. Since you were, you know, the one who destroyed them in the first place."

Indira smacked his arm. Protagonist Preparatory looked the way it had the first time she'd seen it, offering all the promise it had to a young character-in-training. Indira kept thinking Phoenix would let go of her hand, and was glad when he didn't. Instead he led her gently forward.

Off to their left, Antagonist Academy's renovations were coming along just fine. Maxi had been put in charge of everything. All the edits to Fable's most valuable structure had fallen to her, and would be her first assignment as a Senior Editor. She'd taken that promotion in stride, bragging about her newer, fancier sunglasses for days now. It was hard to replicate a canyon of fire, but the renovated school's dark spires were coming along nicely.

Their view of the other school was cut off as they entered Protagonist Preparatory. Phoenix led Indira away from the brainstorms' offices. She felt that giddy turning in her stomach as she tried to guess where he might be taking her. Maybe to where their first class had been? Or out to the Rainy Courtyard, where she'd once ditched class rather than have to tell Phoenix he was her big crush. But Phoenix guided her to the only hallway she didn't recognize. All the stones looked a touch newer, a little less worn. It led to a door that was as bright as a fall apple.

"I wanted you to see this, too."

It opened into a marbled entryway. There were num-
bered classrooms, pristine hallways, brand-new desks.
Her favorite quote was even inscribed in stone by the
entrance.

Loyalty leads to bravery.
Bravery plants the seed
of self-sacrifice. And
self-sacrifice is the highest
call of every character in every story.

"Origin Institute," Phoenix said, sweeping his hands
out. "Walking around this place reminds me of what Iago
did with that wall. He believed a lie enough to make it
reality. The difference is that you believed the truth. You
believed in it so much that *it* became reality. Every stone.
Every door. Every student who walks through here. . . ."

He smiled at her and shook his head in disbelief.

"This world owes you so much, Indira. Do you know
what I said to fill my vial up with truth back in Hearth
Hall? Alice told us that we needed to say something that
was true, down to the very core of who we are. Something no one could deny." He pulled her around so that
they were closer than they'd ever been. Nearly touching
noses. She could feel the fire running through his veins,
pumping in his heart. She liked that warmth. It was like
walking into sunshine. "I told the vial that I loved Indira
Story."

Now, dear reader, it is frowned upon to be too nosy. I

think now might be a prudent time for our attention to be diverted —

EDIT. THIS IS MAXI. I REFUSE TO ALLOW US TO GO THREE BOOKS WITHOUT SEEING THIS KISS. EDIT.

Indira stood on her tiptoes. Phoenix's lips flamed against hers. There was that campfire scent she'd come to love so much. Heat and affection and fumbling. For a brief moment, they were the only two people in the world, and that was enough.

—

When the kiss ended, an inevitable shyness followed. Blushing cheeks. Indira gripped Phoenix's hand tightly, though, because there was no desire in her to stop holding hands. He didn't seem to mind.

"I've got one more surprise," Phoenix announced.

They walked every hall, drank in every classroom, but Phoenix's final stop was an office space similar to the ones the brainstorms used at Protagonist Prep. It was undecorated, except for a desk in the center of the room. The desk had a placard that made Indira stop dead in her tracks.

"But . . . I . . ."

Phoenix laughed. "Underglass couldn't think of a better person for the job. You've been through everything, Indira. You were a side character no one believed in. You've been a hero—in this world and in stories. You've been the bad guy, too, even if it wasn't intentional. We still have to finish the third book in our trilogy, of course. There'll be time for that. But when our books are done, this is what's waiting for you."

Indira walked forward. She used a finger to trace the letters of her name.

"What do you think? Am I really brainstorm material?"

Phoenix smiled. "Well, I'm the one who submitted your name for consideration. So, yeah, I do."

Indira circled the desk.

"It'll be a lot of work."

"Tons."

"And I'll have to deal with upstart first-year fire mages. . . ."

"They're the worst."

She kept circling. "Not to mention evaluating auditions. Tough job."

"Almost impossible."

Indira had circled all the way back around to Phoenix. She reached up on her toes again and planted a kiss on his cheek. "Would you help me? With this one little task?"

"Which is?"

"Changing the world."

He grinned. "Thought you'd never ask."

46

First Day of Classes

Indira hadn't felt butterflies like this since her auditions.

The front doors were opening. The ribbon had been ceremoniously cut. New students were set to arrive any minute. Peeve Meadows had checked in earlier that day. She had taken an advisory role in the neighboring building of Antagonist Academy. Her goal—which had been Iago's pretend goal—was to find bad guys with a heart of gold. She'd agreed to act as a special liaison between schools, evaluating crossover students and such.

Brainstorm Underglass had also stopped by and wished her luck. She was angling for retirement, but wanted to be around for the first few years of Indira's bright new plan, just to make sure the transition went well. Indira had been given the chance to hire a number of fantastic teachers.

Mrs. Pennington and Patch had agreed to teach a course on family dynamics, in case some students were a better fit with an ensemble cast. Indira's other one-time mother, Minerva Deacon, would be teaching some introductory character courses. She'd been brilliant the year before, during Indira's tutorial. Detective Malaprop had agreed to tackle a basic humor course. The sleuth had been rather surprised by the idea that he was funny, but promised to do his best. David was co-teaching a class with Samwise Gamgee on how to grow as a character, no matter what role you were in.

Phoenix had agreed to be her right-hand man during this first year. They stood together now, looking down at a pile of jackets. In their first year, the color of one's jacket had meant everything. It had caused a number of problems for Indira. The side characters sported navy blue. Protagonists wore a lovely gold. Indira could still remember the injustice she'd felt when she finally figured out how that system worked.

Origin's staff had voted to have indigo jackets. It was a salute to the slice of bad that lived inside every good character. It was the touch of good that a bad character might demonstrate, if a story gave them the room to do so. Indira stood there with the hired teachers and staff as the first trickle of students entered, all looking as nervous as she felt. They were instructed to come get a jacket that was the right size. Indira's eyes glittered a little as they tried them on. She stood there like a proud mother until one girl pulled her off to the side.

Her voice was a low whisper.

"What do they mean? The jackets? I had this friend who told me that the different jackets mean different classes. Or something. Is that true?"

Indira shook her head. Her voice did not tremble.

"Welcome. All they mean is *welcome*."

47

Back in the Real World

Deus Ex Machina slipped briefly down the rows of a bookstore in the Real World. He admired the rustic wooden floors and the stacked books. There was an upper level with a curving black railing, decorated with a quote from one of his favorite Authors. He nodded to the words like they were old friends before finding the section he'd come to visit.

Timing—as one might expect with the provider of convenient solutions—was everything. If he made his adjustment too soon, a bookseller would swing by and dutifully reposition the books. Too late and his intended target wouldn't see the alteration.

Always a delicate balance.

He waited until he felt a slight breeze. Someone entering the store. And then he slid forward. His hands drummed along the spines of books until he found the right book in the *G* section. With practiced ease, he wedged his hands there and started to push in both directions. There was just enough room for him to push and push until an empty, book-shaped space remained.

———

Viola Grimsley never *planned* to go to the bookstore. It just happened. Ever since she'd gotten her license, she'd found herself pulling into the parking lot without even meaning to. She liked the emblem for this particular store: a red-painted quail with a book clutched in one talon, quietly reading. She always imagined the bird hosting a book club with feathered friends.

Inside, there was a bookseller waiting with a smile. Viola nodded politely, eyes drawn to the sprawling rows, feet already moving in a familiar circle. She liked to glance at the poetry section first. When she walked through a bookstore, she felt like the tips of her fingers were seeing as much as her eyes did. She'd let them trace the raised words on the spines as she walked.

After the poetry section, she'd check in on fantasy and science fiction. She was old enough now that she'd started dabbling in the adult section. Great door-stopping books with plots as wide as her head. There'd been one series recently that reimagined Atlantis using the tarot deck. Viola had fallen in love with the two main characters and the magic and was waiting for the fifth book to come out. Her eyes found those books on the shelf. Sometimes walking through a bookstore was like checking in on old friends.

Saying *Hello, how are you? Do you remember all the fun we had together?*

Eventually, though, she made her way to the section with all the young adult and middle-grade books. She saved it for last, the way you might save the gooey center of a cookie as your final bite. Her eyes traced covers she'd tried to redraw in her own notebooks, found books she'd written her own fan-fiction spin-offs for. These particular books were the ones she kept in her bones. They were the reason she stayed up late, listening to music, scribbling about other worlds. They'd given her the quiet, if distant, dream that maybe one day she could write a book.

Viola walked up and down that section three times before she noticed it. There was a gap on the third bookshelf, two rows down, halfway across. Her eyes found the spot, and for some reason she couldn't stop staring. She took a step closer, squinting. There were a number of books by an author with the last name *Green* on one side, and a couple by *Grossman* on the other. In between them, a perfectly blank space. Just enough room for one book.

She took a few careful steps back. It wasn't lost on Viola that her name would fit right there between them. *Grimsley.* If lightning could have struck in that store, it would have. Viola felt like she was looking into the future. Her dreams of writing weren't just dreams, but a reality. The gap on that shelf wasn't there because someone had taken a book away. It was an invitation. It was the place where her book would go.

Viola was so distracted that she didn't see the easy-to-miss man slipping around her, making his purchase of the newest Indira Story book and heading out of the store with a grin. Nor did she know that her name had appeared a few moments later on a chalkboard in the world of Imagination.

A new brainstorm was looking at the name, already thinking through characters that might fit in the worlds Viola Grimsley would summon to life. There would be origin stories and plot twists and sequels. She had a great feeling about this one. All it had taken was a single, hopeful moment.

And a little help from an old friend.

———

That, my dear reader, is the end. But only of *my* story. I rather enjoy thinking that it's the beginning of yours.

Acknowledgments

I always want to begin by thanking my readers. I very distinctly remember being at Cary High School as a senior. My creative writing teacher—Anne Dailey—would put a green slip of paper in my hand at the start of class, smile at me, and say, "Go work." I'd head to the library, grateful for that permission slip, which was an invitation to dream.

If you've attended a public school, you probably have an idea of what our library looked like. At the time, there was a circle of computer stations with monitors stacked atop bulky mainframes. I'd take my seat in one of the color-faded chairs with the high backs and the ghostly indentations of former students. I'd type in my password and pull up my document, and I'd chip away at the next scene. If you walked into that library and told *that* kid that readers would one day reach the end of his eighth book— the conclusion of his *third* series—he would have laughed you out of the building.

So thank you, dear reader, for breathing life into what once felt impossible.

My biggest acknowledgment for this book goes out to Emily Easton. Most casual readers don't have a sense of what a modern editor *does*. It gets confused with the equally important task of copyediting. Often, it's assumed that an editor glances through a manuscript and makes sure all the commas are in their rightful places. But these days, an editor wears several other hats as well.

They're the front lines of acquisition, keeping an eye on submissions, trying to find the next great voice. They're in-house advocates for the books they choose—giving speeches and making arguments for why your book deserves a little more attention in the grand machinations of a publishing house. They're big-picture readers who guide the courses of stories. They're nuanced detectives who put their thumb on what was missing in certain scenes. They're often the first people to put enough weight behind our dreams to make them tangible. The first to believe those dreams are worth sharing with the rest of the world.

If you have enjoyed any of my first eight novels, it's because Emily Easton opened an email from my agent back in 2015 and fell in love with a story about a young man from Detroit launching into space. Ever since then, she's been my editor. Which means she's worn all the hats I've listed above, in service to launching my career. I always tell people that writing books is collaborative. It is a team effort. You could say Emily Easton has been our captain this entire time. Thank you, Emily, for your unwavering belief in me as a writer. It has not gone unnoticed, and it is not something I am likely to ever forget.

Speaking of commas, I owe a great deal to this book's personal grammar police, Melinda Ackell and Karen

Sherman. A huge thank-you to Claire Nist for making sure we're always on track and to Josh Redlich for always guiding my books into the right hands. A thank-you to Jennifer Baker for making everything run smoothly, from start to finish. Thank you to Adrienne Waintraub for green-lighting the brilliant trailers that brought this series to life, and to Nicholas Sailer for translating my vision to the screen. Thank you to Carol Ly for directing the vision behind the covers in this series. All the love in the world to Maike Plenzke for the delicate care she put into creating the images that have snagged readers as they passed by and saw the book glinting down from the shelves.

I'm indebted to Kristin Nelson and the entire team at Nelson Literary Agency. If Emily was our team captain, then Kristin was the one who joined the team before it was ever officially in the league. I am always grateful for your faith in me, for your vision, and for your pursuit of excellence on my behalf. These books don't exist without you. Thanks to Brian Nelson, Samantha Cronin, Tallahj Curry, Maria Heater, and Angie Hodapp for their irreplaceable work.

I wrote most of this book in the first few months of my second son's life. Thanks for being a smiley boy who sleeps pretty well, Thomas, and letting your dad sneak downstairs to his office to write books. Thank you to Henry, as well, for giving me breaks from my writing to take funny pictures and goof off. As always, the biggest thank-you in the world to my wife, Katie, for putting up with someone who's constantly running into the room and shouting things like: "I figured it out! The dragons are all dead! And that means . . ." She is a saint. Shout-out to my momma as well, for being the first person to read every book I've written.

To the family and friends who've loved on us and on my books all this time? Thank you. To the readers who do not know me at all but have fallen in love with these characters? Thank you.

I'm honored to get to do this. I'm grateful to God for this strange life I get to live, where dreams come true and stories are loved enough that a person can make a career out of writing them. One of my favorite verses from Isaiah says, "You will be like a well-watered garden, like a spring whose waters never fail." I have a lot of other books I want to write, but eight books into my career, I can tell you that I feel like a well-watered garden. Someone who has gotten to exist and dream and bloom because so many other people took the time to help me grow.

All I can say is thank you.

About the Author

SCOTT REINTGEN is a former public school teacher from North Carolina. He survives mostly on cookie dough, which he is told is the most important food group. When he's not writing, he uses his imagination to entertain his wife, Katie, and their sons, Henry and Thomas. Scott is the author of the Ashlords duology, the Nyxia Triad, and the Talespinners series. You can follow him on Facebook, on Instagram, and on Twitter at @Scott_Thought.

itspronouncedrankin.com